The MINISTRY of UNLADYLIKE ACTIVITY

ROBIN STEVENS

PUFFIN

PUFFIN BOOKS

UK | USA | Canada | Ireland | Australia
India | New Zealand | South Africa

Puffin Books is part of the Penguin Random House group of companies
whose addresses can be found at global.penguinrandomhouse.com

www.penguin.co.uk
www.puffin.co.uk
www.ladybird.co.uk

First published 2022
This edition published 2023

001

Set in 12.5/18.5pt ITC New Baskerville Std and 12/18.5pt Melior LT Pro
Typeset by Jouve (UK), Milton Keynes
Printed and bound in Great Britain by Clays Ltd, Elcograf S.p.A.

The authorized representative in the EEA is Penguin Random House Ireland,
Morrison Chambers, 32 Nassau Street, Dublin D02 YH68

A CIP catalogue record for this book is available from the British Library

Paperback
ISBN: 978-0-241-42987-7

All correspondence to:
Puffin Books, Penguin Random House Children's
One Embassy Gardens, 8 Viaduct Gardens, London SW11 7BW

To my baby. The next generation.

↑ Coventry

Elysium Hall

Abandoned cottage

River

↑ Village

Field

Rose Garden

Orchard

Box Hedges

Anderson Shelter

Well

Walled Kitchen Garden

Victory beds

Stable Yard/Garage

Generator

Elysium Hall

Tree

N
W   E
S

Elysium Hall

Ground floor

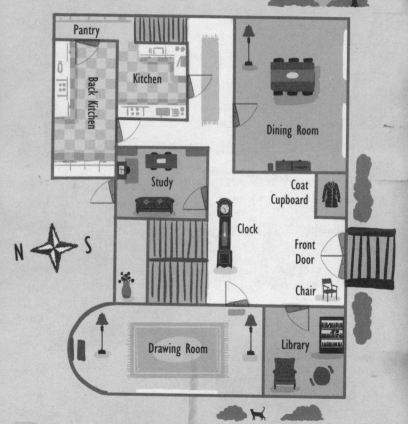

Pantry

Kitchen

Back Kitchen

Dining Room

Study

Coat Cupboard

Clock

Front Door

Chair

N S

Drawing Room

Library

Elysium Hall

First floor

Hugh & Pamela

Spare room

Bathroom

Annabelle-Olivia

Old Mr & Mrs Verey

Sidney

Neil

N — S

Second floor

Eric

Scott

Nuala & May

Mrs O'Malley

Ruth

The Foley–Verey Family Tree

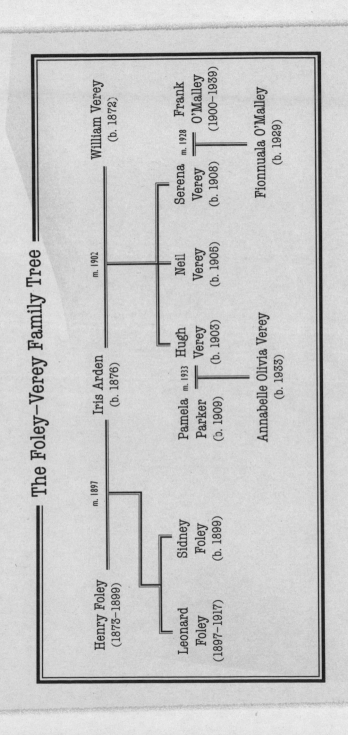

TOP SECRET

From the case files of the WOE
(Women's Operation Executive, also known
as the Ministry of Unladylike Activity)

December 1940

PART ONE

WE BEGIN OUR MISSION

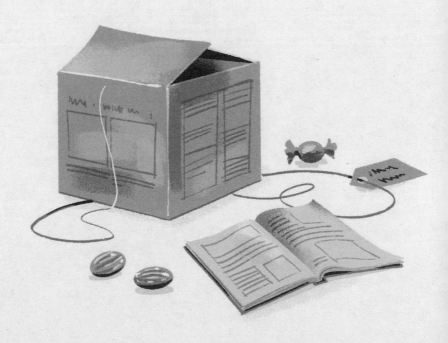

I

My name is May Wong. I am ten years old (nearly eleven), and I have become a spy in order to save the world. That is true and not an exaggeration. *Anything* can happen in a war, and anyone can be a hero.

And anyone can be evil too. When the war began, I thought that Nazis might look like the lizards who used to bask on the steps of our Big House, back in Hong Kong. I imagined them with scaly, flickering skin and yellow eyes. I thought that being evil must make you *look* evil.

But, now that I'm older, I've realized that evil can look like anything. Evil can look like a starchy governess, or a kind old lady, or the warden who comes round to check the blackout.

This is the story of how I – how *we* – uncovered a Nazi spy in England, solved a murder and joined the Ministry of Unladylike Activity. It was much harder than I expected.

We had to be very clever, and, as usual, none of the grown-ups listened to us until it was almost too late. Grown-ups really are hopeless. But they're listening now, at last, and they want to know everything that happened. That's why I'm writing this.

By the way, this is the *official* version of the notes I took during our mission. I'm supposed to be using formal language, the way we're taught at school, but I've decided that this is *my* report, and I'm going to tell it my own way. And that means explaining some things first.

The most important thing to know about me, apart from the fact that I am now a spy, is that I'm not supposed to be in England at all. I'm *supposed* to be living in Hong Kong, where I was born, with my mother and my father and my little brother, Teddy. But I came to England last year with Father and my second sister, Rose, to visit Deepdean School for Girls – the stupid English boarding school that Father planned for us to go to. And, while we were here, the war began.

Father went home as quick as he could to be with Ma Ma and Teddy, but he left me trapped in England with Rose and my biggest sister, Hazel. I can't go back to Hong Kong until the war ends – so obviously the only thing I can do is make sure it ends as quickly as possible. I miss Ma Ma and I miss Teddy (even though he's too small to be very interesting). I think I even miss Father, although he was the reason I got stuck in England in the first place, and the reason I have to go to Deepdean, which I hate.

Or at least I *did* go to Deepdean until I ran away to become a spy.

I ran away because I had to. There was no other choice. Everyone in my family – including Big Sister Hazel – thinks that I'm still a baby, but I'm not. The truth is that I can speak two entire languages and run for ten minutes without stopping and lie well enough to trick Father and the Deepdean mistresses. I can fight with a sword (or I could if someone would give me a real one – all I've practised with is a stick) and with my feet and my fists.

So I was sure that I'd be an excellent spy, if only someone would give me a chance.

You see, I knew a spy already: Hazel.

I am absolutely not making that up. It's true.

And it's hard when your sister has already done all the things you want to do. Hazel went to Deepdean once too, and she's famous there, even now that she's very old (nineteen). She loved school. And Rose, who is twelve, loves it as well. So, when I first decided I wanted to become a spy, I thought I had to love it too. I spent minutes and minutes on my school compositions, and I *tried* not to hit any of the other girls during Games, and I even gave Mariella Semple my jam roly-poly pudding at dinner. (I was sorry about that later – she didn't even finish it. What a waste of jam roly-poly!) But it all just made me notice how much I hated school, even when I was trying.

So I decided to become a spy another way.

I asked Hazel how to do it, but she would never answer any of my questions. She wouldn't even admit she *was* a spy, even though it was perfectly obvious.

And then I found the note in her handbag.

Obviously it wasn't for me – I'm not stupid – and I shouldn't have been looking in Hazel's handbag in the first place. But I was bored, and I was cross, and sometimes I just *do* things without thinking about them. I only feel bad about them later.

It happened like this.

By September 1940, the war had been going on for a year, but you almost wouldn't know it, living in Deepdean. Deepdean Park was full of sandbags, a bomb had fallen on the cinema by mistake (no one was hurt) and there was no cream on the cakes at the Willow Tea Rooms or soap powder at our boarding house to wash with. I didn't care much about the soap, but I did about the cream. But that was really as far as it went. It wasn't at all like war is in stories. The newsreels at the pictures, of cities in Europe falling and German soldiers marching and shooting, felt exciting but nearly as made up as the main feature. It sounds strange now that I know better, but I was . . . almost disappointed.

And then we began to hear stories about the Nazis crossing the Channel to flatten us like a thumb squashing a bug. Planes buzzed overhead every night, and every day the invasion seemed closer and closer. So, when Hazel came to Deepdean to take me and Rose out for tea, one weekend at the beginning of October, I decided I couldn't wait any longer.

I asked and asked and asked Hazel about spying, and what it felt like to be in a real air raid, and how many people were dead in London, and whether it was true that the Germans were about to invade, and if so what were we going to do about it, until Rose got all wobbly and started to cry, and Hazel told me to stop. Rose had to sit down on a bench on Deepdean high street and put her head between her knees, hugging her gas-mask case, while Hazel patted her back and gave her a bullseye to suck. Hazel always has sweets in her pockets, even now they're rationed. Spies get all the best things: another reason why I wanted to be one.

'It'll be all right,' said Hazel, as a man in a Home Guard uniform walked by. 'No one will hurt you, Rose, I promise. We're prepared. We won't let them come here.'

I didn't see how she could promise something like that. It sounded like a grown-up lie. I picked up her handbag to look for more sweets. But what I found, instead, was a note.

It was scribbled all over with crossings-out, but circled at the bottom of it was a very simple message, underlined:

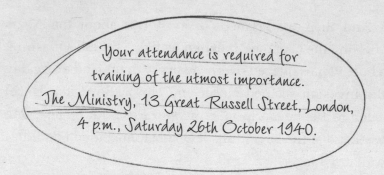

Your attendance is required for training of the utmost importance. The Ministry, 13 Great Russell Street, London, 4 p.m., Saturday 26th October 1940.

This looked important. I shoved it in my pocket just as Hazel turned to look at me.

'Give me that,' she said, and slid her handbag back onto her arm. So she *hadn't* noticed what I'd taken. 'Come on, who wants scones?'

I did, obviously. But, more than that, I wanted to find out what that message meant. It was *spy business*, I was sure of it. I knew that this was my chance to find out what Hazel was really doing, and help her do it.

I just had to run away from school first.

2

From the report of May Wong

The running-away part was easy in the end.

Everyone at Deepdean has stories about how hard it is to get away, and what a bad idea it is (the stories all end with the girl either getting detention for the rest of her life or falling over dead in a ditch). But actually all I had to do was leave our boarding house in the usual Saturday crocodile of girls, wait until we were almost at the park, and then pretend to be ill and have to go and sit down next to some sandbags. Eloise Barnes wanted to stay with me, but I told her that I thought I was going to be sick, and she squealed and scuttled away. As soon as she was gone, I ran as fast as I could to the train station.

I'd filled my gas-mask case with everything I'd need: some sweets, a manual about air raids, extra shoelaces (in case I needed to tie anyone up), a London A to Z, a small torch, and a spare pair of knickers. Once I'd done that, there was no room for my actual gas mask, so I'd hidden that under my dorm-room bed. I also had all the money I could find, most of which I'd had to pinch from Rose's tuck box because I'd spent mine. I felt quite bad about that because Rose is a kind person and would have given it to me if I'd asked – but she's also very honest, so if I *had* asked she'd have told Matron what I was up to.

I bought a half-fare to London, one way (because I was not planning on going back to Deepdean), and ducked into the loos to swap my uniform for my weekend dress, cardigan and hat. When the train came, I pretended to belong to an old woman with a crowd of children. I climbed aboard and sat in the blue half-light next to another woman in a siren suit (these are funny overalls that you're supposed to wear over your clothes in case there's an air raid, which just make people look like they're about to go fix a car), watching out of the edge of the lowered blind as the train crept through the countryside. It was going slowly because there might be bombs on the line, and everywhere it stopped was a mystery, all the signs painted out and no announcements, in case of German spies. It already felt like I was part of a story.

Finally, we pulled into the big dome of Paddington station. I dodged round grown-ups in uniforms, and newspaper sellers, and came out onto a street full of red London buses that had advertisements for OXO cubes and powdered eggs on their sides.

I got on a bus that I knew from my A to Z would take me to Great Russell Street. I pretended to belong to another grown-up – it's useful being little sometimes: no one thinks you could possibly plan anything yourself – and as the bus jolted its way through London I tried not to look shocked at what I saw out of the window.

I'd heard stories about the Blitz, how the whole city was lit up with fire every night, how the Germans had huge great big bombs that could crush whole houses to powder and peel the clothes right off the people who lived in them, but I thought it all sounded too big to be true. Except, now that I *was* in London, I realized the stories might not have been big enough.

The buildings we drove past looked like a giant had been playing with blocks and got bored. Some of them were smashed sideways, and some of them were pancaked flat, and some of them were sliced down the middle – one half gone and the other half a dangling mass of broken beams and drooping floors and doors that went nowhere but the sky. There was glass everywhere being swept into piles by people in uniforms whose faces were pale with dust – and the air was full of dust too, and the clothes of the other people on the bus. I shifted my feet about, and they made dust patterns on the floor.

The bus stopped halfway down Oxford Street, and we all had to get out because there was an unexploded bomb in the road. I didn't understand at first, and tried to keep on walking past shops with shattered windows and signs that said MORE OPEN THAN USUAL, but then a man with a walrus moustache shouted, 'Go away, little girl, unless you fancy being blown up!'

That was when I suddenly realized that it wasn't a joke or a grown-up invention. There was a real bomb, and it might really explode. I felt my face flush, and I couldn't work out whether I was excited or terrified, and whether I wanted to run a mile or sit down right there on the pavement.

Instead, I turned onto a side street and kept on walking towards Great Russell Street. It was warm now in the afternoon sun, and my cardigan itched me – English clothes always do – and my gas-mask case bumped against my hip. Barrage balloons glittered in the sun like fat silver moons, and I stepped over bits of fallen building and reminded myself that I was here to become a spy and put a stop to all this.

When I got to Great Russell Street, it was five minutes to four. I was just in time. I walked down the row of houses, counting, until I arrived at Number 13. It had a red-painted door with a brass knocker shaped like a fox, and standing in front of it was a boy. He had dark skin, a round body, and a round, friendly face surrounded by dusty, curly hair. He was wearing a dusty knitted pullover and shorts, and he had a dusty, cross-looking ginger cat with one white paw in his arms.

The boy and the cat both stared at me.

'What are you looking at?' I asked. 'And what are you doing here?'

'I solved the crossword,' said the boy simply, as though that explained anything. 'I suppose you did too?'

I narrowed my eyes at him, not wanting to admit that I had no idea what he was talking about.

'The one in the paper,' he went on. 'The Junior Championship puzzle. The solution was a message, about *training*, and this address.'

I've learned since arriving in England that when someone tells you something, it's always best to pretend you knew all along.

'Yes,' I said. 'The puzzle. I solved it too, and that's why I'm here. I thought it was easy.' The boy's eyes lit up with respect, and I realized that was probably pushing it a bit. 'Is that your cat?'

'I found her,' said the boy, petting the cat's head gently. 'In the rubble. I think she came from one of the houses that got hit last night.'

I don't like cats. I think they're too clever. But I liked how careful the boy was with the cat. It made me like him.

'I'm May Lee,' I said. 'What's your name?'

'I'm Eric. Er, Eric Jones.' The way he said that, with the pause, told me he was lying too. I respected that. 'Do you think it matters that I'm not thirteen yet?' he went on, frowning. 'I'll be eleven next month.'

'I'll be eleven soon too,' I said, which was not technically a lie because I will, in half a year. 'I shouldn't think it matters at all.'

I still had absolutely no idea what we were talking about. How had the note I'd found in Hazel's handbag ended up as the solution to a newspaper crossword? What other information had I missed?

'I was almost late,' I told Eric, just for something to say. 'There was a *bomb* in the road.'

I was still a bit excited about it, and I wanted someone else to be too. But Eric just stood with the cat in his arms and stared at me as though I'd said something strange.

'Where are you from?' he asked. 'You're not from London, are you?'

I felt myself get all spiky with annoyance, because usually when English people ask where I'm from they're being very rude. But then I looked at Eric's curious expression, and something clicked into place. His accent wasn't quite English. Mine isn't quite yet, either, unless I concentrate, and I can tell when other people are trying as well.

'I'm from Hong Kong, but I go to school in Deepdean,' I said. 'It's in the country, over *that* way. You aren't from London, either, are you? You're—'

I struggled to think what the not-English bits of Eric's voice sounded like. I couldn't hold onto it at first, and then I had it. The newsreels.

'You're *German*!'

Suddenly my heart was beating as fast as it had when I'd realized about the bomb.

Eric had turned almost purple, staring round the street as though someone might pop out at any moment and arrest him.

'Don't SAY that!' he hissed. '*Please!*'

'But you *are*!'

'I'm *English*!' said Eric fiercely. 'I am now, anyway. My family – we came here four years ago. Mama and Papa were musicians in Germany, famous ones. But my mama has dark skin, like me and my sister, and the Nazis hate people who look like us. They think we're not really people at all. So we had to escape to England. We were supposed to be safe here. But then, about a month ago, Papa was taken away by the British government because he's German. They think he might be *a Nazi spy*. I thought that if I could prove that we're loyal, not dangerous, and if I could help end the war, then Papa – then they might let him come home.'

He gave a gasp, his face red and upset. Almost automatically, he reached for his right wrist, for a heavy, grown-up watch that was too big for him. I wanted to know more about Eric's family, and Eric, but I was most interested in what he'd said about ending the war. My breath had caught as he said it.

'I think this is something to do with the war too!' I said. 'That's why I ran away—'

I stopped myself because I wasn't supposed to be saying that, especially not to someone I'd only just met. We were always being warned about careless talk costing lives — and Eric was German, after all, even if he said he was loyal to Britain. But he looked excited.

'I ran away too!' he said. 'I've never done anything like this before. My twin sister, Lottie, is the brave one, not me. But I'm good at puzzles. I even know Morse code! When I solved the crossword and saw what it said, I knew I couldn't just let myself be evacuated, not with Papa taken. Our train left this morning, and I gave Lottie the slip on the platform. I put a note in her pocket to explain, and another letter for Mama for Lottie to post. It should stop Mama looking for me for a few weeks, anyway.'

I was very impressed.

'Won't Lottie tell on you?' I asked.

'We're twins!' said Eric. 'She wouldn't. Anyway, I'm usually the one not telling on *her*.'

As he was talking, the London clocks began to strike four. And then the red door we were standing outside opened.

3

From the report of May Wong

The person who opened the door was a tall, thin woman with pale skin, extremely blue eyes and wavy blonde hair. She stopped still when she saw us and glared at me and Eric. I glared back, my heart thumping. I knew her, and she was the (second) worst person I could have met just then.

This was Big Sister Hazel's best friend, Daisy Wells.

'What are you doing here, May?' she snapped, as she closed the door behind her and stepped outside. 'Why aren't you in school?'

'Hello, Daisy,' I said cheerfully, because I was *not* going to be talked down to, not after I'd gone to so much trouble to be here. 'I solved that crossword puzzle, and it told me to come here.'

Daisy's eyes narrowed and a wrinkle appeared at the top of her nose. 'What do you mean?' she asked. 'Did Hazel put you up to this? You can't be here – you're too young.'

'Hazel doesn't know anything about it,' I said, drawing myself up. 'I solved the puzzle all on my own!'

Daisy groaned. 'I should have known you'd manage to stick your nose in where it isn't wanted. That's quite enough – you have to go back to school. You're a baby, and Hazel would never forgive me if you got mixed up in this business. And you!' She turned to Eric. 'You can't be here, either. Girls only: it said so in the crossword.'

'No it did not,' said Eric, fishing a battered bit of newsprint out of his pocket. 'It didn't say anything about girls.'

'Really?' asked Daisy. 'Bother Hazel. I told her to put that in! This is a nightmare. Well, never mind that. The two of you must leave at once. May's too young, as I said, and you're a boy and – and are you *German*?'

'So what if I am?' asked Eric. His round face was glowing all over again. 'I'm here to *help*. Anyway, I'm English too. I have a passport that says so now.'

'We're not leaving!' I cried. 'We solved the crossword, didn't we?' (I decided I'd better stick with my story about having solved it. It wasn't really important, anyway.) 'And we came all this way. We're here to be trained, just like it says.'

Daisy breathed out loudly. The crinkle at the top of her nose deepened. 'This is exhausting,' she said. 'You're all wrong for the job, both of you. We're looking for older girls who are ready for this.'

18

'We *are* ready,' I said. 'We're perfect. And we're your only options. No one else is here, are they? Oh, *do* let us in so we can learn to be spies. That's what this is all about, isn't it?'

Daisy's eyes flicked from me to Eric to the empty street behind us. I thought, for a moment, that she might be about to give in. Then her expression hardened.

'Absolutely not,' she said. 'Go away! And forget all that nonsense about being spies. You don't know what you're talking about.'

This was clearly yet another grown-up lie.

'Oh, please let us in!' said Eric suddenly. 'I *have* to do something. Everyone else gets to!'

That was exactly it. It wasn't fair that all the grown-ups could join up, while we had to sit about doing nothing just because we were children. Eric, I thought, was quite right and very sensible. I liked him even more.

'This is ridiculous,' snapped Daisy. 'And, May, how did you get here, anyway?'

'None of your business,' I said rudely.

The top of my head was burning through my hat. Eric wiped sweat from his eyes. His knitted pullover looked very uncomfortable. Daisy crossed her arms and glared at us.

'Good grief, did you *run away*? I don't have time for this – I shall have to take you back. Hazel will be furious with me—'

I felt sick. My adventure was about to be over before it had properly begun.

But then the front door opened again, and a ginger-haired woman popped her head out. Her face was tense. 'Daisy,' she said, 'you're needed. It's urgent. *Hurry*.'

Daisy replied with an extremely rude word. 'You two,' she said to us, 'stay there. *Don't* move. I'll be back.'

And she whisked away into the depths of the house, slamming the door behind her.

Eric looked at me. 'Er – should we stay?' he asked.

'Absolutely not!' I said.

My heart was rushing in my chest. If I stayed, Daisy would take me back to Deepdean. The mistresses and Matron wouldn't let me out of their sight again. Hazel would be angry with me. She might even tell *Father*, in Hong Kong, what I'd done.

But if we left now, then Daisy wouldn't find us, and we might still get the chance to be heroes.

What if there was a way we could prove ourselves? I imagined us coming back to Number 13 Great Russell Street having completed a dangerous mission. Daisy and Big Sister Hazel would tell us how brilliant we'd been. They'd absolutely have to let us be proper spies then.

But what could we do to show them?

'I think that's it,' Eric said sadly, putting the cat down. It trotted away towards the red door and sat in front of it expectantly. 'I'll have to go and find Lottie.'

20

'NO!' I said through gritted teeth. 'We can't just give up.'

'But you heard that woman. She said we were all wrong for this. How did you know her, anyway? Who's Hazel?'

'Never mind!' I said. 'And we *aren't* all wrong. We're just right. We simply have to show them!'

'How?' asked Eric.

'We—' I said. 'We—'

I stuck my hands into the pockets of my cardigan and squeezed them desperately, trying to think. And my fingers touched a crackly bit of paper. I pulled it out, and saw that it was the note I'd found in Hazel's handbag, the one that had led me here. I turned it over, frustrated – and caught sight of something I'd missed before.

On the back was a list of place names, some of them crossed through.

~~Foxton Manor, Berkshire~~
119 Parrish Gardens, Berwick-upon-Tweed
~~The Cedars, Glasgow~~
29 Mote Street, Hull
Elysium Hall, Coventry

And a note in Hazel's handwriting:

Information recently received by Berlin must be coming from these addresses! Identify the agents behind it.

I shoved the list at Eric. 'Here!' I said. 'Look at this! It's our mission!'

'What is it?' asked Eric. 'Where did you get this?'

'Hazel's my sister,' I admitted. 'And she's a spy. I got this out of her handbag, only I didn't realize how important it was until now. If someone is sending information to *Berlin*, it means they're working with the Nazis! We have to go to one of these places and work out who it is and how to stop them. Then, when we come back here, Daisy and Hazel and the people they work for will be really impressed. They'll have to let us in. Do you see?'

Eric nodded, his eyes wide.

And that was the moment that our first mission began.

4

It was also quite easy to get out of London again. All we had to do was pretend to be evacuees.

Once we'd left Great Russell Street, Eric took us to a place that was a bit like a sorting office for people.

'It's called the Rest Centre,' he explained to me. 'People come here when they've been bombed out of their homes; they can get help finding a new place to live outside London. If we say we've got somewhere to stay in one of those places on your piece of paper, they won't ask questions. They're far too busy.'

It was true. There were lots of other people crammed in round us at the Rest Centre: children and grown-ups, all dusty and desperate and carrying strange things. I saw a woman with a pram full of dinner plates, and a man holding a cage with a parrot in it.

The tired-looking woman we spoke to didn't even look up at us properly when Eric told her that we were May

Lee and Eric Jones, neighbours whose houses had been hit by a bomb.

'Any relatives?' asked the woman.

'My uncle's in Coventry,' Eric said hopefully. 'Near – Elysium Hall.'

He was turning out to be very useful in this situation, and I felt more pleased than ever to be working with him.

The woman nodded, scribbled something down on a piece of paper and sent us to another room, where a second woman wrote a message on a second piece of paper and sent us to another room again.

This kept on happening, for hours, until we each ended up with an extra set of itchy clothes (why *are* English clothes so itchy?), an ugly suitcase and a large label with our made-up name and address on it. The suitcases and clothes had both been used by someone else before, and they smelled like it. We were also given tickets to Coventry for the next morning. Somehow, what Eric had said had started a strange series of misunderstandings that ended with the woman who gave us the tickets assuming that we were expected at Elysium Hall itself. And that was all right by Eric and me.

Another woman gathered us up, with five other dusty and miserable-looking children, and led us about like Matron for the rest of the day. I had to keep reminding myself that I was not helpless at all, but undercover and on a mission.

*

24

That night we all sheltered in Leicester Square Underground station. I hated it. It turns out that air raids are not as fun as I thought they'd be.

The platform and the stairs and the ticket hall were all stuffed full of people, crammed together like they were playing Sardines. The air was hot, smelly and stale. After a while, we heard distant rumbling explosions, and then the crash of something big hitting nearby. Dust shook from the tunnel arches, and I wondered if one of these shelters had ever collapsed. Our evacuee leader made us all sit in a circle and sing songs, which was awful. But I gritted my teeth, and Eric put his arm round me, and we counted off the minutes on his big wristwatch.

'That's your father's, isn't it?' I said. It was a guess, but a good one because Eric sighed sadly.

'Papa gave it to me just before he was taken away. It reminds me of him. Do you miss your father?'

'No,' I said bitterly because my father was the reason why I was stuck here. And then, after a pause, as I imagined his big, warm hand with its square fingers on my shoulder, his voice rumbling above my head: 'Yes.'

Eric nodded. I could tell he understood.

In the middle of the night, a funny little train pulled up to the platform and some people got out of it and began to serve food and drinks. I sneaked past the evacuee leader and bought us both hot chocolates and buns, and, as we ate them, I realized the bombs had stopped.

'Jerry's gone home,' said someone, and I felt suddenly cheerful. Eric and I had survived the air raid, on our own, without help. We could face whatever was coming the next day.

That following morning we were led through smashed-up, dusty, broken London to Euston station in time for our train.

Some of the evacuees in our group were excited, but others began to cry, which I thought was *wet* (an English word I've learned). I said so to Eric, and he made a thoughtful face and said, 'It's all right to be scared when you're leaving somewhere you know for somewhere you don't.'

I felt a bit ashamed then, because that was how I'd felt when I left Hong Kong. But I didn't feel scared now. I felt full of purpose. I was away from Deepdean, and away from my family, and I was about to prove myself once and for all. Once we'd worked out who was sending information to the Germans from this Elysium Hall place – which sounded easy to me – all I had to do was telephone Big Sister Hazel at the number she'd taught me and Rose ages ago. Then she could come and collect us and take us back to Great Russell Street in a cloud of glory.

I *knew* we could do it, never mind what Daisy said. Eric had already shown how clever he was, and I knew that I was brave. Which was a good thing because I could tell that Eric was nervous now that we were really about to leave London. He'd gone pale, and he was hugging his gas-mask case to his chest.

'Buck up!' I said to him. (This is something else that English people say. I learned it at school.)

'You know, you sound really posh sometimes,' said Eric. 'Like a character in a book.'

'I'm not posh!' I said.

Actually, I think I might be. I think Deepdean is too. I've only realized it since I met Eric, who is definitely not posh at all.

The train came puffing into the station, trailing steam.

'This is it!' I said, lifting up my suitcase. 'Are you ready?'

'No,' said Eric, paler than ever. 'Yes. You're sure this is a good idea?'

'*Obviously*,' I said.

The other evacuees shoved forward as the train doors opened, and I grabbed Eric's free hand and dragged him forward too. We jumped onto the train, the grown-ups on the platform waved – and then they were lost in a swish of steam and the scream of the engine starting up again.

We were on our way.

5

From the report of May Wong

The train stopped at Coventry, and the evacuee leader made us all get off. The real evacuees (the ones who weren't secretly spies like me and Eric) huddled together on the platform anxiously, clutching their suitcases. I decided I did feel a little sorry for them, because they didn't even have an important mission to distract them from missing their families.

A group of grown-ups came towards us, and the evacuee leader got out a clipboard. The grown-ups had expressions on their faces just like my father when he is about to do a business deal, or like Deepdean girls queuing for bunbreak.

An old lady took two tall, strong-looking boys, and then another lady took one of the prettier girls. They both looked at me and Eric and pursed their lips and shook their heads, which made me angry. If they only knew that we were the cleverest and best evacuees out of everyone!

And then the leader beckoned forward a big, craggy man with one eye, wearing worn-out old driving clothes. His beard was yellowed, and he glared at all of us. The other evacuees pressed together in terror.

'Children, this is Mr Scott from Elysium Hall,' she said. 'I've had a message to say that some of you are expected there?'

My hand shot up in the air.

'Such enthusiasm!' said the leader. 'There you are, Mr Scott: your evacuees.'

Eric was squeezing my other hand so tightly it hurt.

'Humph,' said Mr Scott, frowning. 'Ruth told you on the telephone that we're not expecting anyone. I dunno why they think they're coming to us.'

The leader looked tired. 'Well, are you happy to take them, anyway? Mr Verey always does his bit. I'm sure he won't mind.'

Mr Scott looked at us rudely with his one eye, and I held my breath until I almost popped. Then he sniffed and said, 'He'll take them. It's the law, isn't it? Come along, you two. Hurry up. Hope you don't have lice. The last lot did.'

Then he went striding off without glancing round once to make sure we were following him. Eric and I picked up our suitcases as fast as we could and ran after him.

'I told you we'd do it!' I hissed. 'See?'

'*Shh!*' said Eric.

His expression wobbled between terror and amazement. I knew how he felt. Our plan was *working*. I tried not to think about Rose waiting for me back at our Deepdean boarding house, wondering where I was and raising the alarm; or what Big Sister Hazel would say once Daisy told her that she'd seen me. I had to focus on our mission.

We clambered into the back of Mr Scott's car, an old black Rolls-Royce, and tried to behave like ordinary evacuees. Annoyingly, Mr Scott didn't pay any attention to either of us. In fact, he didn't say a word the whole time he was driving us through the flat gold, green and brown (mostly brown) countryside, wide, damp, tilled fields dark under a whitish sky. All he did was point, once, just as we went through a gate, and a building – which had to be Elysium Hall – came into view.

It wasn't very big – not even the size of our house in Hong Kong. It was dwarfed by big dark trees and looked little and sickly. The next thing I thought was how straight up and down it was. It was just a grey stone box with a few funny spiky chimneys and three rows of flat black windows running along its front.

'It's quite small!' I said, just as Eric whispered, 'It's *huge*!' We stared at each other for a moment in confusion.

The car crunched over the drive and then stopped at the front door.

'We're here,' said Mr Scott, and Eric and I both jumped.

'Thank you,' said Eric politely.

Mr Scott sniffed at us, his yellow beard twitching. He had a big nose and a big face, and his single eye was mean and small, almost lost at the top of his cheek.

'Just doing my job,' he said. 'Now, before you go inside, some rules. You answer to Ruth, the maid. Mind your manners and don't annoy her. She's a good girl, but she's had a hard life, coming here alone – so don't add to it. Be polite to the Vereys, and remember Old Mr Verey may be the important one, but it's Old *Mrs* Verey who really runs the show. Best behaviour around her, otherwise you'll be out on your ears. That means no elbows on the table, no running in the corridors, and most importantly: no talking about the war.'

I stared at him, not sure I'd understood properly. We were supposed to be evacuees! How were we meant to not mention the war we'd been evacuated from?

Mr Scott carried on. 'When you're outside, though, you're in my domain. I'm the gardener here, and you'd better treat the grounds with respect. No running riot, no picking flowers and no scrumping apples. Do you hear me?'

We both nodded because he was glaring at us furiously.

'Good. I know what you evacuees are like. Noses in everything. Troublemakers. Well, I'll be watching you – remember that. Now go on – get out before you get more city muck on the leather.'

I was offended. I was perfectly clean (apart from London dust) and so was Eric. If anyone was dirty, it was Mr

Scott – when he took off his driving gloves, I could see black lines at the top of his nails and in the cracks on the palms of his hands. His beard was dirty too.

We got out (I went very slowly to be annoying, and Mr Scott growled at me) and stood side by side on the pebbly stones of the drive. Eric and I both reached for each other's hand at the same time – at that moment I didn't have to pretend to be nervous.

The front door opened. I was expecting to see a grown-up – the maid, the one Mr Scott had mentioned. But the person who stepped out didn't look any older than Eric. She was a bit taller than us, and she had a lot of tangly red-brown hair that hung down round her face. She wore a big pair of glasses, along with (I blinked) a long, flowing pink dress with a plaid waistcoat over it. Her feet were bare.

She stopped in surprise when she saw us, and then stared at us coldly. I drew myself up as tall as I could. I might be little but I'm fierce, and I don't like people looking down on me and judging me.

'*You* aren't the evacuees,' the girl said at last. Her voice was BBC radio English, and she spoke in such a rude, scornful way that I felt my face go red.

'Of course we are!' I said.

The girl's face went even colder and more snobby, and I thought I knew what she meant. Eric and I don't look like most people in England. We stand out, and English

32

people don't like that. I'm sick of it. The truth is that I look perfect, and all you need to do is spend one day in Hong Kong to be able to see that.

'Well, you're stuck with us,' I snapped. 'And, by the way, we didn't ask to be sent here, to this tiny—' I remembered just in time that I was not May Wong, who lived in the Big House on Robinson Road in Hong Kong, but ordinary May Lee, evacuated from her little bombed-out house in London. 'This *big*, ugly house in the middle of nowhere.'

'What's wrong with it?' asked the girl, and her face went red too.

'Nothing!' said Eric, squeezing my hand. 'May didn't mean it. It's nice to meet you. Thank you for having us.'

I wasn't done yet. 'There might not be anything wrong with the house. The people who live in it, though, are really rude.'

I felt Eric squeeze my hand even harder, but sometimes things just come out of my mouth without my being able to stop them. And sometimes I just look at a person and know that I hate them, and this was one of those times.

'Excuse me,' said the girl, looking at each of us in turn as though she wanted to freeze us to death with her eyes. 'I don't want to be here any more.'

And with that she turned and stalked away towards the trees, her long, slightly dirty bare feet pattering across the drive.

I felt breathless with loathing. I despised this girl.

'I hate her!' I snarled at Eric, as soon as she was out of earshot. 'She was so rude! She thinks she's better than us!'

'May!' said Eric. 'She wasn't very nice to us, but you can't just – we have to be *careful*. We mustn't attract attention until we find out what's going on. We're not even supposed to *be* here, remember? What if the War Office works out they've made a mistake? What if the Ministry finds us before we've completed the mission?'

I breathed out like a balloon being squeezed. I knew we'd only got here in the first place because of some overworked grown-ups, and I knew we might be discovered by Hazel at any moment – but that girl had made me so angry I'd forgotten all that.

Eric sometimes reminds me of Rose. He's so kind and sensible, and he's usually right, even when I don't want him to be – and I knew he was right now. Except—

'You can't make me be friends with her,' I said, glaring darkly after the girl. 'I'll never be friends with her, not ever.'

PART TWO

WE MEET OUR ENEMY

6

From the diary of Fionnuala O'Malley, age eleven
(and one month!), Elysium Hall, Coventry,
Warwickshire, England, Europe, the World

Wednesday 30th October 1940

Dear Diary,

I'm back again. I know I've been ignoring you lately, and
I'm really sorry. The last time I wrote anything was pretty
much years ago, when I was only a kid of nine, and the war
was brand new, and I thought we were all about to die any
day. I guess I'm still scared of dying, but the war's been
going on for so long now that I'm mostly just kind of tired.

Imagine, though, dying in *England*, in this cold house in
the middle of nowhere.

I can't stop wishing we hadn't come here after Da died.
Just think, we could still be in America with Orla, Megumi,
Jim and the rest of Da's theatre company, or even with my
Irish grandparents, Nana and Grandda O'Malley. I asked

to go to live with them, but Granny and Grandfather insisted on us moving here instead. And I think Mam was glad to agree. Da always said his family were never happy he married her. It's funny how little all of that seemed to matter when we were in America, but how much it matters now we've left.

Did you know there's no war in America or in Ireland? That means no rationing, no blackout, no planes buzzing overhead at night, no air-raid shelter or rows of vegetables where the lawn used to be. No being so scared you feel sick. In plays, war makes people noble, but in real life it just makes everyone mean.

That's the thing I've been feeling more and more, Diary: that the person I used to be, before the war, has gone away and left a much worse girl behind. For more than a year now, I've been really seriously trying to be nice and jolly and English and *good*, like the kids in an Enid Blyton book. I *did* use to be a good person, I'm sure I did, but now it just feels like I'm playing the character of one, and not even doing it very well. All my trying turns out to be *wrong* – too loud, too rude, too much. Sure, I think I'm not really the kind of granddaughter Granny and Grandfather were expecting.

Da would have said the Vereys have *notions* – they're obsessed with being polite, so I guess they were hoping for someone like my cousin Annabelle Olivia, someone with a nice accent and pretty clothes who always tries to be helpful. My dresses mostly used to be costumes, and they don't really fit, and I keep forgetting whether the words I'm saying are English, Irish or American. I've been trying to get my English accent right by listening to the radio, but I mess up all the time.

Maybe it's not just the war. I don't think being in this house helps. It's *nothing* like the ones in books about the English countryside, where there's plenty of food, and the adults are kind, and the kids get to have all the adventures they want. And the playing-a-character-badly feeling is made worse by the fact that Granny and Grandfather won't use my real name. They call me Fiona. They say it's because they can't pronounce Fionnuala, which is a lie. It's so easy. You just say *Fin-noo-la*, like that, and people in Da's theatre company, the O'Malley Players, used to call me Nuala, which is even easier. But I know the real reason: when they call me Fiona, they can pretend that there's only one part of me, the English part. Fionnuala belongs to the part that's like Da, and they don't want that. They think there's something wrong with being Irish here.

So I feel split in pieces. Sometimes I even imagine that the Fionnuala part of me is a separate person, still on tour with Da's company, in theatres and hotels and on boats and trains, travelling all over America and round the world.

Anyway, there's a reason I decided to write in you again, Diary. Elysium Hall's got two new evacuees, and there's something funny about them. Something not right at all. I swear I'm not making this up.

They arrived by the first train on Sunday 27ᵗʰ October. When I heard Ruth on the telephone, being told that evacuees were coming to Elysium Hall again, I was so excited. We had two evacuees last year, just after the war started and everybody was expecting the bombs to fall any time: Bob and Bert from London. They were both pale and skinny, and they swore very loudly when they saw the sheep in the long field. Granny pursed her lips and said swearing was common, but it made me like them. The sheep had surprised me too when we first arrived.

Once Bob and Bert calmed down about the sheep, they were a lot of fun, even if they hadn't ever been to any London theatres (that was the first thing I asked). They had some great stories about where they lived – a place called Poplar. They knew good games too. We used to go down to the abandoned cottage at the edge of the grounds and play. Sometimes we were kids who'd run away to a secret place to live on our own, and sometimes we were Hitler and Chamberlain bombing each other. Sometimes the pretending got kind of violent, and once we ended up smashing a hole in one of the cottage windows.

When Granny found out, she gave out to me for being bold and ruining family property (even though the cottage was already a ruin!). She sent Scott to mend the window, and he stormed around with his tools for days, so we couldn't play there any more. When Mam was told, she sighed, told me to *be good* (sounding more like Granny than she ever had before: Da would be turning in his grave if he heard her accent now) and went back to bed.

I don't know which I hated more.

But I was still so happy while Bob and Bert were around. They didn't fit in, just like me. I thought I finally had friends in England, and I hoped they'd never leave – but I should have known that it never works out that way. Everyone always leaves.

By Christmastime last year, no bombs had fallen, and so Bob and Bert's mothers wanted them home. I almost didn't have time to say goodbye. We'd made up a festive play together (well, I'd written it and was going to direct it, and they were supposed to act in it) and they didn't even get to stay for that.

So, when I heard there were evacuees coming to Elysium Hall again, I was expecting we'd get Bob and Bert back. I wanted to show them the room in the cottage that I'd set up as a theatre, with chairs I'd rescued from the spare room and done up nicely. I had so many new plays for us to perform. But when I went out to meet them last Sunday, they weren't Bob and Bert at all.

I keep thinking about that moment. I think I might have messed it up, and now it's too late to take it back. I know I was disappointed that they weren't Bob and Bert. When I'm like that, I get shy, and when I'm shy I go all cold and frozen. I can feel it happening, but it's so hard to stop it. And I'm not usually very good with new people my age.

I spoke in my most ridiculous English accent, and I just remember the girl's face getting redder and redder and more outraged. I didn't know how to fix it, so I ran away. I've been avoiding speaking to them ever since.

But maybe it's a good thing that I didn't try to make friends with them. I know if I said this to anyone else but you, Diary, they'd laugh at me. But – and this is the long and the short of it – there's something very, very strange about the pair of them.

They're up to something.

And I want to find out what it is.

7

From the diary of Fionnuala O'Malley, continued

This is what I've noticed about the evacuees. This is why I think something's going on.

The girl's name is May, and she's obviously the leader. She's tiny, and she's fierce and mean. She's always stomping around, glaring at me and saying awful things – she thinks she's saying them under her breath, but she's actually really loud. I *think* she's Chinese. I went to Peking once, with Mam and Da and the Company, but I was only a little kid, so I don't remember much about it.

The boy's called Eric. He's always carrying some animal around – the other day he pulled a grass snake out of his pocket in the middle of lunch. He acts really quiet and serious – until he's talking with May. Then he whispers and whispers and never shuts up. Also, yesterday I went into the library and heard him and Ruth talking. In *German*! I'm sure it was German: I've heard enough of it on that

43

awful radio station Uncle Sidney listens to when he thinks no one's around.

They stopped when they saw me and acted really guilty, so I knew I'd heard something important. Eric has dark skin, so he doesn't look like the kind of blond-haired, blue-eyed Germans you see at the movies – but I've been to Germany too, and I know that not all Germans look the way they do on film.

May and Eric have spent the last few days writing notes to each other in lessons – if you can call them lessons. Granny's been teaching me because she doesn't think it's safe for me to go to school in Coventry in case it's bombed, and since the evacuees arrived she's started teaching them too. Granny's teaching style is mostly telling us to be quiet.

The notes are *absolutely* not to do with schoolwork, and I don't think they're jokes, either – they always look really serious when they're reading and writing them. They're very careful to rip them up afterwards too, so I've never been able to get hold of one.

The evacuees also keep appearing in places they shouldn't be. They spend loads of time hanging around outside the adults' rooms, and whenever any of the family makes a telephone call from the hallway one of the evacuees will always *happen* to be nearby. I caught them coming out of the study on their first morning here, and everyone knows that's out of bounds to kids. Grandfather is really serious about that – it's where he does all his important magistrate work.

When we're allowed outside (only after breakfast and lunch for an hour at a time; if we're longer than that, Granny gets worried), they're always poking into everything and annoying Scott. This tells me they're seriously brave, as well as suspicious, because Scott is scary and doesn't like kids – he thinks we're all trying to steal vegetables out of his Dig for Victory beds and fruit from the orchard.

They even managed to follow Uncle Sidney into the village during our outside time on Tuesday – which, again, was incredibly brave because when Uncle Sidney noticed them lurking by the pub he dragged them both home by their collars and flung them inside the house, roaring that he was going to have their heads. It was a joke, I know, because he was laughing when he said it, and Granny just sent them to bed without supper.

But it also wasn't a joke, in the confusing way that Uncle Sidney's jokes usually aren't. Like when he teases Ruth about light-fingered foreigners and nothing in the house being safe any more. One time, Ruth got so upset that she dropped a vase, and Granny asked Uncle Sidney whether *he* wanted to make all our meals and clean the carpets. Then Uncle Sidney shut up, but sometimes I still come across him whispering nasty things to Ruth. He says mean things to me too, about Irish people and Da. I don't want to write them down here. They're too horrible.

Somehow I've ended up talking more about Uncle Sidney than the evacuees, but they're the ones I need to watch, not my own family. I guess I'm probably wrong about Uncle Sidney, anyway, since he's clever and an adult and a politician, and I'm just a kid.

But this is why I know I'm *not* wrong about the evacuees. Today I came out of the bathroom on the first floor and saw that the door to the spare room across the landing, the one I took the chairs from, was open a little, and voices were coming out of it. I crept up to it and peeked through the crack – and there were May and Eric, crouched over a notebook and whispering together. Eric murmured something I couldn't catch, and May said in her blaring whisper, 'Well, SOMEONE is!'

Eric murmured again – and then I did catch a word, and I gasped because it was the one word that makes me go cold all over: '*Nazi*.'

So the thing they're up to is to do with the war. That's why I've decided I need to act like a detective to work out exactly what it is.

I've watched plays about detectives and read books about them, so I knew exactly how to be one. The first thing I had to do was find the right costume. It's important to commit to the role – Da always said so – and that means looking the part.

There was nothing in the wardrobe in my room that looked right, so after lessons were over today I went digging round Mam's while she was half asleep in bed. Since Da died, she rests after lunch most days. And after breakfast and supper too.

In among her old costumes and party dresses I found the most perfect outfit: a dark blue dress with a patterned scarf that looks exactly like what Nancy Drew wears on the front of *The Secret of the Old Clock*. I put it on and stood in front of the mirror, and – this is the magic of costume – I felt myself *becoming* Nancy: smart, confident, fun and much older than eleven. I even brushed my hair so it curled round my ears like hers.

Then I took a pencil and paper from my room, in case I needed to take notes. I put them in a bag, along with a flashlight and my bar of chocolate, and finally snuck downstairs to steal the magnifying glass out of the library. Ruth went hurrying by, carrying a pile of linen, too busy to notice me, but no one else was around. I worked out why when I heard the rumble of a car out front. I guessed that someone had come to visit, and they were all outside greeting whoever it was.

But I couldn't care about that. I was going to track down my targets.

8

From the diary of Fionnuala O'Malley, continued

I stuck my head out of the drawing-room window and saw
May and Eric creeping away down the garden together.

As fast and quiet as I could, I ran out through the
kitchen door at the back of the house. It was raining
softly, so I could track their footprints in the grass. There
were two sets spidering away across the remains of the
green lawn, between the victory beds, round the grassy
lump of the Anderson shelter, through the dark box
hedges and heading off to the right, into the tangle of
the orchard.

Like I said, kids aren't supposed to go into the orchard
in case we scrump apples. Scott is really strict about that. I
don't know why – the grass is covered with the ones that
have come down in the wind and have little freckles of
worm-dirt spreading out across them. They're falling faster
than Scott can pick up or Ruth can cook up, but we're still
not supposed to have them. I think kids are just not

supposed to have things sometimes, here in England. It makes no sense to me, but nothing does.

I took off my shoes and slipped from tree to tree, following the press of feet. I really was Nancy Drew tracking the bad guys. I stepped carefully and tried to be as cool and in control as possible.

Then I heard a branch crack up ahead, and a voice hiss, '*Careful!*'

I looked round a tree trunk – my cheek brushing against its scratchy greenish bark – and I saw them: May halfway up the apple tree that hangs right over the edge of the orchard, almost into the rose garden, and Eric on the ground below her, his expression anxious. May's hair was caught on a branch, and her face was red with effort as she tried to untangle herself.

Finally, she pulled free and gestured for Eric to follow her up. He climbed more slowly and carefully. I've noticed that everything Eric does is careful, but not like he's afraid, more like he's always paying close attention. When he's concentrating, he folds his top lip over his bottom one and frowns. He looks kind of like a turtle when he does it.

They perched next to each other on the branch, their eyes focused on something over the top of the orchard wall, and then May pulled the little notebook I'd seen before out of her coat pocket and started making notes in it.

I had to know what they were looking at. So I stealthily hauled myself up through the branches of the tree I'd been

49

hiding behind. As Nuala, I get scared of heights, but as Nancy I was fearless. I climbed as high as I could and stopped for a second, leaves turning round me and the heaviness of apples knocking against my forehead and arms.

And then I saw why May and Eric were here.

Two people were in the rose garden. Their shapes were dim in the thickening darkness, but when they spoke I could hear them pretty well. One of them was Uncle Sidney.

'So Mother's prevailed on you to come and stay at last.' He sounded sulky.

'It's not safe in the city at the moment. It seemed prudent for us all to accept her invitation.'

I knew that voice too – it was Uncle Hugh. He's the second-oldest brother, after Uncle Sidney, and he stays at Elysium Hall most weekends. So that was who'd been arriving in the car! Uncle Hugh and Aunt Pam and my cousin Annabelle Olivia live a few miles away, in the centre of Coventry, in a fancy house right by the cathedral. Uncle Hugh owns a factory that usually makes cars, but now that there's a war on it's making important secret stuff for the army. I don't think I'm supposed to know that.

Uncle Sidney snorted rudely. 'Ever the prudent one. Sure it's got nothing to do with money? Struggling to keep Pam in new clothes and Annabelle Olivia at her ludicrously pricy school? Last I heard from Pam, there were . . . difficulties.'

'It's not that! Do stop talking to her about me behind my back. She's *my* wife.' There was a moment of angry silence, then a grumble from Uncle Hugh. 'Although . . . well, if you must know, expenses *have* been piling up. Taxes, you know, and Annabelle Olivia's school fees keep on climbing, and Pamela – she likes the best of everything. And the government are behind with their payments for the factory's work. *Bureaucracy.* If I don't get a cash injection soon—'

Uncle Sidney gave a bark of laughter. 'Good luck trying to wring money out of this ridiculous coalition government!' he said. 'Although it won't matter soon, anyway. The invasion's imminent.'

'Do you really think so?'

'Yes, it's certainly coming,' said Uncle Sidney. 'The only question is when. The fifth column's here already, don't you know? It can't happen soon enough.'

I felt chilled with worry. No one tells kids anything, not to our faces, but I've been hearing more and more adults saying scary stuff – like the Nazis are on their way, and maybe some of them are already here, disguised as ordinary people while they wait for the rest of the army to turn up. That's what Uncle Sidney meant by *the fifth column.*

I'm pretty sure I wasn't supposed to know about that, either.

And I suddenly wondered if that was the answer. Were the evacuees German spies? Were they *fifth columnists*, here to spy on the house and tell Berlin all about us?

But why?

Uncle Sidney went on. 'Anyway, enough about that. What's so important that you couldn't say it in front of Mother and Father?'

'You know perfectly well.'

Uncle Sidney paused for a moment. 'You got my letter, then.'

'I did. Are you *sure*?'

'As sure as I can be. I'm still looking for absolute confirmation, but from what I overheard him telling Mother last week, it's serious. Terminal, I think.'

'So Father's *dying*?' said Uncle Hugh. 'Good grief! How could he not tell us?'

I had to grab the branch I was sitting on. What was he talking about? Grandfather wasn't sick. At least, no one had told me he was. Suddenly secrets were unfolding all around me. I know I'd been pretending to be Nancy Drew, but I hadn't expected to get stuck in a real-life Nancy Drew situation.

Uncle Sidney snorted again. 'God forbid either of them should discuss important things with their family. I shouldn't think Mother will bother to mention it until the day of his funeral.'

'Don't be disgusting, Sid.' Another pause from Uncle Hugh. 'I, ah, suppose you're already looking to the inheritance?'

I dug my fingers into the green mould of the tree branch.

I felt kind of dizzy. I hate thinking about people even getting sick now – and I couldn't believe that my uncles could be so cold about Grandfather dying. *Dying!*

'Why shouldn't I? It's not like he's my real father, after all. It's different for you. But then again you do need money, don't you?'

'This is *Father* we're talking about,' said Uncle Hugh. 'Money hardly matters!' But he sounded unconvincing.

'Just wait until he *is* gone!' said Uncle Sidney, laughing. 'You won't turn your nose up at some cash then!'

How could they be talking like this – as though Grandfather wasn't important? I decided then that I'd be extra nice to him now that I knew. I wish that I'd known what was going to happen to Da. I'd have been nicer to him every single day.

Uncle Hugh grumbled a curse word, and then he turned and stomped away. Uncle Sidney laughed to himself again – he finds a lot of strange things funny, like I said – and then strode after him.

After a couple of seconds, I heard the evacuees in the next tree start to climb down. And that was when I made my mistake. I guess I was too eager – or maybe my mind was just racing from what I'd heard. Grandfather was dying? Uncle Hugh was here to stay, and he needed money? And Uncle Sidney was waiting for the Nazis to invade, and he almost sounded . . . excited about it?

I started to move while May was still hanging halfway out of the tree and Eric was hovering below her, trying to guide her to safety.

'I'm FINE!' she snarled – and then Eric caught sight of me and yelled, and May fell straight out of the tree on top of him.

9

From the diary of Fionnuala O'Malley, continued

Eric didn't cry, even though I know it must have hurt him, and May didn't apologize. She just rolled off him and said, 'What's wrong with you, Eric? Don't shout like that!'

I hated her even more. As soon as I thought that, I felt my Nancy Drew act slipping away from me, because Nancy would never be so mean. But I *feel* mean around May.

'It was *her*!' said Eric, pointing at me with one hand and brushing dirty green mould off his sweater with the other.

'YOU!' May snarled, on her knees in the long grass of the orchard, fists clenched. 'What are you DOING here?'

I felt myself blushing. I can't help it – I blush so easily. Da was the same. I go so pink that my freckles disappear. I didn't know what to say. I suddenly realized that I'd tracked them here, and so *I* looked like I was spying on *them*, instead of watching *them* spy on my uncles. I had that creeping feeling you get when you know you're wrong but you don't want to admit it. So I drew myself up tall and reminded myself what Da always told me: that when I feel shy, or scared, or unsettled, I just have to be someone else. I just have to *pretend*, as hard as I can, until my whole body believes it.

The person I usually pretend to be when I want to be cold and ruthless and fierce is someone called Gráinne Ní Mháille. She was an Irish pirate queen, and she gave no quarter. Da used to say that we might even be related to her, since we have almost the same last name. I imagine her standing with the sea beneath her and the wind in her skirts, afraid of absolutely nothing.

So I gave May and Eric my best Gráinne stare, and I said, as haughtily as I could, 'Why shouldn't I be here, so? It's *my* family's orchard.'

'You're not allowed to be here any more than we are!' said May. 'And what's wrong with your accent?'

'Sure, I always sound like this,' I said, my voice dripping ice.

Maybe that's not totally true – when I'm doing my Gráinne character, I sound more like Da – but May had no right to notice. 'And I'm only here because you were first. What are *you* doing? Are you *spying*?'

'SPYING!' cried May, her face going just as red as mine felt. 'How dare you! As if we ever would! We were playing a game, only you can't join in because we don't allow stuck-up snobs to play. Isn't that right, Eric?'

I thought I'd hit on something. May was raging, the way people get when you've said something true.

'Do you *want* to play with us?' asked Eric quietly.

He was rubbing his chest where May had fallen on it, and staring at me with thoughtful eyes. It made me uncomfortable – as though he could see through my Gráinne act – and so I stood up even straighter, as though there was steel in my spine.

'I'm too old to play games,' I said. 'Games are for little kids. I only want to know what you're doing in *my* orchard.'

I knew I was saying the wrong thing again. It isn't my orchard, and Granny and Grandfather (and Scott) would be furious if they knew I was in it. May was right about that.

'Trying to get away from you,' hissed May. 'Obviously.'

'Then why were you listening in on Uncle Sidney and Uncle Hugh?'

'There was a . . . a bird in the tree,' said Eric. 'We thought it might be hurt. We didn't even notice your uncles were there, and we didn't hear anything, anyway.'

Their stories didn't fit together, and this was also clearly a lie. I knew it, and he knew it, and I was going to tell him so – but then we all heard someone running through the garden towards the orchard, making an awful lot of noise.

'FIONA!' they cried. '*FIII-OHHH-NAA!*'

'Who's that?' asked May, screwing up her face.

'That's my cousin,' I said, my heart sinking.

'Well!' said May. 'Aren't you lucky. *All* your family are here now.'

She said it really bitterly, and I couldn't work out why. There's nothing worse than being surprised by Annabelle Olivia. She's a few years younger than me, and she's a snitch. If you tell her anything, it'll get back to the adults in no time. She's everyone's little pet, and Granny is always trying to get me to play with her – but, if I do, she always just tells Granny every rule I've broken.

'FIONA! EVACUEES! Where ARE YOU?' Annabelle Olivia was yelling, her voice really proud and important. 'Granny says it's TEATIME, and you have to come in AT ONCE otherwise you'll MISS IT. You're not SUPPOSED to be OUT HERE – it's against the RULES!'

May made a horrified face. I caught her eye and almost slipped out of my cold act and smiled at her – but then I remembered that I didn't like her and Eric any more than I did Annabelle Olivia.

'You'd better go in and change,' I said, icier than ever. 'You're all over dirt.'

'Same to you,' snapped May, back to her usual nastiness. 'Come on, Eric!'

She grabbed him by the hand and started to tow him out of the orchard. He looked back at me with the same sharp, serious look he'd given me before, and it was a real struggle to stay aloof.

Once they'd gone, I looked down at myself and saw that my dress had smears of green bark across it.

At least Mam won't notice, I thought – but that made me mad because she *should* notice, shouldn't she?

When we first arrived here, I was really bold, for weeks, to try to get her to punish me. But she never did – she just stayed in bed – and now I've given up. She was never like this when Da was alive. He made her brave enough to act in front of thousands of people and smart enough to help get the Company halfway across the world. But now he's gone and so has she.

I was about to follow May and Eric inside, but before I did I stopped and thought. There's a war on, after all. Things that seemed impossible once are real now every day.

The evacuees weren't just *being suspicious.* They were *actually* watching people at Elysium Hall. They really were *spying,* just as I'd thought. But why? What did they think they were going to find out? And what was I going to do about it?

10

On the morning Eric and I arrived at Elysium Hall, we had barely stepped through the front door behind Ruth the maid (dark hair, pale, thin face and something sharp and angry just beneath her surface) when we met Sidney Foley. He was a tall grown-up, with the sort of nothing-coloured hair that so many English people have, and he stood at the top of the stairs in the wide stone hall and smirked down at us as though he'd thought of a really good joke.

I decided I didn't like him any more than the girl we'd just met outside – and then he spoke, and I was absolutely sure of it.

'Take care of them, Ruth,' he said, quirking an eyebrow. 'They look like trouble. But you'd know about that, wouldn't you? Just make sure *they* put back what they steal, eh?'

Steal? I was furious. How dare he! I've never stolen anything in my life, apart from the things I *needed* to, like

Rose's money. Thinking about Rose made me feel creepingly guilty, and *that* made me angrier than ever.

I looked at Ruth – and saw that she was as angry as I felt. Her dark eyes blazed with fury as she stared up at Sidney, and her thin hands clenched round our suitcase handles. The next second, though, she had smoothed out again.

'Very funny, Mr Sidney,' she said calmly. She had an accent, a little like Eric's. 'Come along, Eric, May. I'll show you to your rooms.'

'We don't steal things,' said Eric earnestly to Ruth as she led us up the dark, curving back stairs. 'We would never steal anything.'

'Of course you wouldn't, Liebchen,' said Ruth, putting down our cases suddenly in the middle of a gloomy landing. We were right at the very top of the house now, where the servants' rooms were, and I was a bit shocked by that until I reminded myself for the second time that day that I *wasn't* May Wong from the Big House any more.

'That was just Mr Sidney's joke. But *stay away* from him.' She turned to us quickly and looked us both right in the eye. 'Do you hear me? He doesn't like people *like us.*'

I glanced at Eric, and we both nodded.

'Good. Now this is your room here, Eric. May, you're next door with Fiona. Fiona is Mrs O'Malley's child – Mrs O'Malley is Old Mr and Mrs Verey's daughter, back from America. Her husband died last year.

'Old Mr Verey is a very important person, a magistrate. Don't ever go into his study. Do you understand? And stay quiet. You must be seen and not heard when he's around.

'Mr Sidney Foley –' I thought I could see her arranging her face carefully as she spoke about him again – 'he's Old Mrs Verey's son from before she married Old Mr Verey. He's staying with the family while London is being bombed. It's *safe* here, you see.'

Ruth began to explain about Elysium Hall's schedule, but I was only half listening. Then she said something that felt important.

'There's one more thing to remember. Old Mrs Verey doesn't like anyone – *anyone* – to talk about the war. She lost her first husband and her eldest son in wars, so it upsets her.'

This seemed very odd – although I remembered Mr Scott had told us the same thing earlier. Was this a clue?

'But what if there's an air raid?' asked Eric.

'Then of course you'd go into the air-raid shelter in the garden,' said Ruth. 'But only for a real raid. The sirens in the village are always being set off by mistake. And I manage the ration books so that she doesn't have to. You lost yours in London, didn't you? We'll have to apply for new ones. Oh, and remember to leave your gas masks under your beds. Now clean yourselves up and come downstairs for lunch.'

Once she was gone, Eric began to obediently wash his hands and face in the basin in the corner of his room.

'Oh, leave that!' I said impatiently. 'Come on, we've got to start investigating!'

What I didn't say to Eric was that I needed to distract myself. If Ruth was going to be applying for new ration books in our made-up names, we'd have to complete our mission before she found out we didn't exist. But something else she'd told us had just fallen into place. *Fiona.* Mrs O'Malley's daughter, which made her Old Mr and Mrs Verey's granddaughter. She had to be that hateful girl we'd just met.

And I was sharing a room with her.

Unmasking the spy at Elysium Hall felt even more hush-hush now we knew that we weren't even supposed to talk about the war. When I saw Old Mrs Verey (she passed us on the stairs, glaring disapprovingly, and said 'Shush!' even though I was walking as quietly as I could), I felt doubly sneaky and a bit curious too.

'I don't think she can be passing information to the Germans,' I said to Eric, 'if she won't even talk about them!'

'It might be a trick,' suggested Eric, but he didn't sound convinced.

Then we suspected Old Mr Verey, especially after he burst out of his study on the ground floor as we were walking past it and glared at us from beneath two enormous white eyebrows. He was big and heavy, with a red, important face. 'Do be quiet,' he said. 'I'm doing *serious* work.'

We managed to slip out of breakfast early and into the study while Old Mr Verey was still eating, so we could investigate him. But we discovered nothing but very dusty, boring piles of legal papers.

'I don't think there are any clues here,' I said to Eric, disappointed. 'What *is* a magistrate, anyway?'

'What are you two doing?' asked horrible Fiona, sticking her head round the door. 'You shouldn't be in here – it's private.'

I made a face at her. We'd managed to avoid speaking to each other for the whole of our first night at Elysium Hall, me staring stonily at the ceiling from underneath my scratchy blanket. 'We're just curious,' I said.

'A magistrate's like a judge, by the way,' said Fiona. 'It's really important. *Grandfather's* really important.'

Pride lit up her face, and I rolled my eyes. 'Teacher's pet,' I said.

'Trespasser,' said Fiona.

'*Bore*,' I said.

'*Sleeveen*,' hissed Fiona. I didn't know what that meant, but I thought it was probably bad.

'Hurry up – he's coming!' said Eric.

We ran.

So we were fairly sure that Old Mr Verey wasn't the spy. He was practically the opposite – he was *too* honest. He went round each night, looking for gaps in the blackout, and made Ruth show him the ration books every week. Ruth told Eric that he didn't even let her barter apples from the orchard for nice things like butter outside the ration.

But Eric and I didn't mind for long, because that evening we finally came upon something extremely suspicious: Sidney Foley's radio programme.

It was after dinner on Monday, and we were supposed to be getting ready for bed while Ruth tidied up. But Fiona was brushing her teeth, and I refused to be anywhere she was, so Eric and I were loitering on the stairs until she'd finished in the bathroom. Then we both heard it: the squeal of a wireless being tuned downstairs, and then a burst of someone speaking *German.*

I jumped. 'Eric!' I hissed.

'I know!' he gasped.

We both crept down the stairs, listening furiously. The noises were coming from the drawing room, and suddenly the German words changed to English. The person speaking was a man with a posh, nasal voice, and he was talking about the fact that Hitler was winning the war, and bombs were hitting London, and people were dying.

As we listened, Eric's face grew bleak, and I remembered that his mother was still in London and so was Big Sister Hazel. I wanted to plug my ears, but I made myself keep on hearing the words, squeezing all my fear up like a fist, because if we're going to lose I want to know about it. I want to see it coming so I'm not surprised. I think being surprised is the worst thing that can happen to a person.

Then Old Mrs Verey came charging down the stairs, awfully quick for someone so old. She rushed past without even noticing us, her face flushed and her eyes glittering, and burst into the drawing room.

'SIDNEY!' she cried. 'Turn that racket off! I told you – I told you – I don't want any of that war talk in this house!'

Then out came Old Mr Verey from his study, looking just as cross as his wife. 'Sidney!' he bellowed. 'Listen to your mother! Turn off that programme immediately! It's unpatriotic filth!'

The awful nasal voice was cut off, and Sidney appeared. He looked sulky and annoyed, like a little boy. 'I don't see why I shouldn't listen,' he said. 'Plenty of fellows think the way I do.'

'I don't want to hear it,' said Old Mr Verey. 'Don't upset your mother, Sidney. You know what we agreed. Don't – mention – the – war.'

And there it was. There was one person here who was very obviously interested in what the Germans were doing, who was sneaky and mean and an all-round excellent

66

suspect: Sidney Foley. If anyone was selling secrets to Germany, it was him.

So we began to follow him.

After lunch on Friday, our sixth day at Elysium Hall, we followed Sidney all the way into the centre of the village just over the river.

We almost lost him in a crowd of people doing air-raid casualty practice, lying about in the road and pretending to be injured while other people bandaged them up. But we tracked his loud voice and his smart suit and hat as he wove through the crowd and fell into step with two men in dark clothes. This was extremely suspicious.

The three of them ducked into a pub called the Rose and Crown, which was very annoying. Children can't go into pubs, not even children on spying missions. But I climbed up onto Eric's shoulders and peered through a little mullioned window to see Sidney and the two men whispering together.

I gasped, and Eric wobbled and said, 'May!'

'Stay still! I'm trying to look!'

'I can't! *Verflixt!* It's Mr Scott!' Eric gasped, and I looked round to see that he was right.

Mr Scott the gardener was coming out of the telephone box at the end of the lane. We both froze in horror, and I slid right off Eric's shoulders and onto the ground. We were waiting for Mr Scott to bellow at us for being out of bounds – but he just clung more tightly to the big bag he was carrying and rushed past us as though he hadn't seen us. But I was certain he had.

We were mystified – and then Sidney Foley glanced at the window and locked eyes with me.

He came roaring out of the pub, dragged us home and we were sent to bed without supper. I thought that was very unfair. But I was also excited because I was sure we'd found our spy. When we'd overheard the conversation between him and his brother Hugh in the orchard, it felt as though our mission was almost over.

And then the hauntings started.

PART THREE

WE ARE HAUNTED

11

From the diary of Fionnuala O'Malley

Saturday 2nd November 1940

Dear Diary,

There's a ghost at Elysium Hall. Part of me is certain it's all a trick – I've seen it done with mirrors onstage all the time – but I know that sometimes ghosts are real. And I think this one might be.

We were at dinner when it happened.

The air-raid siren had just gone off in the village, and we heard it across the fields. A yelp and then a rising howl, up and down, filling the air. We all looked at Granny.

See, the thing about Granny is that she's *terrified* of the war. Her first husband, Mr Foley, died in the Second Boer War (a very old war), and then her eldest son, Leonard Foley (the first husband's son, not Grandfather's), died in the last war. So she doesn't like to be reminded that we're at war again, and, when she is, sometimes she's so frightened that she gets very, very angry.

There's an Anderson shelter in the garden, but we only go in there when we *have* to – and the rule is that we're not allowed to without Granny saying we can. Granny likes to feel safe at Elysium Hall, protected from the war and from the whole world, and the shelter is a reminder that nowhere is safe, not really. She only agreed to have it put up because the air-raid warden told Grandfather that it was against the rules not to have one.

Ruth had just come into the dining room with the main course (beef and onions with no onions because there aren't any right now). She paused, tea towel in her hands, and we all waited to hear what Granny would say.

'Don't get up,' said Granny at last. 'We're safe here. Ruth, the beef, please. As I was saying, Sidney, would you get me some more wool when you go into the village tomorrow? I've almost got through it all.'

'But the siren!' said Aunt Pam, standing up from the table and looking perplexed.

She and Uncle Hugh and Annabelle Olivia have been here for four days now. The house feels much more crowded with them in it.

She wrung her hands together, spinning the ring on her finger round and round nervously. Aunt Pam really hates being here, I can tell. She gets changed five times a day, just to have something to do, and she's always complaining about all the parties she's missing in Coventry. 'What if it's a real raid?'

'Sit *down*,' said Granny. 'This house is quite safe, I tell you.'

'But what if there *is* a bomb?' said Annabelle Olivia, tugging on one of the corkscrew curls that Aunt Pam puts into her hair each night.

'That's enough!' said Grandfather. He knows that Granny's irrational about the shelter, but he loves her, so he backs her up. 'We are not a target. We're quite safe.'

'Do I have to keep on reminding you, Annabelle Olivia, that little children should be seen and not heard? Listen to your elders,' Granny added.

This is the problem with being a kid. Even when you know you're right, and the adult is wrong, there's nothing you can do about it.

'Yes, Granny,' said Annabelle Olivia anxiously.

But, in that way that an idea gets stuck in your head the minute you're told not to think about it, Aunt Pam spoke up again.

'Are you quite sure?' she asked, fiddling with her ring again. 'If we were at home, we'd be in the shelter by now. The government says—'

'Buck up, Pammy,' said Uncle Sidney, laughing at her. 'I've been in enough meetings to know that the government doesn't know *what* it's saying or why. Anyway, it'll all be over soon. The invasion's coming, and then we won't have to worry about bombs any more. Or about undesirables and surplus people using up this country's resources, either. I've said for years that England needs a clear-out, so really we ought to welcome—'

I squirmed in my seat. *Undesirables and surplus people* – I hate it when Uncle Sidney says stuff like that because I know he means people like *me*, Diary, and Ruth, who's from Austria, and even the evacuees. And I just don't think he's right, even if he is clever and an adult.

'SIDNEY!' said Grandfather over the wail of the siren. 'NO war talk at the table!'

We were all turned towards Grandfather – the candlelight (just one candle these days, so the room's almost dark) hollowing out his cheeks and making him look even more imposing than usual – when a plate WHIPPED up off the sideboard and slammed into the wall right behind Uncle Sidney's head.

Ruth's mouth formed an O of shock, and the beef she was holding jumped on its plate. Aunt Pam screamed and Annabelle Olivia shouted, 'A GHOST! MUMMY!'

Granny said, 'Don't be silly!' and Grandfather said, 'Good lord, whoever did that, own up at once!'

Uncle Hugh said, 'If you evacuees are causing trouble—' and Uncle Sidney said something that's a curse word, so I'd better not put it in here.

Another plate went flying then, like a toy plane, skimming over the table and shattering against the wallpaper. Grandfather bellowed, 'STOP THAT!'

'This is preposterous behaviour!' said Granny, as though the ghost was a bold, bad kid.

She was glaring down the table at us, and I think she must have thought it was one of the evacuees throwing things – but I know for sure it wasn't. They were sitting right next to me, and they didn't move.

I looked round the table, and through the gloom saw the shapes of everyone still seated – and Ruth, caught in the candlelight with her platter of beef.

We waited, sitting in silence, but nothing else happened. Finally, Granny said, 'Whoever did that, we will get to the bottom of it, and I can assure you that you'll be punished. Now, Ruth, serve up, please, or the beef will be wasted.'

Everyone else sort of shook themselves and tried to go back to eating (the siren still howling away over the fields), but I could tell that they were all frightened.

I went back down to the dining room later, once dinner was over and Ruth had swept up the bits of broken plate. I was supposed to be in bed, but I couldn't sleep. To trick May, I pretended to be going to the bathroom, and tiptoed down the stairs.

I looked closely where the plates had been thrown. I could still see the scratches they'd made in the wallpaper as they shattered.

I couldn't see how anyone could throw a plate without *looking* like they were throwing it. I couldn't work out how the trick had been done. So the ghost has to be real.

12

From the report of May Wong

I was obviously not afraid of the ghost. Ghosts in England are weak compared to the ones in Hong Kong. Hong Kong ghosts can actually eat you, and they do – I've heard our maids at home talking about it – but English ghosts just howl like dogs and jangle their bones at you, and who's frightened of that?

However, I had to admit that this ghost was doing more than just jangling. On the first night, the night of the air-raid siren, it threw two plates at dinner. The next day it was a teacup, which came flying out of the sideboard during breakfast, and then after that—

After that, it was as though the house was alive.

Chairs keeled over, and spoons flew at people's heads, and paperweights sailed through the air during cocktail hour and made the grown-ups scream.

'But ghosts aren't real,' Eric said to me – which offended me. They may not be real in Germany, but they are in

Hong Kong. He sighed. 'Oh, all right. At least you're enjoying it.'

I was. I *loved* it.

Elysium Hall had felt so stiff and wrong. Everyone had been pretending, all the time, for Old Mrs Verey's sake. I'd never come across a family so obsessed with covering up the truth. But the ghost laid things bare. It made everything suddenly exciting and out of control, full of life and as dangerous as our mission. And it began to show us the real Vereys: angry, frustrated, confused and scared.

Eric and I worked harder than ever. We listened in at doors and to telephone conversations. We heard Hugh Verey speaking to the people at his factory (they always seemed to need more money) and watched him coming back from the village, smelling sourly of beer and looking cross, and Old Mr Verey discussing cases he was trying (people breaking blackout mostly, or stealing things from houses while families were sheltering during raids; there was even one case where someone had attacked their neighbour in the dark because they thought they were a German spy).

We looked carefully round the grounds in case the spy had left any messages for the Germans there, but all we found was a hedgehog in danger of being scorched in one of Mr Scott's bonfires.

'He should have checked before he lit it!' Eric said, cradling the hedgehog in his arms. 'He's not paying attention!'

And then, a few days later, on Tuesday the fifth of November, a new person arrived at Elysium Hall.

Eric and I heard some commotion in the hall just after breakfast and quickly found places to hide – me tucked into the alcove by the front door, and Eric under the telephone table – just as Mr Scott, looking even more sour and resentful than usual, drove up to the front door in the Vereys' old black Rolls, gravel crunching beneath the tyres. Out of the car climbed a skinny, plain-looking man in army uniform with a captain's stripes. He was a bit too small for it – it bagged round the elbows and knees – and his moustache wasn't very well trimmed. He looked like a thin, sad, falling-apart version of Sidney or Hugh – which is how I knew they were all brothers.

Old Mrs Verey put her knitting into the bag she kept underneath her usual chair in the hall and went hurrying out to meet him, gesturing for Ruth to take his case, but this new Verey brother hardly greeted his mother at all. He gave her a brief kiss and then went bounding past her into the house, looking around urgently.

'Neil!' said Old Mrs Verey. 'I'm so glad you could get away, but I thought you wouldn't be here until next week—'

'I couldn't wait, Mother!' said the new Verey, Neil. 'Hugh sent a telegram and told me what was going on. I came as soon as I could get leave. I believe *Leonard is back*. It's been years—'

'Neil!' said Old Mrs Verey, sounding cross and hurt. 'Please. I've told you, I don't – you mustn't – you *know* it's not Leonard.'

'But, Mother!' said Neil Verey, his moustache twitching. 'Who else could it be? You know he appeared to me after his death. If he's back now – and with new powers – it means something. Sidney's up to his old ways, I expect?'

He suddenly sounded bitter.

'*Neil*,' said Old Mrs Verey. 'Sidney means well. I don't want you starting up your rivalry again.'

'*Rivalry!* Is that what he calls it? Well, at least I shall be distracted by the—'

He said a word that confused me then. It sounded like *poultice*, or *poultry*, but I was sure it couldn't be either of those.

He turned and rushed up the stairs, calling, 'Hugh? Where are you?'

Old Mrs Verey trotted after him, her shoulders drawn up with disapproval.

As soon as they were gone, Eric popped out of his hiding place and said, '*Poltergeist!*'

I frowned at him. 'What?'

'He said *poltergeist*! It's a German word for a ghost that causes trouble.'

'Are you sure that's what he said?' I asked suspiciously.

'I know what I heard,' said Eric, shrugging.

*

It turned out that Neil Verey was Old Mr and Mrs Verey's youngest son. Before the war, according to Ruth, he had been a ghost hunter. I hadn't even known that was a job.

Every time our ghost did something new, Neil got wildly excited. Doors flew open, fire irons fell over, earrings came flying out of nowhere into the Vereys' faces, and Neil was there, sniffing all round the mouseholes and hinges and muttering to himself in delight.

'You look a fool,' said Sidney Foley to Neil with a sneer. He'd taken to jumping out at Neil from behind potted plants and chairs, pretending to be the ghost.

'Do go away, Sid,' said Neil coldly, peering at a stain on a curtain. 'We're not children any more, and you can't rattle me. Now, is that ectoplasm?'

'RUTH!' roared Sidney. 'You missed some ectoplasm when you cleaned last! You really must try harder!'

While Sidney Foley sniggered and scoffed at his youngest half-brother's expense, Old Mr Verey was irritated. 'It really is too much!' I heard him say to Neil furiously that evening. 'You know mentioning Leonard brings up dreadful memories for your mother. Can't you be more respectful?'

'Leonard was the only one who ever cared about me!' said Neil. 'It wouldn't be respectful to ignore him now he's trying to speak to us again!'

'Nonsense,' said Old Mr Verey, and he retreated to the study, where he spent most of his time. I remembered what we'd overheard Sidney telling Hugh, and thought he might be feeling ill.

Old Mrs Verey took to her usual chair in the hallway, knitting furiously and staring out of the window. It was such a funny, draughty place for her to be, and I didn't understand why she would choose to sit there, until I happened to look out of the window myself one day and saw two flat grey gravestones at the end of the driveway. I remembered the husband and son she'd lost, and I felt sorry for her, even though she was old and mean.

So we were busy watching the Vereys. But what we weren't expecting was a murder.

PART FOUR

WE DISCOVER A MURDER

13

From the diary of Fionnuala O'Malley

Saturday 9th November 1940

Dear Diary,

I was all ready for the party last night, but I wasn't ready for what actually happened.

I'm going to say what happened here, because I think *someone* should write it down. It's important. And it helps me remember that it's *real*. It still feels like something from a play. When I try to think back to the moment it happened, all I can see is everyone frozen, like a tableau, hands outstretched and staring at – *the murder*.

But I have to write it all down in order. That's important. I've got to be logical, like Nancy Drew, and remember what I saw.

The party was Uncle Sid's idea, though it began as a joke. 'To celebrate the return of our heroic Captain Neil,' he said, sniggering – but Aunt Pam jumped on the idea straight away, and suddenly it was really happening.

I wasn't excited. We'd already missed Bonfire Night (nobody could celebrate it this year because setting off fireworks would draw the German planes from miles around) and the best holiday, Halloween. Halloween is always awful in England. Last year I wrote a play where I was a banshee and everyone else died gruesomely, but I wasn't allowed to perform it. I guess I shouldn't have even tried, but Da and I always loved Halloween. We'd tell stories and dress up and go trick-or-treating (another thing you can't do here because Granny thinks it's *heathen*).

But then Aunt Pam decided that Uncle Neil's party should have a fancy-dress competition. And I just knew that I had to win it. I'm the best at costumes here – I know I am. I spent years in the Company's wardrobe department with Megumi. I'm basically a professional.

So I took all week over my costume. I decided I wanted to be Gráinne, the pirate queen. I found bits of fabric up in the attic, and I sewed a skirt and a cloak, and I even made a sword (not a great one, only out of tinfoil, but it looked OK). As I did it, I *felt* myself getting stronger and braver and more ruthless.

Annabelle Olivia wouldn't shut up about *her* costume, and how she was going to be a bride. May looked as though she wanted to pinch her, and I had to make sure I didn't meet her eyes because I just *won't* agree with May about anything.

The party started at eight. When Granny finally let us all get down from the dinner table at seven thirty, we had to hustle to get changed. It was dark when I peeked outside through the blackout: no moon, all clouds, totally wrong for an air raid. There hasn't been one for the last few days because the weather's been so bad. The German planes can't see anything when it's cloudy.

I went into the bathroom to change so I wouldn't have to talk to May. I didn't want her to see my Gráinne costume before everyone else did.

I was really proud of myself. I looked totally realistic and absolutely fierce. I felt as though I was going into battle – there was ice in my spine, and I knew I was magnificent. But when I came out and went down the stairs into the hall, everything felt like it had when I got off the boat to England, that creep of wrongness, getting bigger and bigger. All three uncles and Granny and Grandfather looked at me as though I was unwell. Even Mam seemed upset, not proud. Now she's around the Vereys again, they want her to pretend that the Company was all just a dream, that she never acted Lady Macbeth onstage in front of hundreds of people, striding about with a prop knife glinting in her hands and Da beaming at her from the wings. When I do theatrical things, I think she feels like I'm disobeying her family and betraying the English side of myself.

'Fiona has come as a savage, I see,' said Uncle Sidney. 'I'm sure her father would be proud.'

Oh, I wanted to smack him! How dare he!

'Fiona, dear, why don't you put on a nice dress?' asked Granny, and Grandfather just looked pained.

'It's my *costume*,' I said, my mouth thick and my accent slipping into Irishness.

It got worse when the evacuees came downstairs. Eric was in an ordinary jumper and shorts, but May was wearing a draped dress of silky greeny fabric that looked like the sea, tied at the waist with a scarf.

'What are *you*?' I asked scornfully because sometimes, when you can't cope with how awful you feel, you want to make everyone else feel just as bad.

'I'm Emil,' said Eric. 'A detective in a book.'

'I've never heard of him,' I said coldly.

'And I'm Ching Shih, the pirate queen!' said May. 'I used the curtains from the spare room.'

My heart was throbbing with rage.

'*I'm* a pirate queen!' I cried, and oh, I sounded like such a kid, but I couldn't stop myself. 'I'm Gráinne Ní Mháille! You can't just – you can't just do that!'

'Of course I can,' said May. 'And who's that? *I've* never heard of her. She can't have been *that* good at pirating.'

'Oh, here's Annabelle Olivia!' cried Aunt Pam. 'Don't you look pretty, my darling!'

I knew she was trying to distract us, but I'll never forget that moment. If there was ever any doubt, I knew absolutely and totally then that May and I were enemies *for life.*

Scott had carved turnips and put candles in them, and they flickered through the house, their faces leering and horrible. I was already feeling creepy when the ghost knocked two of them over with a bang just after nine, making everyone jump. The adults were wearing costumes too, and it was half embarrassing and half spooky. Uncle Sidney was the Devil, with paper horns and a cloak that swished behind him. Aunt Pam was Marlene Dietrich, with her hair pinned back and a top hat over it. Granny was a hopeless Queen Victoria in a black dress and a doily on her head. Grandfather was Winston Churchill in a stiff, crackly new siren suit, Uncle Neil was a monk, and Uncle Hugh was Charlie Chaplin.

Annabelle Olivia won the costume competition, of course – it was judged by Aunt Pam – and then we all played games that I mostly didn't know the rules of. There was one with flour in a heap, which we had to carve away at without upsetting the penny on top of it, and then we bobbed for apples.

Aunt Pam put a record on the gramophone, and Uncle Hugh said, 'None of that stuffy classical stuff tonight, Pammy! You know I can't stand it. Let's have some jazz!'

Eric was fiddling with that old watch he always wears. 'Hand it over, young man,' said Grandfather at last. 'I shall put it away until you can take better care of it.' Eric looked horrified, but Grandfather took it from him and went off to the study, telling Eric sternly that he was going to lock it up in his desk.

Aunt Pam had set up the drawing room with black drapes and weird lights, and she sent us in one by one to look in the mirror and have a vision of the person we were going to marry.

I knew how to do that trick. You just stand a little way back from the mirror and hold up photos behind a veil, and from a distance they look like real people. I was just impressed that Aunt Pam knew about it too. She looked happier than she had for weeks now the party had started, really swanky in her beautifully cut suit. It's funny to think about an adult feeling trapped here the way I do.

Then, while I was pretending to be excited about the picture of an ugly man with a black beard that Aunt Pam was holding up, Uncle Hugh came to stand by her. I swear I wasn't trying to hear what they were saying, but I couldn't help it.

'You look nice,' Uncle Hugh said. 'But I hope you can return that suit now that you've worn it?'

'I shan't!' said Aunt Pam. 'I look wonderful in it.'

'Pammy, come now – you know money's . . . a little tight at the moment.'

'And whose fault is that? If we could just go home—'

'We certainly can't go home. It's not safe – you know that.'

'I do not! There hasn't been a bomb in weeks – anyway, they wouldn't bomb the cathedral, so we're perfectly all right. Please, Hughie, I was talking to Sid, and he says—'

'NO!' snapped Uncle Hugh, suddenly furious. 'Will you STOP listening to Sidney?'

'He's more fun than you are these days!' said Aunt Pam nastily. 'You hardly made an effort with your costume this year. Sidney helped me with mine – and I lent him those black trousers of yours.'

'You WHAT?' roared Uncle Hugh.

Aunt Pam jumped, and so did I. That made them remember I was sitting right there.

'Oh, Fiona dear,' said Aunt Pam weakly. 'Did you see your future husband?'

I honestly don't want a husband if we're just going to end up yelling at each other like Aunt Pam and Uncle Hugh, but I said, 'Yes, thanks.'

I got up and went out into the hall, and saw Uncle Sidney looking pleased about something. He grinned at me and checked his watch. Ruth came by with a tray of drinks, and Uncle Sidney lunged at her, flapping his cape. She startled, and one of the glasses fell over and smashed on the floor.

'Go on, clean it up, unless you think the *ghost* can do it,' said Uncle Sidney, snickering, as Ruth knelt down with a cloth, her face pale. She'd been looking upset all evening, and I wondered if Uncle Sidney's teasing was the reason.

'Stop it, Sidney,' said Uncle Neil, coming out into the hall too. 'You oughtn't to joke about the spirit.'

Uncle Sidney let out a bark of laughter. 'You really are a credulous little fool, Neil!'

This evening he was being even crueller than usual. It made me kind of scared of him, even though I don't know why, when I think about it now. He was just being Uncle Sidney – but maybe that was scarier than I'd ever let myself notice before.

Uncle Neil flushed and drew himself into the long sleeves of his costume. He muttered something and turned away – and, as he did, I saw another expression on his face, a very angry one. I really don't think he liked the way Uncle Sid talked to him.

I looked down at where Ruth was still mopping up the water and glass, and saw she was staring up at Uncle Sidney as though she wanted to hurt him too.

And then Uncle Sidney said, out of nowhere, looking at his watch again, 'How about a round of Murder in the Dark?'

14

'What's Murder in the Dark?' asked Annabelle Olivia, perking up at once. Everyone was in the hall with us by now.

'We played it when we were children,' said Uncle Hugh. 'But I don't really think it's appropriate—'

He glanced at Grandfather – of course, Grandfather was sick and wouldn't want to be reminded of death. I felt really anxious, and I wished Uncle Sid would drop it.

'Of course it's appropriate,' said Uncle Sidney, smirking at Grandfather. 'It's perfect. Just promise you won't arrest the murderer, Father.'

'Very funny, Sidney,' said Grandfather, frowning. 'Surely there are less disruptive games?'

But Uncle Sidney wouldn't budge, and finally Granny sighed over her knitting and said, 'Whatever makes you happy, Sidney dear.'

I'd always thought that Murder in the Dark was just walking round a room and pinching the people that you wanted to kill, if you were the murderer; but Uncle Sidney said no, not the way they did it. Their version was played through the whole house. The murderer was chosen by being drawn out of a hat, and then they went around in the pitch-dark, sneaking up on people and whispering 'You're dead!' in their ears. This sounded creepy to me, and I didn't really want to do it – I know it's all pretend, and usually I love pretend, but there's something so spooky about a dark house and someone breathing in your ear.

Uncle Hugh grumbled and said, 'All right, all right. But lights out, all the way out. No cheating. I know you, Sid.'

'And I know you too, Hughie. Better and better, in fact,' said Uncle Sidney, winking at him, and Uncle Hugh frowned. 'We'll have Scott turn off the generator to stop anyone using the lights.'

Several people made horrified noises, and Granny said, 'Really, Sidney!'

'Level playing field, Mummy,' said Uncle Sid. 'It's only fair. Neil, go and get Scott. Ah, Scott, there you are. Give us five minutes to draw names, if you please, then turn off the generator in the stables.'

'Yes, sir,' said Scott, his creepy beardy face all lit up by the jack-o'-lanterns.

'If you're doing this, then I'm going to bed,' said Mam. 'I'm too tired.'

'Don't be a spoilsport, Serena!' said Uncle Sid.

Mam's face flickered for a moment. But then she shook her head, and I knew that she just didn't want to be part of anything that was even a little like acting. As she turned away up the stairs, I saw her take out a sleeping pill from the little pillbox that she keeps in her purse and put it in her mouth. There'd be no way of waking her up until morning.

I was mad at her all over again then. But now – now I guess I'm glad she did that, because of what happened next.

Anyway, by then, Uncle Sid was digging out an old hat from the coat cupboard and a black pen from his pocket, and Aunt Pam was folding slips of paper and dropping them in the hat, and Grandfather was passing the hat to Granny to choose first. Aunt Pam blew out the candles, and everyone went quiet as the hat was passed round, and we all took a folded piece of paper.

'The murderer's paper has a black dot on it,' said Uncle Sidney. 'If you have it, don't say anything. Once the generator goes off, you've all got one minute to hide before the game begins.'

I unfolded my paper, and it was blank. I was glad.

And then all the lights went out.

15

From the report of May Wong

When the lights went out, I was annoyed because I wasn't the murderer. My piece of paper was blank. I'd been looking forward to creeping around, telling all the stuck-up Verey grown-ups (and horrible Fiona!) that they were dead.

But then I realized that it was good that I wasn't the murderer because I had a job to do. We'd been looking for a chance to examine Sidney Foley's room, and this was perfect.

In the dark, there was suddenly a press of people pushing past us. I grabbed Eric's hand.

'I'll watch Sidney,' he whispered in my ear. 'You go upstairs to his room.'

'All right!' I whispered back.

Eric squeezed my fingers, which meant *OK*, and I was off.

*

Elysium Hall is hard to move around even in the light. It's a box on a box on a box with the kitchens sticking out of the back of it. It was built ages ago, before my Ah Yeh was even born, and hardly altered since. Inside, instead of the cool, uncluttered rooms of our Big House, it's full of tables and chairs and vases and statues and sofas leaking stuffing. I don't know why English people like to have so many *things* around them.

Of course, in the dark, everyone was banging and thumping into furniture, giggling and whispering.

I stood in the hallway and *paid attention* as hard as I could. There was a click off to my right, something thin and metal – Old Mrs Verey's knitting needles, which she'd stuffed into her Queen Victoria costume. I could smell Sidney Foley's disgusting cologne to my left – so he was still somewhere on the ground floor. Someone was pacing heavily up the stairs with a rustling noise that I knew was Old Mr Verey's siren suit. And then, on the first floor, right above me, I heard heavy footsteps.

I went sliding up the stairs, fast and quiet. I've been practising moving silently. Usually, I slam my feet against the floor because I can hardly bother thinking about where they are, but when I'm being a spy I can move like air. I darted round Old Mr Verey, who was moving too slowly, and was sure that he didn't notice me.

There was someone at the turn of the stairs, behind the potted plant there – I listened and caught their breathing going fast and light. Either Annabelle Olivia or Fiona, not a grown-up at all.

Now I was up on the first floor. I paused for a moment and heard the heavy footsteps again in front of me – and then voices. It was Hugh and Pamela, by the door to their room, and they weren't bothering to keep quiet. I heard Pamela say, 'I'm not in the mood for this game, Hughie. I'm *leaving*!' and Hugh say, 'Just be patient, for God's sake! *Don't* go anywhere.'

Then there was an angry pause, followed by the slam of a door. As I stood there, trying not to breathe too hard, I heard more footsteps behind me and rustling – Old Mr Verey stomping across the landing and going into *his* bedroom.

I pressed myself against the wall, hearing all this go on around me, and glad as anything for the blackout. And then I heard someone else, someone smaller and lighter, climbing the stairs. Next, only a few feet away, a voice said, 'You're dead!' and Old Mrs Verey gasped, a high, fluttering old-lady noise.

'Go downstairs, Mother. I've caught you,' said the first voice – it was Neil Verey, and now I knew who the murderer in the game was.

As quickly and quietly as I could, I went across the landing and pushed open the door to Sidney Foley's room. I took off the scarf I'd tied round my dress to hold it in place and pushed it against the gap at the bottom of the door, and then, when I knew no light could escape and give me away, I clicked on my torch.

The room was very tidy. His bed was neatly made, his suits were hanging up in his wardrobe and his shoes were in a row beneath the window. The space under his bed was clear, and his drawers were full of carefully folded shirts. That made what I found on his desk seem particularly strange. It was a pile of *things* – a cufflink, a shard of teacup, a brooch, an eggshell, a pen lid, string and a shilling. Had Sidney stolen them? But what odd things to steal.

And then I pushed them aside and saw . . . a folded piece of paper.

I held my torch up to the paper and squinted at it. And my heart began to race. On one side was a drawing, a doodled plane in flight. And next to it was a map – buildings sketched from above, with different bits labelled in German. A heading at the top read *Verey Industries*. This was Hugh Verey's factory.

This was important – I knew it. This was what we'd been looking for: actual information, and actual proof that Sidney Foley was sharing it with the Nazis. This must have been what he was showing those men in the pub! We had him at last! I had to tell Eric. Our mission was about to be over. I could telephone Hazel tomorrow, and then we'd be out of Elysium Hall forever.

I shoved the piece of paper in my pocket, clicked off my

torch and crept out of the room. I knew I'd already been in there far too long.

Back out on the first-floor landing, I paused anxiously. I thought I heard something downstairs. I stayed stock-still, taking in little sips of air and doing my best to blend into the dark wallpaper – and, after a long pause, I started to walk down the stairs, floating my steps so as to remain absolutely silent.

Time seemed to have stretched out in the darkness or gone a strange shape. The clock had struck ten just before we began the game, and I couldn't tell what time it was now. I suddenly wasn't sure what I should be doing. I stood at the turn of the stairs above the main front hall, and got a funny, unscientific feeling – I was sure there was someone near me. I was so nervous I almost yelled, and I had to press my hands against my mouth and dig my nails into my cheeks to calm myself.

I stood motionless again, and the clock in the front hall struck half past ten while I was still panting into my palms, telling myself I was being absolutely stupid.

Someone banged into me then, and knocked me backwards, and together we half fell up the stairs. I bit my tongue and felt it sting, my mouth full of salt.

'OW!' I cried.

'UGH!' said the person who'd hit me, their bony elbow digging into my chest, and I twisted in fury. I knew from their voice that it was horrible Fiona. So that must have been the person I'd felt before. I hissed and struck out at her, and she gasped. 'Ah, here! I didn't do that on purpose!'

'Well, I did!' I snarled, and she snapped, 'Oh, I'm tired of this!'

She grabbed at me, her fingers twisting into my hair, making my eyes stream. I balled up my fists and struck her in the chest, knocking all the air out of her (she made a *whoofing* noise, and I felt her breath on my face) – and then a voice below us said, 'May.'

It was Eric, and something about how he sounded made me freeze. Fiona got one more hair-twist in, and then she stopped too. Even though we'd been fighting, we'd still been trying to stay quiet until that moment. It's funny how only something really serious or important can make you break the rules of a game like this one – and Eric had just broken them.

'May,' he said again, in the same dead-calm voice. 'Are you there? I can hear you. Listen to me. I went into the study. There's something on the floor. I fell over it. My hands are wet. Can you help me?'

I fumbled for my torch, which was stuffed into my sock, but it was Fiona who got to a light first. There was a hiss, and a match flared in her hand. She lifted it up, and it lit Eric, who was standing in the hallway below us. His face was drawn, and his hands were held up in front of his chest.

And they were completely covered in blood.

16

From the diary of Fionnuala O'Malley, continued

When I saw Eric and all that blood, I remembered *Macbeth* again, and Mam playing Lady Macbeth with *her* hands covered in blood. I kind of wanted to laugh. My chest was full of bubbles – although that was maybe from the punch May had landed on me. It hurt so much and it made me so mad I felt like I was floating. I made a noise that was kind of a snort and kind of a scream, and both of the evacuees said, 'Shut UP!'

'Where did you get all that blood?' I asked. 'Are we playing a new game?'

You can tell from that how I was thinking. It just didn't look *real* – or it looked so real that I couldn't believe it, like when prop designers are *too* clever in their designs. It has to look a little fake for the audience to buy it, Da always said. The match burned out against my fingers then, with a little hiss, and we were left in the dark.

Then I remembered all my suspicions about the

evacuees, and that May had just attacked me when, sure, all *I'd* done was walk into her by mistake. I took a deep breath and tried to put the steel back into my spine.

'Who did you hurt?' I said, and I grabbed hold of May's hair again just as another light came on – a little flashlight that she'd pulled out from somewhere. She said, '*OW!*' but I didn't let go, and I dragged her downstairs to where Eric was standing.

'I didn't hurt anyone!' said Eric. His red hands were trembling, and I saw that his whole body was shaking like he was a puppet with someone twitching his strings. 'It's blood, isn't it? I've got blood on me. It smells so bad.'

I know I should have been suspicious, but the frustrating thing is that I actually believed him. If it'd been May, I wouldn't have, but he just looked so scared. I stopped twisting May's hair.

'Get *off* me,' she snarled. 'Something's wrong! Can't you see that?'

'How do I know you won't hit me again?' I asked, which seemed reasonable.

She hissed: 'Because, as much as I'd *like* to, there's no time for that now. Eric has blood on his hands, and it's not his.'

'It's not mine,' agreed Eric, teeth chattering.

'So we have to go and find out whose it is, obviously,' said May.

103

'I'm not coming with you,' I said, which was silly because by then I absolutely wanted to.

'I didn't ask you to,' said May. 'I meant the two of us. You're not invited.'

'Grand – I'm coming along, then,' I said.

'Please stop arguing,' said Eric. 'Please. There's *blood* on my *hands*, and I don't know why.'

'Why is there a light on?' called Annabelle Olivia, coming down the stairs behind us. 'Is the game over? Oh – is it the ghost?'

'Ghost?' asked Uncle Neil, sticking his head out from the library. 'I've been looking – did one of you see it?'

'WHO TURNED ON A LIGHT?' called Grandfather from somewhere upstairs.

'There's something wrong in the study, Grandfather!' I called back.

'Fiona, what are you doing?' asked Granny. She was sitting in her usual chair in the hall by the front door, knitting the same ugly scarf she'd been working on all day – in the pitch-black, which tells you how good a knitter Granny is. She got up and came towards us with her lips pursed angrily. 'Why are you being so loud? OH MY GOODNESS, child, are you hurt?'

She'd seen Eric's hands in the glow from the flashlight.

'Is it a nosebleed? Have you been fighting?'

'It's not his blood, Granny,' I said, but she didn't listen to me. She pulled out a handkerchief from somewhere in her Queen Victoria costume and started dabbing at Eric, getting blood all over her dress and her knitting. Someone lit a lamp – it was Aunt Pam, and I can't remember where she'd come from, but that was how the next few minutes were. Everyone was buzzing round the three of us, asking questions that didn't make sense and telling us off for no reason, the way adults like to do. Granny called Ruth to bring bandages, but it was Scott who turned up with them from the kitchens – his coat still on – and when he saw the blood he exclaimed and dropped them so they unravelled all over the floor.

'Excuse me,' Eric kept on saying. 'Excuse me. EXCUSE ME.'

'You children really mustn't fight with each other!' Granny was muttering crossly.

'But it's NOT MY BLOOD!' said Eric, louder than I'd ever heard him say anything. Everyone froze. 'I was in the study. Something's in there. *Someone*. That's where the blood came from.'

'Nonsense,' said Aunt Pam shrilly, dabbing at him. Annabelle Olivia burst into tears.

Uncle Hugh said, 'Frightening my girl!' in an angry way, like it was Eric's fault for telling the truth.

'Ruth, go and look in the study, please,' said Granny. 'Take the lamp.'

'Yes, Mrs Verey,' said Ruth, who'd finally come rushing down the back stairs, looking flustered, and she went floating away across the dark hall, her face haloed by the lamplight. The study door opened, and Ruth disappeared inside. There was a long pause.

And then Ruth screamed.

17

From the diary of Fionnuala O'Malley, continued

That was when I knew that something was truly, honest-to-God wrong.

There was a moment's hesitation before everyone ran towards Ruth's scream. Later I thought how weird that was, that you hear someone yelling and you don't immediately rush to them. Da always used to tell me that if you're ever in trouble you should scream *FIRE*, not *HELP*.

Everyone was crowded in the doorway to the study – May wriggled by me and ducked under everyone's arms to have a look – and there was a lot of exclaiming and yelling and crying, and then Granny staggered to one side and, in the flickering of the lamplight, I could finally see it.

Uncle Sidney was lying on the study floor, face down, and he was dead.

I could tell he was dead because the back of his head was the wrong shape, and also because of the pool of blood that had leaked out of him and spread like a fan round his body, from under his Devil's cape.

I'm sorry, that's revolting, I know, but I have to say it. I already keep wondering whether I've just made all this stuff up, but seeing it written down on the page makes it clearer. Every time I read those words, I can see it all over again.

Uncle Sidney is *dead*.

Even though I wasn't really thinking like Nancy Drew then – I was feeling like I wanted to vomit – sometimes your eyes and ears and nose do good detective work on the spot anyway. So this is what I observed in the room.

Uncle Sidney was lying very close to Grandfather's big desk, next to the French window at the other end of the room from the door we'd come in. His arms were stretched out in front of him, his fists clenched and his legs bent, like he'd fallen to his knees and then slumped forward onto the rug.

The desk was clear, no papers on it at all, which was unusual – Grandfather's desk is always piled high – and a couple of the drawers were open. The fireplace looked wrong too, and I couldn't work out why until I realized that the poker that usually stood beside the hearth was on the rug next to Uncle Sidney, its thin point covered with blood.

And (this was actually the first thing that I noticed – it was impossible *not* to – and it was almost as scary and wrong as Uncle Sidney being dead) the heavy blackout curtain that should have covered the French window was thrown back, and the window itself was open, gusts of cold air blowing through the room and whipping my hair round me.

Everyone else saw that at the same time I did.

'Shut that curtain!' snapped Granny. 'Put out the lamp!'

Ruth gasped. 'I didn't go near the window! I didn't touch him!' And the lamplight dipped and then flickered out totally.

Uncle Hugh went striding over to the French window and pulled it shut, hurriedly closing the curtain. Everyone breathed out with relief.

'Who the bloody hell broke blackout?' growled Grandfather. He's ferocious about checking it and always makes sure each window has been done properly, with not even a strip of light showing at the edges. 'I closed that curtain myself before the party. Don't you understand how important this is? If Jerry sees the house—'

We all know that even a tiny light can be seen thousands of feet up in the air, and if there's a German pilot up there he'll use any target he can find. I could feel all the adults shifting nervously.

'It's closed again now,' said Granny at last. 'Ruth, turn the lamp on again, and Scott, go and put the generator back on. We must be able to see.'

There was a pause, and then a match flared. The lamp's wick caught and flamed, and then Ruth put the glass dome over it, and it guttered down to a soft glow. I could see spatters of blood on her white apron. Her hands were trembling, and her lips were shaking as she leaned against the door.

Once again, the figure on the floor was visible.

Granny knelt down very slowly on the rug and put out her hand towards Uncle Sidney. It didn't quite brush his cheek, but it trembled like a drop of rain about to fall off a leaf.

'This house was supposed to be *safe*,' she said quietly. 'I was sure it would be safe for you all. How can this be happening again?'

I've seen plenty of death scenes. Ones in plays, I mean. People in plays take lines and lines to die, and are always getting up again so they can die even more, and then their loved ones throw themselves over their bloody corpses, screaming and yelling and rending their hair. So it surprised me when I found out that real death isn't like that. When Da had his heart attack, and Mam told me, I burst out laughing because I was sure she was making it up. He'd been sick, but I never thought he'd *die*.

Lookit, what I'm trying to say is that if you were expecting a scene from a play, Diary, you wouldn't get it. Granny just sat on the rug, crying. Grandfather bent over her, looking haggard, covering his eyes with his hands.

Uncle Hugh kept on saying, 'There, there, there, there,' to Aunt Pam, who was whimpering softly. Even Annabelle Olivia didn't yell. She just seemed glazed over.

Ruth was still leaning against the door, panting, until Uncle Hugh cried out, 'Telephone the police, Ruth! Don't just stand there! Quickly!'

She rushed out, and when she was gone I saw the two evacuees whispering together. I had believed Eric when he said he hadn't hurt anyone, but now I got suspicious all over again. What were they up to?

Then Uncle Hugh suddenly gasped. He let go of Aunt Pam and ran over to the desk. 'Oh my God,' he said loudly. 'Oh my God!'

He started to rummage through the open desk drawers, *thump, thump, thump*, each thump making Granny twitch a little as she wept.

'I knew it,' he said. 'I knew it. *I knew it.*'

'What is it?' asked Aunt Pam.

'My papers!' said Uncle Hugh. 'I had some papers – important documents. I stored them in here for safe keeping this afternoon and now they're gone!'

He kept on opening drawers, *slam, bang, slam*, until Aunt Pam said, 'Please be quiet! My *head*!'

This was so obviously the wrong thing to say that everyone instinctively turned to stare at Uncle Sidney's body.

'This is serious, Pammy,' said Uncle Hugh. 'I left them all here, and now – my God – they're gone! This is a crisis!'

'So does that mean – thieves?' asked Aunt Pam.

'Thieves,' said Uncle Hugh grimly. 'It's obvious what's happened. They jemmied the window lock and came in here, looking for loot. Sid must have walked in and surprised them, and they – well, they stopped him from raising the alarm. And they made off with my papers! Father, you were only telling us last week about a gang operating in the area!'

I know I said that everyone reacts differently, sometimes very strangely, when something terrible happens, but even then I thought it was weird that Uncle Hugh was worrying about these papers, whatever they were, instead of his own brother lying dead on the floor.

There was a hum, and then the lights flicked back on, and we all started and blinked. Scott must have switched on the generator. Out in the hall, I could hear Ruth speaking on the telephone. 'Hello? Yes? Murder – Elysium Hall – come at once, please.' Her voice sounded jittery and strange. Suddenly everything felt more real-life and more made-up all at once.

Uncle Hugh obviously remembered the rest of us then, and said, 'Children, to bed! This is no place for you!'

Annabelle Olivia was crying now. 'He's dead!' she sobbed. '*Mummy!*'

Aunt Pam and Uncle Hugh both ran to her, the way they always do, and then Aunt Pam rushed her up to her room on the first floor, next to Aunt Pam and Uncle Hugh's.

Grandfather barked, 'You three! To bed!'

You don't ignore one of Grandfather's commands, so me and Eric and May had to troop out of the study together. I felt like we were being shoved offstage.

But, I realized, I was the only member of the household who suspected that the evacuees might not just be innocent bystanders. Eric had found Uncle Sid, after all. I knew that often the person who claims to have found a body is actually responsible for the crime. Uncle Hugh thought that it was thieves, but I wasn't sure I believed that. Not when there were two almost-strangers in the house – almost-strangers who I'd already caught spying.

I waited until we were up past the curve of the stairs and then I turned to them, being Nancy Drew, and said, 'OK. *I know.*'

'What are you talking about?' snarled May.

'I know you're spying on our family,' I said. 'And I think you might have killed Uncle Sidney.'

18

From the diary of Fionnuala O'Malley, continued

I was looking right at them, and I saw the start Eric gave. I thought I might have worked it out – but whether I was just right about the spying or about the murder as well I couldn't be sure. I was impressed by May, though. She didn't flinch at all.

'You're spying for *the other side*, aren't you? And you killed Uncle Sidney. You were stealing Uncle Hugh's papers in the study, and he caught you, so you turned round and murdered him.'

My throat felt tight. I suddenly realized (after I'd said all that, pretty much working it out as I spoke) that if I was right I was alone with two murderers, and all the adults were downstairs.

But May, instead of lunging at me again, burst out laughing.

'You think we're working for the Nazis?' she gasped. 'That's rich! When it was your *own* precious uncle!'

'May!' said Eric warningly.

'What?' I said. 'What do you mean?'

'I'm sorry,' said May. 'She's just so *stupid*! I mean, what can you expect from a horrible stuck-up English idiot like her?'

'I'm *not* just English! I'm Irish and I'm American too!' I yelled. 'How dare you! You don't know anything about me, but I know all about you. You're German spies, I know you are – horrible fifth columnists here to help the invasion, and I'm going to *tell everyone*.'

'Stop!' said Eric. 'Just stop! Please *don't* do that. You have to listen to us. We can explain.'

That's the annoying thing about Eric, Diary. He doesn't talk that much, but when he does he sounds like someone you should pay attention to. Unlike May.

'You're right that we're here for a reason,' he went on.

'ERIC!' growled May, but he ignored her.

'But we're working for the British government, not the Nazis. At least, we're trying to. We're here because someone at Elysium Hall has been passing information to the Germans.'

I shook my head. It all sounded so wrong. 'Who?' I asked. 'No one in my family would do that!'

'Yes, they would,' said May. 'It was your uncle Sidney. We've been watching him, and tonight I found proof in his room!' She brandished a ripped-up piece of paper in my face, too fast for me to see anything.

'Let me look!' I said.

'No!' said May. 'This is *classified*. We don't trust you.'

'You have to understand that we were here to *watch* Sidney, not *kill* him,' Eric went on. 'I went into the study and tripped over his body. He was already dead. And that's not all. You saw the way the French window was open when we all went in together afterwards. Well, it wasn't before.'

'What?' cried May.

Eric nodded. 'When I went into the study and tripped over Sidney's body, that window wasn't open. It was pitch-dark; there was no breeze and the room was stuffy, as if it hadn't been opened all evening. I could smell Sidney Foley's cologne, and – and the blood, even though I didn't realize then what that smell was. But by the time we all ran back in to see what'd happened, the window was open and so was the curtain – and you all felt the breeze. The only way that what I saw and smelled makes sense is if the window wasn't opened until *after* Sidney Foley was dead. And that means what Hugh Verey said about thieves breaking in can't be true.'

He took a deep breath and stared at me and May.

'Sidney was killed by someone who was already inside this house.'

19

From the diary of Fionnuala O'Malley, continued

'That's not true,' I said. 'It can't be.'

'Eric doesn't lie,' said May, bristling.

'Well, the police will find out,' I said. 'Sure, they'll be here soon, and they'll work out what went on.'

'Let me tell you what'll happen once the police arrive,' said May, looking at me pityingly, which made me mad. 'Your grandfather's a magistrate. If he tells the police that thieves broke in and killed his son, they'll believe him. If Eric tells them that the window wasn't open when Sidney died, they'll just ignore him. *You* know the way English people work – you're one of them.'

'I'm *not* just English!' I said again through clenched teeth. 'Stop saying that! I hate it here!'

May blinked at me. '*Do* you?' she asked.

'Of course I do! I wish I was anywhere else.'

'Don't be stupid. You've got your whole family here.'

'They aren't my real family! I mean, Mam is. But I've

been trying to sound English to fit in with the Vereys and it isn't *working*. If Da hadn't died, we wouldn't be here in the first place. I'd be with the Company in America, and everything would be the way it should be. I *hate* it!'

I felt tears prickling at the back of my eyes and blinked furiously. I was *not* going to cry in front of the evacuees.

'Huh,' said May. 'Interesting.'

She was staring at me, like she was seeing me for the first time, and it made me uncomfortable.

'Anyway, if you *are* right about it being someone in the house, *I* might be the murderer,' I said. 'So I don't know why you're telling me all this.'

I kind of liked that thought. I imagined myself dressed as a villain, creeping through the house with a dastardly purpose.

'You're not the murderer,' said Eric. 'You were fighting with May when I came out of the study, and I didn't lose sight of you until we all went back into the study together. You didn't have the opportunity to open the window.'

This was so logical that it knocked all my murderer imaginings out of my head.

'Oh,' I said. 'I guess so.'

'And we're telling you so that you understand what's going on,' Eric continued. 'We need you on our side.'

'If you tell anyone what we're doing here, we *will* kill you,' put in May. 'Horribly. Because, you see, we're going to solve the murder.'

Eric and I both looked at her, and I think we had exactly the same expression on our faces.

May glared. 'Eric, I've told you before: I'm a detective.'

'You're a kid!' I said. I mean, I know I'd been pretending to be Nancy Drew, but I didn't think that pretending was going to help us work out what happened to Uncle Sidney. 'We're all kids.'

May drew herself up. Her hands were on her hips, her cheeks were scarlet and her eyes blazed. 'I *am* a detective,' she said. 'I was one before I became a spy. I've helped my big sister solve two murders, and I solved another one entirely on my own. I know exactly what I'm doing, and I know that we can work this out *without* help. All I need is for you to believe me.'

'But kids can't be detectives!' I said. 'Even Nancy Drew is almost an adult.'

'Of course they can,' said May. 'Maybe they can't in the books you've read, but this is real life. Look at me and Eric. We've run away from home and school, and now we're here, on our own, on a dangerous mission that may just change the course of the war—'

I still wasn't sure if I believed that was true. Also, had they really run away? Their story sounded more and more made up.

'—and so why shouldn't we also solve a murder?'

'Because you can't,' I said.

'Yes, we can!' flared May.

'Even if we can,' said Eric slowly, 'should we? May, if you really have proof that Sidney *was* sending information to Germany, our mission's over now. He's dead. We telephone the Ministry tomorrow and tell them where we are and what we've found. Why should we stay and try to work out who did it? I mean – does he deserve justice? My family had to leave Germany because of people like him. And we're lucky to have escaped. People are dying there, thousands of them, because of men who think the way he does.'

His cheeks had got flushed as he spoke, and he was breathing heavily. *What's the Ministry?* I wondered, but May spoke before I could.

'We wouldn't be doing it for *him*. We'd be doing it because we can't call the Ministry until we work out who killed him. The mission's only half over. Until we know who did it, we won't know *why*. What if he was killed because someone else knew what he was doing, and decided to put a stop to it? The Ministry would want to know about that.'

Eric nodded slowly. 'You're right. Fiona?'

'She doesn't get a say in this!' said May. 'She's not part of it!'

But Eric was looking at me, waiting. I thought about it. I thought about how much I hated May. I thought about the fact that I'd been right that they *were* spies, and how I still didn't have any proof that they were the good kind. I thought about how they were accusing someone in *my* house of being a murderer.

120

And I thought about how miserable I was here, and how much I wanted anything, absolutely anything, to happen.

'Grand,' I said. 'I'll help.'

'Oh, FINE,' said May.

'*Grand*,' I said. 'But this doesn't mean that we're friends.'

'Of course not,' said May.

'Of *course* not,' I said.

Eric sighed. 'You have to be nice to each other,' he said, 'otherwise there's no point.'

May and I both made a face.

But Eric smiled at me. 'And if we're going to work together, we should introduce ourselves properly. My name is really Hans Erich Schlossbauer, not Eric Jones – but you can call me Eric. I can't be Erich here in England.'

'I'm Fionnuala O'Malley,' I said. 'Nuala for short. Fiona's just what the Vereys call me. It's not my real name, either.'

May looked furious. 'I – I'm Wong Mei Li,' she spat, glaring at Eric. 'But you can call me May.'

And that's why I'm writing this, Diary – because I've just become a detective. I'm going to help solve Uncle Sidney's murder – *me*, not even me playing a part. It feels weird, and I don't know if I trust it yet. I sure don't trust May. But I do want to solve the case. I want to know what happened to Uncle Sidney.

Because, if May and Eric are right, there's a *murderer* here at Elysium Hall.

20

From the report of May Wong

I could not believe that we had to work with Nuala. Eric tricked me into it. I was furious with him. I couldn't tell him so out loud at the time because she was *right there*, and although I'm rude, I'm not *that* rude (usually), so I had to tell him with my eyes. We had a murder case, an actual *murder* to solve, my first for a whole year, and we had to share it with *her*.

I said before that I've solved other cases, and I have. You can read about them if you want – not in these files, but in Big Sister Hazel's notes. You'll see that I'm not lying.

And I knew that Eric wasn't lying, either. He's good at puzzles and noticing things – that's why I'm glad he's here on this mission with me – and he'd never have missed anything as big as whether a French window was wide open or not. If it hadn't been open the first time he went into the study and fell over Sidney Foley's body, but it was when we all went back in a few minutes later, then it didn't seem as though thieves had really broken in. Someone was just pretending they had. And that meant we really did have a murderer at Elysium Hall.

'What are we going to do now?' asked Nuala.

'You're going to follow our orders,' I said to her because she might be helping, but she wasn't in charge. Eric and I were here first (sort of), and so it was up to *us* how the case was detected.

Nuala narrowed her eyes at me, and I narrowed mine right back at her, crossing my arms for good measure.

'Someone needs to go downstairs and find out if the police are on their way,' said Eric. 'We don't want to miss them when they do get here.'

'*You* do that,' I said to Nuala. 'They'll mind you going back down less than if it was us. You can say you're scared or something.'

'I'm never scared,' sniffed Nuala.

I knew she was lying because even I'd been a *bit* scared when I'd gone into the study and seen Sidney Foley lying there with his head knocked in. But only a bit.

I held my glare and at last Nuala sighed, pushed her glasses up her nose and went rushing off downstairs, her straggly browny-red hair flying behind her.

'Ugh!' I said, as soon as she was gone. 'Thank goodness it's just us for a minute.'

'Give her a chance, May,' said Eric. 'She's nice. Were you telling her the truth about finding proof that Sidney was the spy?'

'I always tell the truth!' I said, stung. 'Here. This must be one of the papers Hugh is missing.'

Eric looked at the paper with the labelled sketch of Hugh Verey's factory buildings on it, and then up at me. 'You really did,' he said wonderingly. 'May, we did it. We worked out who the spy is.'

I grabbed his hand, and we both started to giggle because we *had*. It felt like us again, just the two of us, which I liked best.

'We've only done half of it, though,' I reminded him. 'Now that he's been murdered, we have to find out who did it. All right. You said when you went into the study that you tripped over Sidney. I'd imagined him right next to the door, but he was all the way over by the desk, near the French window. What were you doing over there?'

Eric wiggled his shoulders in the way he does when he's a bit embarrassed.

'I – needed to get something from the desk.'

'*What?*' I asked.

'Don't look like that, May. I wasn't stealing anything! I had to get Papa's watch back. Old Mr Verey took it and put it in the desk in his study. I thought I could go and get it during the game.'

If I hadn't known that Eric was absolutely trustworthy, I'd have felt sick with shock. I glared at him. 'You abandoned the mission? You were supposed to be watching Sidney! What if he'd found me when I was going through his room? And what if you'd stuck with him properly? You'd have seen who murdered him!'

Eric hung his head. 'I know. I'm sorry. But Papa's watch is all I have to remember him by. And I thought Sidney was safe in the library. He went in there at the beginning of the game, and he didn't seem to be leaving. He was looking through books, I think. I left him there after about ten minutes and sneaked off to the study. But then I heard someone coming down the stairs, and I had to run away.'

'Do you know who it was?' I asked.

I was so cross. Eric had been a terrible spy, and now our suspect was dead. It was a horrible mistake to make.

Eric shook his head. 'A grown-up. They were taller than me, I could tell. I went back to the library to find Sidney, but he'd gone. I went into the drawing room and all round the ground floor. And then I heard voices in the study. One of them was Sidney. I was stuck – I couldn't go in because the door was shut. So I stayed outside. I heard voices and saw torchlight under the door. I think the person I'd heard before was still in there – with him.'

'How long were you there? *Who was it?*'

'Not long, I think, but I didn't have Papa's watch so I can't be sure. And whoever was with Sidney was talking too quietly for me to hear. But then there was a noise like someone slapping a hand down on a table, and after that the voices stopped, and the torch was turned off. I waited for a few minutes, but I couldn't hear anything at all. So I stuck my head round the door and listened – it was so quiet inside. I thought I must have missed Sidney leaving, somehow, so I waited another minute, just in case, and went in, over to the desk – and that was when I fell over him in the dark. There was no one else apart from me in the study. No one alive.'

I felt sick. 'But, Eric, that can't be true. If no one came out of the study door before you went in, but the French window was open by the time everyone else came in to see Sidney's body, then there's only one way the murderer could have gone – out of the French window, after you'd left. They must have been in the room with you, hiding.'

Eric's eyes got very wide. 'Oh no,' he said. 'You're *right*.'

'And – wait. Did you get your watch?'

'No,' said Eric miserably. 'I *know*.'

I should have felt sorry for him because he'd been in a room with a murderer, and he might have been killed himself, but I was just cross with him. That watch had his father's full, real German name engraved inside it, not the made-up last name Jones that Eric was using. It was a stupid thing to bring, and I'd been anxious about it for ages – and now it was part of a crime scene, and the police were on their way. At any moment they'd find it and open it up, and, once they'd done that, what was to stop them from suspecting Eric? He'd been found with Sidney Foley's blood all over his hands, after all. The investigation was going wrong almost before it had really started.

21

From the report of May Wong

Nuala came back then, looking excited. I was sure all over again that we'd made a mistake involving her. She couldn't even pretend to be calm and ordinary and not on an important spy – now detective – mission.

'The police are on their way,' she said. 'But they'll be half an hour. There was a scare over at Little Hanfield – one of the tower-watchers thought that they saw someone come down in a parachute, so they had to search the area.'

'Did they find anyone?' asked Eric.

Nuala shook her head. 'They think it was only a cloud.'

I sighed. 'I *told* you the police wouldn't be any use,' I said. 'If they're bothered about clouds, they can't take a murder seriously.'

'They are taking it seriously!' said Nuala. 'Apparently, they think it sounds like the gang that's been robbing people all around us. They force windows open and take jewellery and stuff. Sure, I heard Grandfather talking about it last week.'

'And does the gang kill people?' I asked. 'Because, unless they do, they don't sound right at all.'

'Of course they don't!' said Nuala. 'Or, I mean, they hadn't until this evening. I'm just telling you what everyone's saying downstairs.'

I clenched my fists and tried hard not to shout at her. In spite of what Eric had said, she still believed thieves might have committed the murder.

'If we've got half an hour before they arrive, we've got time for a detective meeting,' I said stiffly, trying to be calm and grown-up. 'We need to get our facts straight before we forget anything.'

I've learned this from Big Sister Hazel, although I would never admit it to her. If you see something, write it down *immediately*. Everyone trusts their memory, but the further you get away from something, the more you forget, or mix up what you did that day with what happened the day before. I remember as clearly as anything taking Rose's doll and ripping its head off when we were little and I was angry at her – but that doll is perfectly all right. Rose still has it, and it was never torn at all, not even torn and then mended.

I asked her once, and she looked at me as though I was mad. 'You tore my *dress*,' she said, 'the purple one with the blue trim.' And then the sewing amah told us that

Rose never had a purple dress with blue trim, but a purple dress with white trim, and that was what I'd ripped. So you see, you can lie to yourself while thinking that everything you're saying is the perfect truth, and that was why I knew how important it was for us to make notes absolutely at once.

I turned to Nuala. 'Now,' I said, 'we're letting you work with us, but I want to be clear that it's *only* for this case, all right? Once it's done, we'll leave, and you'll never see us again. Do you see?'

Nuala sniffed. 'I get it,' she said. 'You'll leave. Everyone always does. Look, I'm not going to tell anyone, OK?'

'Good. Come on, to the night meeting room.'

I meant the spare room on the first floor, which is full of old broken furniture and next to the poky back stairs. None of the grown-ups go in there, which is very useful for us, and so Eric and I identified it as a meeting room for our mission almost as soon as we arrived at Elysium Hall.

'Do you swear not to breathe a word about this?' I asked Nuala when we got there. 'Because, if you do, you'll be helping Hitler. It's like you're going right up to him and whispering in his ear, and if he wins the war it'll be your fault. Do you want that?'

Nuala made a face. 'I don't know if that's true,' she said. 'But have it your way. I swear, OK?'

I looked at Eric, and he nodded at me.

Then Nuala smiled. 'This is kind of exciting,' she said. 'I mean – lookit, you know what I mean.'

'Ugh, stop making a fuss!' I said, even though I did know. 'We've only got half an hour. We have to write down what we saw.'

22

From the report of May Wong

I turned to a fresh page in my notebook and wrote:

WHO KILLED SIDNEY FOLEY?
Time of death: between 10:10 and 10:28 p.m., 8th November 1940.
(We know this because Eric heard Sidney going into the study
after the game had begun, and then he discovered Sidney's
body there just before the clock struck ten thirty.)

People in the house when the murder happened:
— Sidney Foley (dead)
— May Wong (detective)
— Eric Schlossbauer (detective)
— Nuala O'Malley (witness but also a detective now)
— Hugh Verey
— Pamela Verey
— Annabelle Olivia Verey (not a suspect)

- Neil Verey
- Ruth the maid
- Mr Scott the gardener
- Iris Verey (Old Mrs Verey)
- William Verey (Old Mr Verey)
- Serena O'Malley

'Why isn't Annabelle Olivia a suspect?' Nuala asked, looking at my writing upside down.

'Because she's not a grown-up,' I explained, trying to be patient. 'Eric heard someone coming down the stairs and going into the study, someone who was taller than him. And, anyway, Annabelle Olivia was hiding behind the potted plant on the turn of the stairs almost the whole time. I heard her, and she came out of her hiding place when Eric called out. But her size absolutely rules her out.'

'Oh!' said Nuala. 'I see. What about my mam? She's not a suspect, either.'

'Of course she is!' I said.

'No, she isn't,' said Nuala. I was ready to shout at her until she said, 'I saw her take one of her sleeping pills after supper, on her way up to bed on the second floor. They always send her to sleep almost immediately, and it's impossible to wake her up for hours. She couldn't have killed Uncle Sidney, so.'

'Then we have seven suspects,' said Eric.

Suspects:
— Hugh Verey
— Pamela Verey
— Neil Verey
— Ruth the maid
— Mr Scott the gardener
— Iris Verey
— William Verey

Underneath our list of suspects I wrote:

Observations:
— Sidney went into the library just after the game began, at ten.
— Eric heard Sidney in the study with someone else (the murderer?) later in the game.
— May heard Old Mr Verey go upstairs and into his bedroom at the beginning of the game.
— May heard Hugh Verey and Pamela Verey talking outside their room on the first floor just after the beginning of the game.

'What were you doing on the first floor?' asked Nuala.
'Spy stuff,' I said shortly.
'That's not fair!' cried Nuala. 'You have to tell me!'
'I told you already,' I said, a little rudely. 'I was looking for proof that Sidney was a spy, and I found it. All right, what did *you* see?'

134

'I was in the drawing room,' said Nuala. 'Hiding. I've this little spot in one of the cabinets. I heard a couple of people in there, later in the game. One of them was pretty quiet, but one of them was crying – I think it could have been Aunt Pam. I snuck out when I heard that and started up the stairs, and that's when I bumped into you, May – just before Eric came out of the study with bloody hands.'

'Well, that's no use!' I said.

'What about after that?' asked Eric. 'When you turned on your torch, May, and then Old Mrs Verey lit the lamp.'

'It wasn't Granny who had the lamp!' said Nuala at once. 'It was Aunt Pam – at least, Aunt Pam had it at first, and then she handed it over to Ruth. Granny was by the front door, I remember, in her usual chair, knitting that horrible scarf in the dark. Grandfather came down the stairs, Uncle Hugh came out of the dining room and Uncle Neil came out of the library.'

Very annoyingly, she was right, and that made *me* remember something. 'I know who the murderer was,' I said. 'The one in the game, I mean! It was Neil. I heard him catch Old Mrs Verey on the first floor and send her downstairs. So she'd been caught – she must have just sat down and begun knitting.'

I started adding that to my observations list.

'Are you sure you're laying it out right?' asked Nuala, peering at it. 'Aren't we going to get confused when we look back at this later? It all feels a little . . . messy.'

I turned on her furiously.

'She's not wrong, though,' said Eric, putting a hand on my arm. 'Isn't there a better way?'

I grumbled. The truth is that, even though I'd wanted to try out my own method first, I do know a better one: the way Hazel taught me.

Suspects:
- Hugh Verey. May heard him talking angrily to Pamela Verey outside their room on the first floor at the beginning of the game. Nuala saw him come out of the dining room as the alarm was raised.
- Pamela Verey. May heard her talking to Hugh Verey outside their room on the first floor at the beginning of the game. Nuala thinks she heard her crying in the drawing room just before Eric stumbled across the body. She turned on the oil lamp after Eric raised the alarm.
- Neil Verey. May heard him talking to Old Mrs Verey (Iris) on the first floor at the beginning of the game. He was the murderer in the game. (Was he the murderer in real life?) Nuala saw him come out of the library as the alarm was raised.
- Ruth the maid. Came rushing down the back stairs after the end of the game. She found the body and telephoned the police.
- Mr Scott the gardener. Came from the kitchens with bandages after the end of the game. Still wearing his coat.
- Iris Verey. May heard her talking to Neil Verey on the first-floor landing close to the beginning of the game.

She went downstairs and was still by the front door, knitting in her usual seat, when the alarm was raised.

— William Verey. May heard him go upstairs and into his bedroom at the beginning of the game. Nuala saw him come downstairs after the alarm was raised.

'I've remembered something else from the study!' said Nuala. 'Once we were all in there, looking at Uncle Sidney. The poker was off its stand and on the rug, and it had blood on it. I think that must have been the murder weapon.'

'Did Sidney make a noise?' I asked Eric. 'When he got hit, I mean. And did you see anything else?'

Eric hunched his shoulders and grimaced.

'Not much,' he said. 'Just that noise I told you about – I thought someone had slapped their hand down on the desk. And I didn't see anything else, but – oh, wait! When I went in and fell over Sidney, I found something on the floor. Here, look.'

He held something small and dark out to me. 'It was on the rug by the desk.'

'It's a Kirbigrip,' I said. 'Women use them to pin up their hair. Not me, obviously.' It's true – my hair is short, cut just below my ears because I can't bear it getting in my eyes and annoying me. Rose says it makes me look like a boy, but that's stupid. I know I'm a girl, so I must look like a girl whatever my hair is like.

But I knew who *was* wearing them. Pamela Verey had pinned up her hair to look like Marlene Dietrich. I told the others.

'She must have been in there at some point during the game!' Eric said.

And there it was. Our first clue.

'Do you think the murderer got gory?' I asked. 'I mean, Sidney's head was all knocked in, and there was blood everywhere, so it stands to reason—'

'Don't!' said Nuala.

I sighed. Having Nuala on the case was going to be so boring.

'*Someone* has to say it,' I pointed out. 'The murderer must have got blood on their clothes. So had anyone changed when we saw them after the end of the game?'

Nuala and Eric both frowned. I squeezed my eyes shut and tried to remember. I saw the lamp going on, and Mr Scott arriving with the bandages, and everyone shouting in the dark, shadowy hall—

'Blast,' I said. 'Eric, you've confused things.'

'What, by finding the body?'

'No, not that – but when you were covered in blood and all the grown-ups crowded round you. The murderer could have used that to disguise the fact that they already had blood on them. Old Mrs Verey and Pamela were trying to clean you up, remember, and they both got blood on their clothes. And the light wasn't bright enough to tell whether they already had blood on them. So, even if we do find blood on them when we go looking, we won't know whether it's from the murder or from you.'

'But Neil and Hugh and Old Mr Verey shouldn't have blood on them, at least,' said Eric.

'Oh,' said Nuala.

We both looked at her. 'What?' I asked.

'When I went downstairs, Grandfather and Uncle Neil and Uncle Hugh were moving the body out of the study,' she said. 'They were going to put it on the dining-room table so the police could look at it when they came.'

'WHAT!' I shouted. 'WHY?'

'Uncle Hugh thought it was a good idea,' said Nuala. 'And Grandfather agreed, so they moved him.'

I wanted to tear my own hair out. I must have hissed *stupid!* out loud because Eric shrugged and said, 'Or clever. Now no one will be able to tell who was near the body.'

'Wait,' said Nuala. 'I've remembered something else. I know someone who wasn't near Eric but still had blood on their clothes. Ruth did, on her apron.'

'But she found Sidney,' I said.

'Yes, but she told us she didn't touch the body,' said Eric slowly. 'So she was lying? Why?'

'I think that might be important,' said Nuala, pleased. 'We should write it down.'

Eric beamed at her, and I felt cross because *I* was the detective. The others were still only supposed to be learning. 'Nuala, how were your family acting when you went downstairs?' he asked. 'Are they upset?'

'Aunt Pam is,' said Nuala at once. 'And Granny and Grandfather. But Uncle Hugh's more worried about his papers, and Uncle Neil – I don't know. He was talking about the ghost. He's sure it's my uncle Leonard, who died years and years ago.'

The doorbell rang then, far away downstairs, but the noise of it went stinging up through the house like electricity.

'That must be the police,' I said.

'I'll go have a listen to what they say,' said Nuala. 'Why don't you two look for evidence – and for the papers that were stolen, if you think they're still in the house?'

We had only just let Nuala be part of this investigation, and she was taking it over already. But the truth was that if we were right, and this was an inside job, all the stolen papers *should* still be somewhere in the house, at least for now. If something or someone gets taken, the quicker you start looking for it, the more chance you have of finding it again. The more time that passes, the more places it could be, like a road that splits and splits again in the middle of a city.

'All right,' I said crossly. 'But you had *better* take good notes. You're not just playing about.'

'Don't worry,' said Nuala. 'I'm great at memorizing lines. It'll be grand.'

Which was not the right attitude *at all*. I fumed. Eric grabbed my hand and squeezed it calmingly.

'Come on, May,' he said. 'She's right. The quicker we look, the better.'

I breathed out through my nose, and, just as I was opening my mouth to say *all right*, Nuala turned back to us.

'What if – what if Leonard's ghost did it? The poker was right there, after all. What if the poltergeist just spun it into the air and whacked him with it?'

I was very glad I'd been clear that, no matter how the investigation went, Nuala O'Malley and I were *never* going to be friends.

PART FIVE

WE CONSIDER THE CASE

23

I thought that the police would fix everything, Diary. In plays, they always come in and save the day – sure, that's their job.

So I was shocked at what actually happened. I guess I shouldn't have been. Except I really wanted May to be wrong. I really wanted the case to be solved quickly. I was kind of hoping that, after all this, Mam would decide to take me back to America, to the Company.

Anyway, that was what I was thinking as I came downstairs to see a short man in a tall blue hat and a blue uniform stepping inside. The uniform was dirty, especially round the ankles – it must have been raining outside again – and he looked shattered. He introduced himself wearily as PC Cuffe, and then the adults all crowded round him, talking in his face.

I knew where they'd end up – the drawing room. That's where guests are always taken when they come to Elysium

Hall. So, while the policeman was led away to view Uncle Sid's body in the dining room first (which I didn't want to see ever again if I could help it), I snuck off and hid inside my secret cabinet.

The cabinet is a good find of mine – it's very comfortable, and it's almost empty. It's usually used to store drink, I think, but there's not much of that around right now. I have a pillow that I sit on in there, and my notebook and pen. When I'm inside, I can see and hear everything if I just open the doors a crack. That's where I'd been hiding during the game, thinking about a new play I was planning.

I drew a line under the last thing I'd written in my notebook, and I smoothed the paper down on my lap and waited.

After a few minutes, I heard a rising hum, like people getting ready to take their seats in an auditorium, and the drawing-room door opened and everyone filed in – Granny, Grandfather, Uncle Hugh, Aunt Pam and Uncle Neil, with the policeman following.

They all sat down in their usual chairs – the policeman stood there awkwardly because no one had offered him a seat. He tried to lower himself down into Uncle Sidney's chair, but Granny gave a gasp, and he jumped up again like he'd been stung.

'Many apologies. I'll try to make this as quick as possible – I have to get to Kenilworth this evening on another case.

Mr Verey, I am so sorry for your loss. If you could just repeat what you said to me earlier, for my notes—'

There was a pause as everyone waited for Grandfather to speak. He's the kind of person you want to listen to, with a voice any actor would envy. I guess a magistrate is a little like an actor, only with a courtroom instead of a theatre.

'My wife's son, Sidney – *my* son, I took him and his brother, our poor dead Leonard, in after the loss of their father – has been killed,' he said, and I heard the sorrow in his voice. I felt so bad for him. He's sick already, and now Uncle Sidney's dead too. 'We discovered his murder just after ten thirty this evening. The body, as you saw, had been struck with – in my professional opinion – *two* blows to the back of the skull. I saw something similar in a case in twenty-six – a very bad business: a burglary that went wrong. The homeowner was killed in much the same way. And, as you know, we have been plagued with a spate of burglaries in the area in recent weeks.

'When we found Sidney, the French window in the study was open, and the blackout curtain had been pulled back. My son Hugh then discovered that several important documents had been taken from the room. We must assume that the thief or thieves entered through the French window and were robbing us when they were startled by Sidney. They hit him with the fireplace poker, which was found on the floor next to my son's body, and then fled the same way they arrived.'

'Mmm,' said the policeman, nodding as he wrote. 'Thank you, this is very helpful. We're short-staffed at the moment, as you know, so it's lucky there's a professional on the scene. And when this occurred you were all—'

'Inside the house,' said Grandfather. 'We were holding a costume party to amuse my grandchildren and the evacuees we are currently caring for. The lights were all off, as we were playing—' He grimaced.

'Murder in the Dark,' said Uncle Neil. 'I – I was the murderer. Not in real life, of course,' he went on hurriedly as PC Cuffe looked up, startled. 'In the game, I mean.'

'Mmm,' said PC Cuffe again. 'And there was no break in blackout *before* you discovered the body?'

'Not at all,' said Grandfather severely. 'I'm strict about that. It's important that we all obey the rules.'

'Interesting that the thieves chose this evening to attack. As you said, there's been a string of similar burglaries in the area over the past few months. Always happens the night of an air raid. The thieves wait for night to fall, the air-raid siren to sound and the family to go to their shelter, and then break in – always through a ground-floor window – taking all the valuables they can find. And not just valuables, either. Man over near Canley had plans stolen – what they were of, I can't say: that's top secret – and a family in Kenilworth had some *extremely* important documents pinched. Tonight seems very similar, but of course there hasn't been a raid for several days now.'

'Perhaps the thieves got tired of waiting,' said Uncle Hugh.

'Mmm,' said PC Cuffe for the third time, nodding and blinking. 'It's possible.'

It *was* possible. But it was weird that it didn't fit with the pattern, I thought uncomfortably.

'If I could just take brief statements from each of you as to where you were during the time the crime occurred. Just to build up a picture, you understand. One of you may have heard or seen something that could help lead us to the thieves.'

'Of course,' said Grandfather. 'I shall go first, though I'm afraid I saw nothing useful. I went to my room on the first floor during the game, on the other side of the house to the study – the party was feeling rather too much for me and I needed to rest. I only came downstairs when I heard the commotion.'

'I spent most of the game in the hall,' said Granny. 'I was on my way up to my daughter Serena's room on the second floor to say goodnight to her when I was caught by my son Neil. He sent me downstairs, and so that is where I was until the little evacuee raised the alarm.'

'Ah, of course. Mr Neil Verey, you were the "murderer",' said PC Cuffe, nodding. 'You must have been moving round the house rather more, sir. Did you see anything?'

'Well,' said Uncle Neil, 'I caught Mother, but then I was distracted. The house is haunted, and I saw—'

'NEIL,' said Grandfather.

'I mean,' said Uncle Neil, going red, 'that no, I didn't see the thieves. I didn't go into the study. And I couldn't *find* anyone else. I did look!'

'I didn't, either,' said Aunt Pam loudly. 'I was – I – anyway, I didn't see a thing.'

'Pamela was in our room, with me,' said Uncle Hugh. 'Isn't that right, Pam?'

Aunt Pam shot him a look that I couldn't understand. 'Oh yes, of course,' she said. 'We forgot about the game. We were talking. And we went downstairs together to find Sidney dead.'

But that was a lie! I knew it was, Diary. Uncle Hugh had come out of the dining room alone, and Aunt Pam – hadn't she come out of the drawing room? I thought I'd heard her crying in there just before I left it. They were *lying*, just like Ruth had lied. The policeman was too tired to notice, but *I* wasn't. And that meant – well, that meant they all had something to hide.

24

From the diary of Fionnuala O'Malley, continued

PC Cuffe just noted it all down in his book and kept asking questions, trying not to yawn.

'You, sir, Mr Hugh Verey – the missing documents belonged to you, did they not?'

'They were classified,' said Uncle Hugh, and I could hear him puffing himself up angrily. 'My factory, which usually makes car-engine parts, is currently being used for important war work. I'm not at liberty to say what exactly, but I can tell you that it is *crucial* to the war effort. The documents that were stolen involve that effort.'

'Thank you,' PC Cuffe said, nodding. 'It won't go further. Well, this certainly fits the pattern.'

But it doesn't! I thought again. There hadn't been an air raid, and we were all in the house.

'Who do you think the thieves are?' asked Aunt Pam. 'They aren't . . . Germans? What if they're part of the *invasion*?'

I heard Granny gasp.

'That's enough, Pamela!' Grandfather said warningly.

'Well, it's going to happen soon, isn't it?' said Aunt Pam shrilly. 'And there's nothing we can do about it! I don't see why we're wasting our time in this dusty old house – God, I wish I was anywhere else. I wish I was *gone*—'

I'd never heard her sound so upset and angry.

'PAM!' snapped Uncle Hugh. 'I told you we need to STAY HERE! It's safe!'

'Mrs Verey, as your husband says, you are safe here. We've no evidence that any of the rumours about enemy parachutists are true. We have to investigate each one carefully, but so far every single lead has come to nothing. But – well, there certainly are German citizens in this country who are trying to help the Nazis. And it's not just Germans. It's the Italians and Austrians – and the Irish too. Our nearest neighbour's neutrality looks very much like nothing more than a front, and we do suspect this gang may have connections to Dublin as well as Berlin.'

I could feel myself flushing in shock.

Granny gasped again. 'But there aren't any Irish people around here!' she said. 'We'd have noticed them!'

'Well, there is Fiona,' said Uncle Hugh.

'Who's this Fiona?' asked PC Cuffe. 'The maid? That's often the way in—'

'My niece,' said Uncle Hugh. 'Her father was Irish, unfortunately, and he certainly taught her a lot of anti-English nonsense. She's only a child – but, well, you never know.'

My eyes were stinging. I wanted to burst out of the cabinet and scream at him. *How could he?*

Grandfather cleared his throat. 'Hugh,' he said, 'no one in this family would do such a thing. That's enough.'

At least Grandfather still trusted me.

Uncle Hugh harrumphed and muttered, 'Well, what *about* the maid? Ruth's Austrian, so she might be a collaborator. What if she's working with the gang? And what about that evacuee boy? Where's *he* from?'

'I'm sure he's not German, Hugh dear,' said Granny. 'The authorities would have told us! And Ruth was thoroughly checked by the government before she arrived here. We wouldn't have allowed her to work for us if there were any questions.'

'Well now, thank you for all this,' said PC Cuffe. 'As I said, I have another case in Kenilworth, so I really must go. Now I've taken preliminary notes, I shall keep you up to date with developments. The only other thing I need this evening is a quick look at the outside of the French window that the thieves used to get in. We'll have to wait until the photographer can stop by tomorrow to record the scene, of course, and I shall interview this maid of yours then, just to make sure. Could someone show me the way from the front door?'

'I'll take you,' said Uncle Neil.

'Thank you, sir,' said the policeman.

They went out into the hall together, and everyone else was quiet for a while.

Then Granny began to sob.

'Stay calm, my dear,' said Grandfather. 'It'll be all right.'

'It *won't*,' wept Granny. 'Sidney is dead. My second baby! Oh, will our troubles never end?'

Grandfather put a hand on her shoulder and bent his head to hers.

'Are the papers you lost really so important?' said Aunt Pam quietly to Uncle Hugh.

'Vital,' said Uncle Hugh sharply. 'It'll be all over for me if they fall into the wrong hands. God! What a mess!'

'But they'll know it's not your fault, surely! We were robbed!'

'I'll be for it if the information turns up anywhere else, that's for certain.' Uncle Hugh jumped up and began to pace back and forward in front of my cabinet.

And I couldn't help thinking again that, after their initial shock, some people didn't seem particularly upset about Uncle Sidney.

25

From the report of May Wong

The problem is that it's very hard to conduct a proper search of a house when there are grown-ups and police buzzing round it like flies.

Logically, the best place for the murderer to have hidden the stolen (not really stolen) papers was somewhere on the ground floor. I looked back at my notes and saw that almost all the grown-ups had been there when Eric raised the alarm.

So, when everyone had filed into the drawing room, Eric and I crept down the back stairs, as quietly as we could, and began to hunt round the *most* likely place, the one nearest to the study: the hallway. We looked inside cupboards and behind the cushions of Old Mrs Verey's chair and under the rugs and in the umbrella stand, but we didn't find anything. It was very annoying.

I was kneeling down, looking inside the big old grandfather clock next to the main stairs, when the drawing-room door opened and a square of light burst out into the hall. I scrabbled sideways, and Eric dragged at my shoulder and, as fast as we could, we got across the hall to the servants' little staircase.

It was the policeman and Neil Verey, and they walked to the front door without noticing we were there, talking seriously together. The door squealed open as loudly as always and slammed behind them, and we both breathed again.

And then we heard something else. Someone was pacing back and forth, and muttering anxiously to themselves – and it was coming from the kitchens. 'I didn't touch him,' I heard Ruth say, and, 'I don't know anything. I keep myself to myself.'

The hairs on the back of my neck prickled as we crept back upstairs to the night meeting room.

We got there just before Nuala did. She was flushed and frowning.

'The family gave the policeman their alibis,' said Nuala. 'I wrote them all down – I think Uncle Hugh and Aunt Pam *lied*.'

'We haven't found the papers,' I told her. 'We were in the hall when Neil and the policeman went by – they nearly caught us. And then we heard Ruth – she was talking to herself in the kitchens. I think she's lying as well!'

Nuala was still frowning, and I noticed that she was having trouble meeting Eric's eyes.

'What's wrong?' asked Eric.

'Nothing,' said Nuala quickly. 'No, that's not true. I'm really sorry. The policeman – he thinks it's just a burglary gone wrong. You were right that he'd say that, May. And – well, he reckons the gang of thieves could be German or Irish.'

'WHAT?' I yelped.

Eric just stared at her.

'I know!' said Nuala. 'Uncle Hugh told him about me being half Irish. It's a good thing they don't think you're German, Eric – but Uncle Hugh told the policeman to look at Ruth because she's from Austria. They think that someone in the house might have helped the thieves.'

'But there aren't any thieves!' I said. 'And it's not fair that Hugh says you might be to blame!'

I know I didn't like Nuala, but some things are just wrong, and when you hear about them you *have* to say so.

'Only Grandfather stuck up for me,' said Nuala miserably. That's why I don't like it here. English people might *seem* nice to you, but they'll never really trust you, not when it matters. I found myself feeling sorry for Nuala, having to learn that like this. I told myself sternly to stop it and focus on the case.

'So, what now?' I asked because Eric was still pale with terror. I knew he couldn't think about anything but the fact that the police might connect him with the murder if they knew his real name.

'Uncle Neil and PC Cuffe are outside now, examining the French window,' said Nuala, still looking nearly as unhappy as Eric.

'Well, that's good!' I said. 'If the break-in was faked, which it was, there aren't going to be any marks on the outside of the French window, are there? It'll show that the story is a lie, and there's no gang of Irish and German people roaming the countryside.'

'Oh!' said Nuala, cheering up. 'Of course!'

I had a thought then. 'The loo is just above the study window. If we open the window, we can hear what they're saying,' I said.

Nuala made a face. 'We can't break blackout!' she said.

'Oh, come on! We won't turn on any lights, will we? And *I* don't care that it's the *loo* if you don't.'

I practically had to drag them in, which was frustrating. But of course, when we were there, they were both glad I had. We could hear someone saying, 'Mmm ...' ('PC Cuffe!' Nuala whispered), and Neil Verey's voice saying, 'Golly, look at that!'

We all stuck our heads round the sides of the blackout curtain and peered down into the darkness.

'It's been jemmied from the outside,' said PC Cuffe. 'Very clear. And very fresh too. It all fits. And what's this! A wristwatch – look, here, in the mud. A clue!'

Next to me Eric gasped, and then coughed as I shoved my hand over his mouth.

'Now, Mr Verey, be assured that we won't abandon your family. The work your father does – he's locked more criminals away than we can count, and we're all very grateful. Between you and me, we're very stretched at the minute, but we will make you our priority. I'll be back tomorrow as soon as I can.'

'Thank you,' said Neil. 'We appreciate it. Although we may have someone inside the house who can shed more light on all this.'

'Who?' said PC Cuffe, surprised.

Neil's voice crept higher with excitement. 'My late half-brother Leonard – I saw his ghost tonight. It's been bothering the family for the past few weeks – poltergeist tricks – but tonight I *saw* him. He floated out of the spare room on the first floor – his old room – and down the front stairs, a small patch of whiteness, floating high in the air – my brother's ghost! You see why I was distracted from the game. Leonard was always my protector when he was alive, especially when S— I mean, when other boys in the village were cruel to me – and I now believe he was trying to protect me from the thieves. I'm going to attempt to contact him to see if I can get anything else out of him. *We* may not know anything, but I believe Leonard does!'

There was a pause. 'Sir,' said PC Cuffe, 'I – *really*. Half our calls are from people who think the little old lady living next door is a Nazi spy. I don't think that I can manage a ghost as well.'

'But ghosts are as real as you or I! I must insist—'

The two moved away, and we couldn't hear them any more.

Neil Verey was even stranger than I'd thought if he believed he'd seen his dead half-brother coming out of the spare room we'd been using to hold our meetings. Or was that another lie? After all, he'd just stopped himself from admitting to the policeman that Sidney used to be cruel to him. Was he just trying to distract from the real story – that he'd hated his brother enough to kill him?

And I was also wondering about what PC Cuffe had said: there *were* marks on the outside of the French window, and Eric's watch had been found outside. If Eric was right – if the murderer was from inside the house, and the burglary was all just made up – why on earth had they gone out of the French window? And how had they had time to jemmy the *outside* of it before the murder had been discovered?

Was Eric wrong after all?

26

From the diary of Fionnuala O'Malley, continued

When I opened my eyes this morning, Saturday, I thought for a minute that it'd all been a dream. But then May sat up in the bed next to mine with a snort, her black hair sticking to her forehead sweatily, and said, 'Ugh, why are you writing things down? You'd better not be planning any detecting without us. I've told you: we're leading this investigation, and you're just helping us.'

'Uncle Sidney's dead,' I said experimentally.

'*Obviously*,' said May.

It *is* all real.

I've got to remember, though, that this won't last. Sure, I might be working with May and Eric now, but I'm *not* friends with them. When we find out what happened, they'll leave, just like Bob and Bert did (I mean, Bob and Bert weren't also spies on a mission, but you get my point), and I'm still hoping that Mam will take me away too.

There's no point being *too* nice to either of them. You're the only one who'll stick around, Diary, and that's why I'm talking to you. I finished my entry from last night, and hid this book safely under my bed. When Ruth rang the breakfast gong, May and I went downstairs together (not *together* together, just side by side, trying not to look at each other in case it seemed like we were friendly).

We couldn't eat in the dining room (there was a dead body there) so breakfast was in the drawing room, on a table that I think is usually in the kitchens and looked weirdly out of place among the nice upholstery and fancy paintings. The curtains had been pulled back and it was raining outside, harder than yesterday.

I heard May sigh when she saw that, and realized what she must be thinking – that now we wouldn't be able to check for footprints in the grounds. I guess I really am thinking like Nancy Drew.

I spread a tiny rationed scrape of butter on my bread, took a lumpy ladle of porridge and sat down next to Mam, who was blinking and yawning and asking, 'Whatever happened last night? Why are we in here?'

Everyone went very quiet and still. I'd forgotten that the sleeping pill meant she didn't know.

'Serena, dear,' said Granny, 'I'm afraid something's happened.'

And you know, I felt so mad at Mam right then. I'm eleven and she's ancient, at least thirty, but I was there last night and she wasn't. I should have been happy, because her being asleep meant that there was no way she could have hurt Uncle Sidney – but, as Mam's face crumpled up like a kid given out to for being bold, I couldn't stop myself. Sometimes I think that I'm really the adult and she's the kid, having to be looked after and protected and petted. She was never like this before Da died – or maybe she was, and I just didn't notice because Da took care of her, and I didn't have to.

So I was still raging inside when upstairs there was a shout, and then the drumming of footsteps down the stairs.

'What has got into everyone!' said Granny faintly. 'This is all too much!'

The dining-room door opened, and Annabelle Olivia came in. 'I saw the ghost!' she said. 'I did! Last night! But Daddy won't listen to me!'

'Really?' asked Uncle Neil, leaning forward in excitement. 'When you say—'

'NEIL,' said Grandfather. 'Now is not the time. Annabelle Olivia, you certainly did not see a ghost. Ghosts do not exist.'

'Sorry, Grandfather,' said Annabelle Olivia. 'But—'

More footsteps, heavier, and in came Uncle Hugh, looking pink and out of breath.

'Annabelle Olivia, please stop spreading nonsense!' he said. 'Apologies, Mother, Father. I did try to explain to her.'

'But I saw—' Annabelle Olivia began, and then she looked at Uncle Hugh and shut her mouth with an effort.

'I think we ought to have a seance,' announced Uncle Neil. 'I think it could be important.'

'*Neil!*' said Granny. 'Please.'

'Mother, if we're able to speak to Leonard's ghost, he may very well tell us the details of Sidney's death. He could have crucial evidence that will help the police catch the thief! There's Hugh's papers to think about, after all.'

'I should never have mentioned them!' snapped Uncle Hugh. 'They're *classified.*'

'Hugh, please. Neil dear, this is upsetting me. I don't like it when you talk about Leonard, you know that. And, with poor Sidney lying dead in the dining room, I wish you'd have some decorum. Why can't this family be *nice* to each other?' Granny said with a sigh.

'I should think it'll be easier now Sidney's dead,' said Uncle Hugh. 'He was always the one who started it.'

'And you let him!' said Uncle Neil. 'You never lifted a finger to stop him! I blame you as much as him!'

They glared at each other, and I wriggled in my seat.

'Really, you are all very disappointing,' said Granny sharply.

She stared around at the room, and I knew she was partly thinking of me. Mam wasn't supposed to run away to America, or meet Da and marry him (just like Da wasn't supposed to marry a Sassenach like her).

That's when I really decided that I was going to show Granny that I wasn't disappointing. I was going to solve the case, and get Uncle Hugh's papers back, and make Granny feel safe again.

'I shall be holding a seance as soon as possible,' said Uncle Neil determinedly. 'The rest of you can come along if you like.'

Everyone sat in silence for the rest of breakfast.

'I'm going to go to the seance,' I whispered to May as we left together. I know what Da would have said: that we needed a priest, not a seance. The thought of summoning the ghost scared me – but now that I was a detective I had to follow the clues.

'Seances are silly!' May whispered back – not very quietly, but then she never does anything quietly.

'It might help us solve the murder!' I hissed at her. 'But grand, so – do whatever you want.'

'Fine!'

'FINE!'

'Please stop doing that,' said Eric. 'May, I know it's raining, but I think we should take a look at the study window ourselves. Nuala, would you like to come?'

'All right,' I said. After last night, I was certain that whatever was going to happen today couldn't get more exciting.

I was wrong.

27

The grass was wet, and the rain got inside my gumboots. I was right when I'd guessed that any footprints from last night would have been pretty much washed away – the ground was mud, and our feet slushed around and left big ugly pawprints that didn't look anything like our shoes.

May was humming, a little grumbling noise in the back of her throat that I've noticed her making sometimes when she's not paying attention, and Eric laughed and poked her. He was finally looking more cheerful.

'May,' he said. 'Careless talk.'

We went round the side of the house so we could see where the policeman and Uncle Neil had stood last night. There was a narrow path leading up to the study's French window, but the beds on each side were all disturbed – Scott had been in the middle of digging up a crop and planting something else – so mud lay all across the path.

We stood and squinted at the mess. If I really tried, I could maybe see a print or two in the dirt, but I couldn't tell who had made them.

'Look at the window!' gasped May.

The French window had a catch halfway up, and someone had gone at the wooden frame around it with some kind of tool. It was neat work – and it had definitely been done from outside.

'I don't understand!' said Eric. 'The gang isn't real!'

'Maybe you made a mistake,' I said – and then I felt really bad because Eric looked wounded, and May scowled furiously.

'What if they arrest me and Ruth?' he asked. 'How can we prove we're not working with the Germans?'

I stared down at my gumboots, their toes slushy with mud. And then I guess I had a Nancy Drew moment because I suddenly *knew*.

'*The rug*,' I said.

'Er, we're outside,' said May.

'No, I mean last night! Lookit, we all saw Uncle Sid lying on the rug. There was blood all around him, but it was *clean*. It wasn't muddy. But it's been raining for days. If someone had come *in* through the French window, their boots would have left mud on the rug. Don't you get it? They only *left* through the French window. And they dropped Eric's watch where they knew it would be noticed, to trick the police.'

167

Eric laughed. 'Of course!' he cried. 'I should have seen it. Well done!'

'Yes, all right, don't overreact, Eric,' said May – but I knew from how wide her eyes had gone that she was impressed. 'Eric, draw the scene,' she snapped. 'For our notes.'

Eric got out a notebook and pencil and made a quick sketch of it. 'May can't draw,' he said to me, 'so I get to do this.'

'I can so draw!' said May. 'I just don't want to, that's all. It's boring.'

'*She can't,*' whispered Eric. 'All right, we have to hold a meeting. Let's go to the Anderson shelter.'

But, as we walked towards it, Annabelle Olivia came running out of the house.

'What are you doing?' she called. 'Are you ghost hunting? Can I help?'

'Nothing doing,' said May. 'We're looking for worms for Eric's hedgehog.'

'I found Emil in the garden,' said Eric matter-of-factly, as though we hadn't just been discussing a murder mystery. 'He lives under my bed.'

'Oh!' said Annabelle Olivia. 'Er – I can help with that too.'

'You look in the shelter,' May went on, 'and we'll look in the mud out here.'

Annabelle Olivia took a deep breath, nodded and dived into the Anderson shelter.

'Quick!' whispered May. 'Run!'

So we ran. I felt kind of bad, but I knew we had to talk about what I'd just worked out.

We went as fast as we could through the garden – the part with those square dark rows of box hedges and curving stone paths, then into the rose garden looking stark and pathetic with all the roses from this summer gone and the bushes cut back. English people are so weird about their gardens. I don't get it. They're just plants, after all – who wants to take care of *them*? Before last year, I'd never stayed anywhere long enough to watch plants grow and die and grow again, and seeing it now makes me feel weird, like they're growing over *me*.

Once we were out past the rose garden, and the orchard, we hopped the fence into the field.

'Where are we going?' said May crossly, as we tracked through the brown grass.

'The abandoned cottage,' I said. I guess that should have been a sign to me that I was starting to really trust them, that I'd think to take them there.

We were almost all the way across the field when Eric froze and held up his hand.

'Quiet,' he said sharply.

'What?' asked May after a long minute.

'I thought I heard rustling,' said Eric.

We were really close to the cottage now, its crumbling stone walls dark before us. It's only one storey, with a roof that's flaking and falling off. Inside, one room is open all the way to the sky, but there are two more that are still intact – including the one I've been filling with chairs for my theatre. But other than that it's completely empty, apart from rat droppings and something that I think could be to do with an owl.

'A fox probably,' said May.

'Bigger than a fox, and it's the wrong time of day,' said Eric. 'There! Listen!'

I couldn't hear anything, and I could see from the look on May's face – scrunched up and sceptical – that she couldn't, either.

At last, Eric sighed. 'It's stopped,' he said. 'Perhaps it was a fox.'

'Oh, come on!' said May. She bounced forward again round the side of the cottage – she really does move in bounces, like she's got too much energy to walk normally – and then it was her turn to stop and yelp. 'Hey!' she cried. 'Come and look!'

Eric and I followed her and both gasped in surprise.

Someone was living in the abandoned cottage.

PART SIX

WE DISCOVER SOME SECRETS

28

From the diary of Fionnuala O'Malley, continued

The abandoned cottage's empty main room wasn't empty any more. A fire had been banked up against one wall, just where the rain couldn't get in. There was a neat pile of cans stacked against another wall, and through the dark doorway into the next room I could see a bedroll. Footprints marked the mud and dirt, and – worst of all – whoever it was had found one of the old chairs I'd brought over from the house to sit on. And they'd *cracked* it.

'My chair!' I yelled.

'SHH!' said May and Eric together.

'They broke my chair!' I said, quieter.

'That is not important!' hissed May. 'This place is supposed to be empty. Who's living here and why?'

'It must be someone who's been bombed out,' said Eric. 'Coventry had a bomb a few weeks ago, didn't it? Perhaps they lost their home and had to go on the road.'

'You're too soft-hearted,' said May. 'Why would they be here *now*? No, I don't like it.'

'Do you think this has something to do with . . . Uncle Sid?' I asked.

'They couldn't have killed him, could they? We just proved that! But they could be an *accomplice*. Or they might be helping Sidney with his spying! They can't have gone far – that fire's still smouldering.'

'Well, the police are going to find this eventually,' I said, kicking at the ashes of the fire with my toe. 'And then we'll see.'

'Why would the police come here?' said May. 'As far as anyone knows, it's been abandoned for years. All right, let me think.'

She started pacing round the room. I got nervous then – we didn't know how far away the person who was living here was, or when they might be back. And hadn't Eric heard rustling in the bushes? I felt unprotected. We might be detectives solving a case, but we were also kids, and I didn't think we'd be much use against a dangerous adult.

'What are you at?' I hissed at her.

'Looking for clues!' she whispered back in that foghorn-blare voice that's basically louder than when she speaks normally. May is not subtle.

'We should leave! The person might come back!'

'I can fight them. Oh, come on – let's look around!'

I thought this was a stupid idea, but I was still so mad about that chair that I felt like I had something to prove. I wanted to know the identity of the person who'd come into *my* cottage and messed it up.

Here are the things I noticed while May was pacing around like a wild animal and Eric was sketching a layout of the cottage.

The fire was definitely still warm. It was banked down carefully – whoever it was knew how to handle a fire – but right in its tender heart it glowed. It couldn't have been left more than a few hours.

The cans had been dented a bit, and their labels were peeling. And some of them weren't in English. They had words on them that I'd never seen on any of the cans in the Elysium Hall kitchens.

I picked one up and stared at it. 'Is this French?' I asked.

'Yes,' said Eric, glancing up. 'So does that mean the person hiding here has come from France?'

'If they have, that's bad news,' said May. 'France is occupied by the Nazis.'

The footprints were big and heavy, way bigger than any of our feet. They definitely belonged to an adult, one who was wearing boots.

The bedroll had been done up very neatly, much neater than I could do. And it was a dirty khaki colour.

'May,' I said quietly (*actually* quietly), 'I think this person—'

'Is a soldier?' asked May, coming up behind me.

That annoyed me because it was *my* discovery.

'Yes,' I said shortly.

'So do I,' said May. 'I've thought it for ages – minutes and minutes. So what's a soldier doing out here? And are they on our side or the enemy's? Remember what I said about France. They could be an English soldier who's come from there, but they could be a German one from there too.'

Eric stuck his head into the darkness of the second room.

'If it is a soldier,' he said, 'he's out here on his own. That means he's probably deserted.'

Deserting's when you run away from the army because you don't want to fight. According to Grandfather, it's a crime, but I think I understand why someone would do it. Sometimes you just can't be a hero any more. But, if the soldier had deserted, then he *really* wouldn't want us finding him. He'd be in a lot of trouble, and that made me feel more scared than ever.

There was another rustling in the bushes outside, and a crack like a stick had snapped. I jumped, and Eric gasped.

'We need to leave, May,' he said. '*Quickly.*'

'But – oh, all *right*,' grumbled May.

She looked mad, like *we'd* disturbed her, but I noticed that she walked faster than she usually does, her back very straight, and I knew that she was just as scared as me and Eric.

176

As we stepped out of the abandoned cottage into the field, it began to rain again. I could feel spits of it sliding down my hair and sticking to my cheeks. I tried not to shudder.

We tracked back through the wet grass, my gumboots squelching and water tickling down my neck, and I really started to wonder. What if this person – whoever they were – *was* working with someone from the house? Maybe they'd killed Uncle Sid together? Or what if they really were part of the invasion that everyone said was coming? What if they'd parachuted down here on a mission to find out everything they could about England? Maybe they'd come to Elysium Hall to get information from Uncle Sidney. Now he was dead, would they come for the rest of us?

29

From the report of May Wong

We got back to the house, panting and soaked through, just in time for lessons. While we waited for Old Mrs Verey, I thought as hard as I could about what we'd just discovered.

I didn't understand how the soldier hiding in the abandoned cottage fitted into the mystery. He might be a German parachutist, but if he was, then why did he have a soldier's bedroll with him? Enemy invaders are supposed to fly in dressed like vicars and farmers and old ladies, not wearing uniforms.

But one thing I did know was that he couldn't have been the one to kill Sidney. We'd proved that the broken French window was a trick. I hated to admit it, but what Nuala had realized about the rug was smart. The murderer *had* to have been in the house with us.

I also knew that the police were going to go off on the wrong track. They had Eric's father's watch now, and all they were going to think was that the Germans were behind it.

So we couldn't stop detecting. It was up to us to work out who the *real* murderer was, and the only way to do that was to be completely logical and move as quickly as possible.

It was already a day after the murder. As soon as lessons were over, we could get on with the case. But Old Mrs Verey didn't come in. After fifteen minutes, Pamela Verey arrived, looking upset and distracted. She didn't even notice that all our socks were damp, and our hair looked like we'd been out in the rain. So had Annabelle Olivia, but somehow, by the time we got back to the house, she'd already changed out of her wet things.

'I couldn't find you,' she said reproachfully. 'I found lots of worms, though.'

I felt a bit bad then, for tricking her – but not too bad. We couldn't tell anyone else what we were doing, after all, and especially not Annabelle Olivia, who can never keep quiet about anything.

'What are you all doing here?' Pamela asked.

'Waiting for Granny to give us lessons,' said Annabelle Olivia. 'She's *late*, Mummy.'

'Oh, good heavens, lessons are cancelled today,' said Pamela, wringing her hands. 'They don't matter! Go and play if you want.'

'What are *you* doing, Mummy?' asked Annabelle Olivia. 'Can I help?'

'Don't worry, darling,' said Pamela. 'I'm just looking for something. It must be around here somewhere. I'm sure I had it last night—'

Eric, Nuala and I backed out of the room as quietly as we could, leaving her shuffling the cushions about on the library chairs and Annabelle Olivia piping questions at her.

'What do we do now?' Eric asked in a whisper.

'Keep looking for those missing papers first of all,' I said firmly, sticking my chin up. 'Last night was a washout, but we've seen how distracted the grown-ups are today. And we have to watch the policemen when they come back. I want us to know what they think they know, so we can prove them wrong.'

Someone pounded on the front door.

'The police!' said Eric. The scared look was back on his face.

'All right!' I said. 'We have to split up. Nuala, you follow the police around. Ask questions and generally be annoying – you're good at that. Eric and I will hunt for the papers. Agreed?'

Obviously this was me trying to send Nuala off so Eric and I could detect together. I also didn't think Eric should be on his own or near the police. I wanted to protect him.

Eric and Nuala nodded.

'Grand, so. And if anyone asks what we're doing,' Nuala said, 'tell them that we're putting together a play. Rehearsing and getting costumes and props and stuff. They're used to that from me, after all.'

This was clever of her. 'Humph,' I said. 'Not bad. And remember: *constant vigilance*. That's what my sister says, and it's good advice. We meet this afternoon in the shelter to discuss findings. *Don't* let Annabelle Olivia follow us. Now go!'

30

From the report of May Wong

Eric and I began on the second floor. Eric kept watch while I went into Nuala's mother's room (she has her old room still, from when she was a child) to collect a few scarves to look like props for Nuala's made-up play in case anyone asked. Not that they would: grown-ups get bored if you even mention something like a play or a game, but it made sense to be prepared.

I pushed the door open very quietly and peeked in. There was a rustle, and a springy turning-over-mattress noise, and then a snore. I crept forward.

The room was in a horrible mess, and it smelled of ten different sorts of scent, with stale grown-up underneath. Mrs O'Malley couldn't be the murderer, but for a moment I wondered whether the papers could be hidden in her room. Then I noticed that some kind of powder lay scattered across the dressing table like fingerprint dust – face powder, I realized, spotting a compact and brush.

A fine layer coated the bottles of pills on the table, and the rug on the floor, and in it were only the pads of Mrs O'Malley's bare feet and a smaller set of bare feet that looked like Nuala's.

I crept out with the scarves, but instead of feeling pleased to have ruled out a hiding place I just felt sad.

I met Eric on the landing. 'Ruth's room?' he whispered, and I nodded. Together we pushed its door open and crept in. And we found enough there to get me out of my funk.

Ruth was downstairs, of course – she's always behind on her work because she's really being three people at once: two maids and a cook – so the room was empty. We still tiptoed, though. Isn't it funny how people do that, like you might disturb the memory of the person, even when they're not there?

It was awfully bare – no pictures, and only a pair of gilt candlesticks on the bedside table, the candles half burned down in them.

There were three dresses hanging in the wardrobe. Two were brownish and boring, but one was deep red and silky, a beautiful grown-up party dress – something my sister Rose would have loved. Thinking that made me feel uncomfortable because it reminded me that I'd left Rose behind at Deepdean. I suddenly wondered whether she was worried about me. Had Big Sister Hazel told her that I'd turned up at Great Russell Street and that she was looking for me?

As I was thinking all that, I was digging at the back of the wardrobe. My hands suddenly bumped into something that crackled and bent. It was a roll of papers.

I pulled it out, exclaiming, and peeled it open – but, instead of the stolen documents that I was expecting, I was looking at a collection of playbills and posters. They seemed old – they were all frayed at the edges – and they showed pictures of tigers and acrobats and men lifting weights. The words on them were in lots of different languages, and I couldn't read any of them.

'What are these?' I asked.

Eric came to look at what I was holding out. 'Circus posters,' he said after a pause.

'How do you know that?'

'That one's in German,' said Eric, pointing. 'It says: *Hoffman's Circus, Vienna, the first to the twenty-second of June 1935. Come and discover the most magical, the most mysterious, the most dangerous acts in Europe! Tightrope walkers, the amazing Wolf Boy, Europe's Best Medium, Harpo the Clown and many more!* The others are all the same, look, but different dates and locations and languages.'

'Why d'you think she has them?'

'Maybe she worked there,' said Eric, shrugging. 'It makes sense. I asked her where she lived before she came to England, and she said she didn't stay in one place because her family travelled all the time.'

'But she's a maid!' I said. I didn't ask Eric how he knew that. I'd heard him talking to Ruth in German when they both thought no one was listening. Eric is too friendly sometimes.

'She's a maid *now*,' said Eric sharply. 'But she might have been something else before the war. Look at that dress! Mama and Papa were famous musicians back in Germany. Our house was nice, and we had lots of good things, but we had to leave them behind when we left. I had a pet chicken called Glockenspiel, but Papa said she wouldn't like the weather in England. When we came here, Papa had to give piano lessons, and Mama cleaned houses. So you see, people change who they are when they come to a new country.'

I thought about that. I was sure I was still the same person I'd been in Hong Kong. But I'd left things behind too. The Big House with its beautiful gardens, my maids and amahs, and Teddy and Ma Ma, the heat and smell of Hong Kong – they all suddenly seemed even further away than usual, and I felt hot with panic. What if I couldn't get back for years? What if I couldn't get back at all?

'Look at this, though,' said Eric.

He'd been going through Ruth's suitcase, which sat under her bare little bed.

'*These* aren't hers.'

He'd uncovered a small wrapped bundle containing a strange mixture of things. There was a tiny blue brooch, a pen without a lid, a little pot of lipsalve, a comb, a china figurine and a medal.

'I've seen Old Mrs Verey wearing that brooch,' said Eric. 'And the figurine is from the drawing room – I know it is.'

'So Ruth *is* a thief?' I asked.

This was surprising. I remembered how Sidney had teased her about it – I'd been sure that he was just being cruel. And there was something familiar about this bundle. I'd seen something like it before.

I thought for a moment, and then I had it. 'Eric!' I said. 'When I was in Sidney's room last night, he had a pile of things like this. I think the lid to this pen was there!'

We stared at each other.

'That's strange,' said Eric. 'Why? What was he doing with them? What's *she* doing with them? Was he trying to frame her? Ruth isn't a thief!'

I wasn't so sure. I knew Eric liked Ruth, so he wanted to trust her, but I didn't have to.

'Humph,' I said. 'We'll have to think about it. Where should we look for the papers next?'

'Mr Scott's room,' said Eric, putting the bundle in his pocket. 'He's outside too. I saw him going towards the orchard as we were coming back from the cottage.'

As we crept out of Ruth's room, I couldn't help thinking that we were uncovering more mysteries than we were solving.

31

From the report of May Wong

Mr Scott's room was even barer than Ruth's. The bed was made up tightly; there was a single extra shirt in the wardrobe, and some disgustingly holey (though clean) underwear in the drawers beside his bed. I bet they were older than Eric and me – they absolutely looked it. This was funny, but not a clue.

There was only one picture on his bedside table: an old faded snap of a woman with two children pressed against her skirt and another in her arms. They were all scowling at the camera as though the sun was in their eyes. One of the children was carrying a bucket, and another wore a bathing suit, and there was a seagull ogling in the background.

'His family,' said Eric, picking it up and turning it over. '*Susie with Edmund, Clarence and Arthur in Blackpool, July 1910.* I wonder what happened to them all, for

Mr Scott to be living here on his own now. Do you think they might be dead? Wouldn't that be sad?'

'I suppose,' I said, even though it was. Mr Scott seemed even lonelier than we were.

I knelt down and peered under the bed. It was swept clean – but then I noticed that the mattress itself was bulging strangely. I yelped excitedly and pushed at it, and it lifted up to reveal a wheel of cheese and a jar of pickles.

'Oh!' I said, sitting back on my heels. 'That's not the papers.'

'He might be trading food on the black market,' said Eric. 'That stuff's not on the ration, is it?'

'He might,' I said, 'but it isn't anything to do with this case. I don't see how it can be, anyway.'

Eric sighed. 'You're right,' he said. 'Come on – let's keep looking.'

Neil Verey's room was messy, which I thought was funny – he was in the army, and aren't soldiers supposed to be tidy? But it was a good thing for us. Messy people show so much more of who they are. His spare uniform was flung over a chair, a big grease stain on its jacket lapel, and scattered round the floor were ghost-hunting books: *Haunted England*, *Speaking to the Other Side*, *Mediums and What They Can Reveal*, *English Lore* – piles and piles of them. There were stacks of notebooks underneath the bed too. I flicked through them, and they were full of the most dreadful scribbles.

For a while, I thought that the papers might be somewhere in the mess. After all, if you wanted to hide something like that, burying them among a larger pile of papers is a good idea. But they weren't. Eric and I shook out each notebook, and furled through the spiritual guidebooks, and there wasn't anything. There was nothing hiding inside all the bundled-up, musty-smelling clothes, either.

I picked up one more notebook, a thin little school-exercise thing, and flicked through it. 'Oh!'

'What is it?' asked Eric.

'He's recorded notes about the poltergeist,' I said. 'And look, here—' I held the page out.

Sid is the centre of the occurrences, I'm sure of it.
He has a very bad aura.

Crash from first floor at 10:42 a.m. and found Sid
rushing out of his room, looking startled. Said that the
cup of tea he was drinking had smashed, and when he
looked on the floor he found one of Mother's brooches
among the shards.

Met Sid on the landing at 3:47 p.m., very angry. Said
that he'd suddenly been bombarded with objects,
eggshells and cufflinks and so on, some of which struck
his face. I hunted carefully and found Father's cufflink
and a shilling on the floor – although both of those

might have simply fallen there at an earlier point and been ignored by Ruth's slapdash cleaning attempts.

Convinced that Leonard is trying to say something by all this poltergeist activity. It's all because of Sidney, I'm sure of it. His negative energy. The house would be calmer if he wasn't here.

'What if this is Neil's motive?' asked Eric. 'He hated Sidney and wanted to get rid of him. Saying he saw Leonard's ghost last night might be an excuse to stop the police suspecting him. Or perhaps he did think he saw it, and it told him to kill Sidney?'

I frowned and nodded. And I'd realized something else. The objects in Neil's notes – they were some of the things I'd seen in Sidney's room, and they were like the things we'd found in Ruth's bundle. I said this to Eric.

'Oh!' he said. 'You think Neil was behind the hauntings, and Ruth and Sidney worked it out?'

'Yes!' I said, excited. 'Blast, no, he can't be. They started before he arrived.'

Eric groaned. 'You're right! Shall we go downstairs?'

I was getting frustrated, and things only got more annoying the more we searched. The fact was that the papers weren't anywhere. Not in Old Mr and Mrs Verey's stuck-up, tidy room with its cases and cabinets full of awards and medals, not in Pamela and Hugh's room (messy, clothes everywhere, things hanging out of drawers and tossed across the floor, which surprised me – I'd thought that Pamela would be starchy and clean, but there was even dirt on the carpet).

We looked behind the cistern of the loo, under the tables and inside the big vases on the first-floor landing, and I even patted down the stuffed deer head hanging beside the stairs (ugh!). Then we went downstairs and ducked into the library to avoid Ruth, who was going towards the kitchens with several pairs of men's shoes to be cleaned, and I suddenly caught a faint whiff of Sidney's disgusting cologne. Bending down under the library table, I saw it: a little black pocketbook sticking out from under the rug.

Of course! Eric had heard Sidney in the library during the game, hadn't he? He must have dropped this without realizing. I nudged Eric, whose eyes got very wide, and together we crouched down and opened it.

On the title page it said *Sidney Foley – appointments* in looping cursive. There was something funny about the handwriting, but I couldn't think what.

Then I turned to the eighth of November, the day of Sidney's murder, and saw only one entry: *10:15 p.m. Study.*

My heart was pounding.

'He had an appointment at ten fifteen?' asked Eric. 'Then why start the game at ten?'

That was exactly what I was wondering. If Sidney Foley had agreed to meet someone at 10:15 p.m., why had he suggested the game of Murder in the Dark just before ten? Unless the game was just a cover . . .

'What was he doing in here?' I asked Eric, practically fizzing with excitement.

'I couldn't – oh!' said Eric. 'What if he was looking for a particular book? Or what if he'd hidden something *inside* one of the books – some papers or something – and he wanted to fetch them for the meeting?'

'Yes! And just think! If he *planned* a meeting, then he wasn't in the study by mistake. He was there to see someone. I'll bet you *anything* that was the person you heard him talking to, Eric – and the person who killed him.'

But who was it? And, if Sidney had taken some papers with him when he went into the study, what were they – and where were they now? It wasn't just Hugh's classified documents that were missing, it was whatever Sidney had had with him.

Eric and I beamed at each other. We'd found something really important. This had to help us solve the case. It *had* to.

I could hear the police moving around near us now. I didn't want them to suspect us, and I knew we had to behave as though we weren't interested in the case at all. So I gave Eric the pocketbook for safe keeping, put my shoulders back and stuck my chin out. Then we crept into the hall.

32

From the report of May Wong

The police were in the dining room. I could see bright flashes from the doorway as their cameraman took snaps of Sidney's dead body.

Eric and I scuttled across the hall and went to lurk halfway up the stairs where we could watch everything. We were next to the enormous potted plant Annabelle Olivia had been hiding behind during the game.

'What if Annabelle Olivia did see something?' Eric asked. 'The murderer coming down the stairs, I mean.'

'Hmm,' I said. 'If she had, wouldn't she have told everyone already? She's no good at keeping quiet.'

'That's true,' said Eric, nodding. 'And look. If you get behind the plant like this, you can't really see – *hey*!' He'd crouched down and tucked himself behind the pot, his whole body covered by the plant's leaves. 'There's something shiny in here!'

'What is it?' I whispered.

'It's – hold on – it's a *ring*.'

Eric wriggled out and held it up to me. It was a thin gold band.

'What's it doing there?' I asked, which was a stupid question, but I really wanted to know. This was definitely a clue.

Eric shrugged and put it in his pocket. Now we had to be *extra* un-suspicious.

I noticed that Nuala was lurking in the hall, just next to the dining-room door. No one had told *her* about not being suspicious. I grimaced at her. She was supposed to be watching the policemen, not behaving like a suspect! She saw me glaring at her, pushed her glasses up her nose and made a horrible face back at me. I was impressed against my will. It was a good face – I don't think I could have done a better one.

Then the flashes stopped, and after a pause the door opened all the way and the policemen – PC Cuffe, the one from last night, and a new one, tall, skinny and carrying a camera – came out.

Nuala immediately surged forward. I winced.

'May I carry anything for you?' she asked in the same posh English accent she'd used when we first arrived.

PC Cuffe sighed and nodded at her. 'Very good of you. Take my jacket, will you?'

'Of course,' fluted Nuala. She took the blue jacket that

the policeman held out, and stood waiting for them to walk ahead of her out of the front door.

She had her back to us, and, as I watched, her left arm came round her back, with something clutched in it.

I'm not easily surprised, but I was then because what Nuala was holding was *the policeman's notebook*. She was quite still, and after a moment her hand twitched, beckoning us – it *must* be us – towards her.

This was extremely stupid and dangerous. I loved it.

I ran down the stairs and up to Nuala. I snatched the little red notebook out of her hand and, as quick as I could, stuffed it into the waistband of my skirt.

'Got it?' breathed Nuala, still without turning round.

'Yes!' I said.

'Shh!' said Nuala. 'I'll follow them outside. You've got five minutes to copy it down and give it back. OK?'

In answer, I flicked her hand, hard (possibly a bit harder than I'd needed to, but I was so impressed with her that it made me cross).

'*Ow*,' said Nuala.

And she folded her arm away under PC Cuffe's blue jacket (which smelled of him – it clearly hadn't been washed in ages, which was disgusting) and trotted after the police out of the open front door.

There was almost no time to even think. My hands were shaking. I gestured to Eric, and together we ran into the coat cupboard.

Spies can *never* be without a pencil and paper – but we can't just write confidential things down normally. Anyone could read them. Eric's the one who's careful and good at codes, and I'm not. (I don't care: I'm good at lots of other things, and anyway who wants to be perfect?) So we've made up a good system for when we want to take down notes quickly and secretly. *I* say the words we want to encode, and then Eric translates it into code on the page – one he's made up that's all his own. He's very fast. It's impressive.

Anyway, I folded open the notebook, took a deep breath and began. Next to me Eric squinted in concentration, face all screwed up as he worked.

At the time, I was reading so quickly that I barely understood what I was saying, but for this account I have Eric's coded version – decoded by him – and this is what it says:

Elysium Hall
8.11.40
Report of death – Mr Sidney Foley. Body found 22:35. Telephoned 22:40. Attended 23:20.
  Death occurred during game (?). Present were family, servants and some evacuees.
  Body found in study, on ground floor of house.
Head beaten in – weapon poker, found on floor beside body.

Signs of entry from outside study – French window forced with tool. Watch discovered outside French window – engraved with German name: Hans Schlossbauer. Indicates German gang.

Papers missing. Hugh, half-brother of deceased, indicates that these papers were hush-hush. Seems distraught.

Family did not see anything.

Likely theft gone wrong – connection to similar cases?

Younger brother is a fantasist.

<u>9.11.40</u>

10:32. Interview with maid, Ruth. Foreign (Austrian), sullen. Refugee. Possible spy? <u>Make enquiries</u> when time. Showed her watch, denied knowing it, but had clearly seen it before. <u>Liar</u>. Said she was in kitchens at time of death – did not take part in the game and did not see anything until she went into the study to find the body, which she did not touch. Must be investigated further – does she have connections with gang?? Seems the most likely suspect at this stage.

Examination of study – photographs and samples of blood taken.

Body examined in dining room, photographed by PC Hare. Victim's hair brown, skin fair. Dressed in costume. Two blows to back of head, strong strikes – considerable damage caused. No other injuries. Victim clearly surprised – made no effort to fight back although he was a strong man of 41. Had been holding paper when struck – small piece torn off in his fist. Handwriting apparent on it reads 'Ed Warburton MBBS'. Body to be sent to coroner for further study, though when he'll be able to get to it is another matter.

And that was where the notes stopped. I'd read as fast as I could, but I knew I'd been more than five minutes. I was hopping with nerves.

'I'll finish writing!' hissed Eric. 'You go and put it back!'

I nodded, trying to look confident, but I didn't feel it. How was I going to hide the fact that we'd pinched PC Cuffe's notebook? How was I going to put it back without him seeing?

I slipped out of the coat cupboard and tried to work out what to do next.

33

From the diary of Fionnuala O'Malley, continued

I stood with Granny and Grandfather and watched PC
Cuffe as he stared at the scratches on the wood of the
French window. The photographer took a shot of them,
his camera tripod sinking down into the mud, and PC
Cuffe, even more wrecked-looking than yesterday, rubbed
his eyes and said, 'Looks professional, doesn't it?'

Ruth had brought him and the photographer cups of
tea, and they steamed and smoked in the cold air. Little
raindrops fell on the policemen's helmets, like fingers
drumming, and I shivered.

I don't know why I'd done that – taken the policeman's
notes and given them to May. It was so dangerous. I was
expecting him to ask for his jacket any minute, and I didn't
know what I'd say when he did. I was trying to make up a
story – had I tripped and dropped it, then the notebook
fell out? – and not really getting very far, when I heard a
noise above me.

There was a face pressed against the bathroom window on the first floor. It was all squished out of shape and looked demonic. I got a shock until I realized that it was just May. She was acting the eejit, and I wanted to laugh at her. Then she pressed her hand up against the glass too, and I saw the little red notebook in it.

I finally got what she wanted me to do. I pulled myself together and imagined that I was about to step out onstage. Funnily enough, right at that moment, I swear I heard Da say, 'Break a leg,' and it made me steely enough to perform.

'OH!' I cried. I put my left hand to my mouth and made a sweeping motion with my arm that took in the garden and the hedges and the field beyond. I made sure to make my accent as English as possible. 'Gosh! I saw someone! Someone in the trees! There! LOOK!'

Everyone swung round to follow my pointing finger.

'Where?' cried PC Cuffe, blinking. 'Where?'

'I can't see anything!' said Granny.

Obviously she couldn't because I'd just invented it, but I made my face wrinkle up with confusion. 'I was *sure* I saw someone,' I said, letting my voice wobble just a little. 'I know I did! What if it was – *the murderer*?'

I was scared that part was too much, but everyone was eating my act up. Granny gasped and fluttered, clutching Grandfather's arm, and the policemen drew themselves up in excitement.

'Go and look!' PC Cuffe said to the one who'd been taking photographs. '*Hurry!*'

And out of the corner of my eye I saw something winging its way downwards, and heard a *thump* as it hit the ground.

'Did you really see someone?' Grandfather asked breathlessly, taking hold of my shoulder. 'Be honest, Fiona.'

I looked up into his stern, craggy face, its big eyebrows scrunched together and his mouth turned down. I really had to act then. I hated that part.

'Yes, Grandfather,' I said, feeling like a worm. 'I promise I did! I wouldn't lie to you. And I wouldn't hurt this family. I *wouldn't*.'

So I'd thought my act would be good to get attention away from May, but maybe it was also to remind everyone that, if there *was* a gang, I wasn't part of it. It still stung, remembering how quick most of my family had been to think I might have helped Uncle Sid's murderer.

'That's a good girl,' said Grandfather.

I felt myself puff up with happiness. Maybe I *could* be the kind of granddaughter he and Granny deserved. Then Grandfather winced, and I felt a stab of panic.

'Are you OK?' I asked.

'Of course,' said Grandfather. 'Don't be silly.'

'And don't say *OK*. It's common,' Granny put in.

And that was the end of me feeling proud of myself.

'Ruth, take her to the kitchens, won't you?' asked Granny. 'Fiona dear, you shouldn't be out here if there is someone trespassing. Give the policeman back his jacket and go.'

'Yes, Granny,' I said, and I let Ruth take my arm. Her skin felt cold and a little damp from the rain, and her fingers were tight round my shoulder. 'Oh! I'm sorry. That book – I think it must have fallen out of his pocket.'

I pointed to the ground, where the notebook May had thrown was lying in the dirt. I could see the dent it had made in the soft mud, but no one noticed that – PC Cuffe just made an exhausted noise, picked it up and knocked the muck off it.

I didn't flinch, but inside I was yelling. I'd done it! *We'd* done it, May and I. That was a weird thought.

But then Ruth murmured in my ear, 'I saw what you did. I know you lied.'

34

From the diary of Fionnuala O'Malley, continued

It was like there was ice water pouring down my spine.

'Saw what?' I bluffed, pushing my glasses up my nose, but I knew I was blushing, and I knew Ruth could see. In my defence, I'd been a detective for less than a day, so I couldn't be expected to be great at it yet. I knew that I should be able to withstand interrogation, but I didn't exactly know how.

'May dropped that notebook,' said Ruth.

'Did she?'

I glanced at her, trying not to move my head too much, and saw that she was looking at me with that hard stare of hers. Her face seemed sharp and drawn, like she hadn't slept properly. I reminded myself that we *knew* she'd lied last night. She'd got blood on her apron. How?

'I saw her,' said Ruth. 'And I know there wasn't a man in the trees. You need to stop lying before you get yourself into more trouble.'

I was so scared, for real this time. I felt like I'd messed everything up. Ruth was one of our top suspects, and she was threatening me. Then I had a brainwave.

'May wanted to get me into trouble,' I said. 'She's been trying for days. I – I upset her. She doesn't like me, and I don't know why. I had to get everyone to look away, otherwise she was going to pretend that I'd stolen that notebook.'

Da always used to say that you need to find something true in every scene you act, otherwise no one will believe in you.

'You don't know why she doesn't like you?' asked Ruth. 'I think it's obvious.'

I wasn't expecting that. I must have made a face.

'She's jealous of you,' Ruth went on. 'You've got your whole family here, and she's missing hers.'

'Oh!' I said, surprised. 'Do you really think that's true?'

Was May jealous? Was that why she'd been so mad at me since she arrived?

'I know it is,' said Ruth. 'I think about mine every day.'

'But *Da's* not here,' I said, without even thinking. Then I realized what Ruth had said, and I felt bad.

'I'm sorry about your family,' I said. 'Are they still in Austria? Couldn't they come with you?'

'Yes,' said Ruth shortly. 'And no. There was a quota. I got a visa to work here, but the rest of them had to stay.'

'I'm – sorry,' I stammered. 'But why—'

204

'Because *foreigners might overwhelm this country* otherwise,' said Ruth, cold as ice. And I knew who she was mimicking. It was how Uncle Sidney used to talk. I felt sick. Did Ruth blame Uncle Sid for her family being stuck in Austria? Was that her motive – to take revenge on him? I was desperate to ask, but I couldn't.

'As though they're not people just like the ones here! Never mind that I love them, and they love me, and they deserve to be safe. They *should* be safe, here, and *some other* people should be – ah, but never mind.'

And then Ruth shook herself and the icy, angry look just fell off her face. 'Come on, I'm taking you to the kitchens. I made biscuits.'

I almost felt like I'd imagined the last few things she'd said. But I knew I hadn't.

What I've noticed about those of us here at Elysium Hall who don't really belong is that everyone has to push back against it in their own way – even when that way is very tiny. I've got my stories and plays, even though Granny thinks it's unladylike of me to dress up like a banshee or a pirate queen. May has her rudeness, of course, and her mission. Eric has his animals. And Ruth – Ruth has her cooking. Ruth's a great cook, but nothing she makes tastes *English*. Granny gets mad at her all the time about it, but obviously she can't do anything because there aren't exactly a lot of maids right now, and if Ruth left they'd have no one.

Ruth's biscuits are definitely not English, nothing like the dry-crumb ones that make my tongue feel like all the moisture's been sucked out of it. They're crescent moons that burst in your mouth with almond sweetness. We went on tour to Vienna once, and I remember going to a cafe and eating them there. I love them.

'This is the last of the sugar,' said Ruth. 'You'd better enjoy them.'

'Did your mother teach you to make kipferl?' I asked as I ate, and Ruth moved round the kitchen, polishing and wiping and peering at a bowl full of clothes she was soaking. Grandfather's and Uncle Hugh's shoes were clean and lined up ready to be taken back upstairs.

'I watched my oma making them,' said Ruth shortly, patting down her apron pocket as she hunted for something. It crackled, and Ruth frowned. 'Not there – ah, there the pegs are, on the draining board. She'd never tell me the recipe, but I worked it out. You can work out most things if you pay enough attention.'

I looked at the clothes as she began to pull them out of the water and hang them up. I realized that they were the things that had got bloodstained last night. I could see Aunt Pam's blouse and Uncle Hugh's jacket and Granny's black dress and Grandfather's white shirt and Eric's jumper and Ruth's own apron – the apron that shouldn't have been bloody, but was.

Looking at it made me feel sick and also worried. Wasn't

it evidence? Shouldn't the police have seen it? Did it matter that Ruth was already washing the blood off?

'Like the murder?' I asked round a mouthful of biscuit. My heart was pounding.

Ruth bent over the washing. 'Like the fact that you and May and Eric are playing with what doesn't concern you,' she said. 'Stay out of it, can't you? Before you put yourselves – and especially little Eric – in danger.'

'But if it was a gang—' I started.

'There is no gang,' said Ruth. 'You know that. *No one* was outside. The danger's here, now. If you're smart, you'll see nothing and hear nothing. I was in my room, and the first I knew of the murder was when I heard the noises downstairs. Do you see?'

'Maybe,' I said slowly.

'When your grandmother told me to, I went into the study, I saw Mr Sidney and I came straight back out again. I never touched him, and I didn't see anything else. That's what I told the policeman, and, if you're smart, that's what you'll tell him too if he asks.'

I felt so scared then. Ruth was still lying. Was she warning me because she wanted me to stay safe – or threatening me because she was the murderer?

35

From the report of May Wong

'There's no need to look so smug,' I said to Nuala. It was after lunch; the police had gone, and all the grown-ups were scattered round the house, still distracted. We were in the air-raid shelter – we'd managed to persuade Annabelle Olivia that we needed her to stay inside and make costumes while we wrote the (made-up) play, so we could hold the meeting to discuss what we'd found out.

Don't tell anyone, but I hate air-raid shelters. They're dark and small, and they smell of rust and old water. Your feet squish into the mud at the bottom of them, and you can *feel* all the earth piled up above you, ready to come squashing down at any moment. They're good if you want to go somewhere private, but I always have to grit my teeth and remind myself that it's worth it.

'Yes, there is,' said Nuala. 'I found another clue.'

Her freckly face was flushed in the light from the little storm lantern, and her glasses were glinting, and, if I didn't already know that she was rude and stuck-up and only helping us because we'd forced her to, I'd have thought at that moment that she looked quite nice. I was almost not listening to her at first because I was sure that what she'd found out would be rubbish, and also because I was trying not to think about being in the shelter. But, annoyingly, it wasn't rubbish, and by the time she got to the end of her story my head was buzzing with questions.

'Ruth really said all that?' I asked.

'Yes!' said Nuala. 'Sure, don't you think it's suspicious? What if she's the murderer, and she did it because the British government stopped her family coming to England, and she took revenge on Uncle Sid for being part of it?'

'Maybe,' I said. 'All right, it could be. It fits with the clue about her apron – and is it suspicious that she tried to tell you there wasn't anyone outside? Does she know about the soldier in the abandoned cottage? Is she trying to hide him? Eric, show her what you found in Ruth's room.'

Eric put his hand in his pocket and pulled out a collection of items wrapped in his handkerchief, including the brooch and pen we'd found in Ruth's room. 'But I still don't think she did it,' he said. 'She wouldn't. She's too kind.'

Nuala leaned forward and picked through all the things – and then lifted something up with a look of surprise. 'Ah, here – that's Aunt Pam's ring! Did Ruth have it? *Why?*'

I wanted to kick myself. Of course! The ring! It must have been what Pamela was looking for earlier that day. I should have realized that at once.

'No! We found it in the plant pot on the stairs,' said Eric. 'That's interesting.'

'She's always playing with it on her finger,' said Nuala. 'I think it's too big for her these days. Maybe it just fell off by accident.'

'Perhaps,' I said. 'But – in the plant pot? She wasn't hiding there last night. Annabelle Olivia was.'

I was thinking. I remembered Pamela and Hugh's raised voices during the game, and then I thought about the dirt on the carpet when we'd gone into their room this morning. The two things stuck together in my head, but the idea stayed just out of reach. I do my best thinking when I'm moving, but I couldn't move in the air-raid shelter. It made me feel stifled.

And then I looked again at the collection of things in Eric's handkerchief, and saw the hairgrip he'd found in the study. That was when my idea filled out in my head and became impossible not to say.

'Pamela and Hugh argued last night,' I said. 'I heard them. She kept saying she wanted to leave.'

'Ah, so did I!' said Nuala. 'They were yelling at each other about it during the party.'

'All right, what if Pamela *did* decide to leave the house last night during the game? She's not happy here, and she wants to go back to Coventry. We all know that. So she packed a bag and crept downstairs. She wanted to leave quietly, but the front door creaks, so she tried the French window in the study. But when she went into the study Sidney came in behind her, ready for his meeting.

'She thought he was a burglar, so she grabbed the poker from the fireplace and whacked him with it – dropping a hairgrip at some point – and then got scared when she realized what she'd done. She ran outside and back in through the kitchens, taking off her muddy shoes. She had to get rid of them, so she stashed them and her bag in the plant pot – her ring slipped off her finger too, only she didn't notice – and went *back* down the stairs to the drawing room, pretending everything was normal. Then the body was found. When she put her shoes back upstairs later, she got mud on the carpet – that's what we saw this morning!'

I was proud of myself.

But of *course* Nuala was shaking her head. 'Sure, why would she think Uncle Sid was a burglar?' she asked. 'What about the person he was supposed to meet? Eric heard them talking before Uncle Sid was killed. Aunt Pam didn't have bare feet when the alarm was raised. And how would Eric's watch have ended up in the mud outside?'

'She's right,' said Eric. 'It doesn't fit. Hey, a frog!'

'Oh, BLAST,' I said, as Eric gently picked up the frog that was hopping by my feet. It was true – the facts didn't fit with my idea at all. But I knew that we'd still worked out something important. Pamela had been in the study at some point when she shouldn't have been.

I updated the suspect list.

Suspects:
— Hugh Verey. May heard him talking angrily to Pamela Verey outside their room on the first floor at the beginning of the game. Nuala saw him come out of the dining room as the alarm was raised. He says he was in his room for the whole game, but this has to be a lie! He is in need of money. Could this be his motive?

— Pamela Verey. May heard her talking to Hugh Verey outside their room on the first floor at the beginning of the game. Nuala thinks she heard her crying in the drawing room just before Eric stumbled across the body. She turned on the oil lamp after Eric raised the alarm. She says she was in her room for the whole game, but this has to be a lie! Her ring was in the plant pot and her hairgrip was in the study — she must have been in there at some point on the night of the murder! Did she try to leave the house and was caught by Sidney? Did she kill him because of that?

— Neil Verey. May heard him talking to Old Mrs Verey (Iris) on the first floor at the beginning of the game. He was the murderer in the game. (Was he the murderer in real life?) Nuala saw him come out of the library as the alarm was raised.

He says he saw his dead half-brother's ghost just before
Sidney's murder. Is this a lie, to throw the police off the
scent? Or does he really believe this – and did he kill
Sidney as revenge for Sidney's cruelty to him as a child?

– Ruth the maid. Came rushing down the back stairs after the
end of the game. She found the body and telephoned the police.
Her apron had blood on it, even though she says she
didn't touch Sidney, and she did not help clean up
Eric, either. She says she was in the kitchens during the
game – is she lying? Her room had items stolen from the
Vereys – why? Could the murder be revenge on Sidney – a
politician – for not allowing her family to come to England
with her?

– Mr Scott the gardener. Came from the kitchens with
bandages after the end of the game. Still wearing his coat.
Motive as yet unclear!

– Iris Verey. May heard her talking to Neil Verey on the
first-floor landing close to the beginning of the game.
She went downstairs and was still by the front door, knitting
in her usual seat, when the alarm was raised. Motive still
unclear – why would she kill her own son? She seems sorry
that he's dead!

– William Verey. May heard him go upstairs and into his
bedroom at the beginning of the game. Nuala saw him come
downstairs after the alarm was raised. Motive still unclear – why
would he kill his own stepson? He seems sorry that he's dead!

Questions:
— Who was Sidney meeting in the study at 10:15 p.m.?
— Sidney had a piece of paper in his hand with 'Ed Warburton MD' written on it. Who's that?
— How does the soldier fit into the mystery?

'So what do we do now?' asked Nuala.

'Find out who Ed Warburton is,' I said at once. 'And find out who Sidney had the appointment with.'

'Isn't that just finding who the murderer is?' asked Eric.

'Yes, all right,' I said, scowling at him.

From inside the house, the tea gong rang. We jumped up and hurried out of the shelter as quickly as we could. We'd found a lot of new evidence — it felt as though we were on the right track at last.

PART SEVEN

WE LOSE SOME SUSPECTS
AND FIND SOME PAPERS

36

From the diary of Fionnuala O'Malley, continued

When we got to tea, which was in the drawing room again, Granny was already there, waiting. She always does that – gets there early and then looks at us as though we're late when we come in.

'Your face is grubby,' she said to me. 'You must take more pride in yourself. Look at Annabelle Olivia, always so nice and neat.'

Annabelle Olivia, who had changed into a pristine white dress, beamed. May made a disgusted face.

Granny had a new piece of knitting in her hands, and as we all helped ourselves to scones she click-click-clicked away with her needles. She doesn't even need to look at them, which ncvcr stops being creepy.

'Finished the other scarf, Mother?' asked Uncle Neil, in the click-clacking silence.

'It got . . . dirty last night,' said Granny shortly. 'I shall have to unpick it and dispose of part of it, but I can't quite face it yet. So I've begun something new. Where is Ruth? She's late with the sandwiches. Ah, here she is now. Ruth, where have you been?'

'I'm sorry, madam, I've been busy with the—' Ruth began, coming in with a plate.

Grandfather cleared his throat fiercely. He hates hearing that people haven't managed to do something they were supposed to yet.

'Many apologies, Mr Verey, Mrs Verey,' said Ruth, wincing.

'Accepted,' said Grandfather, and then everyone ate their scones in silence. Ruth had put some kind of spice in them, and they tasted great. Of course, Granny looked offended when she tasted one and barely nibbled it afterwards.

But what Uncle Neil had said had given me a really good idea, and I couldn't wait to be allowed to test it out. It made me feel kind of dizzy, like I was running late for something important. You know the feeling you have when you see something that has to be yours, like the nicest cake, or the book you really want to read, but you're in a line of people who all might take your thing before you can pick it up? It was like that.

I don't even remember eating the rest of tea. It was only when I looked down at my plate that I realized it was clean.

'May I get down, please?' I asked politely, putting my knife neatly in the middle of my plate.

Granny nodded at me, and I pushed my chair back really gently and trotted out of the drawing room, trying not to even breathe.

Then I ran.

Granny's knitting basket is always kept in the front hall. She likes to sit in her big chair by the window, where she can see the graves of her first husband and son, and knit all afternoon. She makes scarves and balaclavas and gloves and so on, to lift everyone's spirits – even though everything she makes is weirdly scratchy, and I don't think she lifts many spirits at all. That's where I was headed.

The thing that I'd realized, Diary, was that I remembered Granny knitting the night before. She'd been halfway through another one of her scarves. It had grey and brown stripes, and when everyone began to talk about Murder in the Dark she was just beginning another stripe of grey.

We were looking for alibis for everyone in the house, weren't we? And I'd just realized that I might be able to work out Granny's without any help.

I knelt down next to her chair and started digging through the wool basket. I found what I was looking for quickly, pulled it out – and I was *right*. The half-finished scarf from last night, Granny's neat work – and, if I couldn't already tell that this was what she'd been knitting, I'd have worked it out by the fact that one end of it was all speckled with darker brown stains.

I thought about Granny rushing forward to wipe Eric's hands, getting blood on her dress and her knitting, and shuddered.

But could I be sure that was when the scarf got bloodstained? What if Granny had been caught by Uncle Neil, gone into the study to meet Uncle Sid, killed him, got the scarf dirty and then come back out to sit by the front door?

I looked at the scarf again, and I realized I *could* be certain. Each stripe takes Granny about twenty minutes – I've watched her enough times when there's nothing to do and nowhere to go and nothing to say. She'd definitely started the grey stripe when the lights went out for the Murder in the Dark game – and now, on the end with the blood, was that full stripe of grey, almost ready to have another stripe of brown added to it.

Granny's good at knitting, but I don't think you can do it while you're killing someone. But, if she was just sitting by the door, clicking away, after Uncle Neil had caught her the way May said she'd heard him do, the evidence of the scarf would make sense.

I was so pleased with myself. I'd ruled out one of our suspects – the first person that we absolutely knew couldn't have done it. I mean, it's not like Granny was ever really a suspect. Why would she kill her own son? She loved Uncle Sidney. But now I could say for sure that she hadn't.

The drawing-room door opened, and May's angry little face came poking round the side of it, Eric's just behind her, looking curious.

'What's happened?' he asked, coming over to where I was kneeling. 'You left quickly.'

'We lost you!' complained May. 'You can't *do* that! And what are you doing with that basket? We know the papers aren't in there.'

'Lookit! I've found an alibi!' I said.

37

From the report of May Wong

It's always nice to be able to cross off a suspect, but it was annoying that Nuala got to do it first. Eric said that it didn't matter who did it, and obviously that's right, but that's not how it *felt*.

So I was frustrated with Nuala, and that explains what happened next.

'I was thinking,' said Nuala, her eyes screwed up behind her glasses, 'that we should do a re-enactment of the crime. It might help rule some other people out!'

'Humph!' I said. It was a good idea, but knowing that just made me crosser with her. 'Why would it?'

'Sure – the play's the thing,' said Nuala, which was exactly the sort of nonsense she would come out with. She blushed pink to her freckles. 'I mean, sometimes you can get to the truth by telling the right story.'

'*How?*' I asked.

This didn't seem right to me. Investigations work when

you get proper evidence, and make your suspects talk, not when you mess about with *pretending*. You have to *do* things if you want to catch the criminal.

'Because stories help,' said Nuala. 'If you can see yourself in a story, you can – oh – understand the world, I guess.'

'*You* can make up stories,' I said. 'I'm going to go and *do* something. We still have to find those papers, don't we? *I'm* going to do that. *You* can stay here and pretend.'

I stuck my chin out and went marching away, my fists clenched.

Marching felt good, so I kept on going, all the way out of the front door and onto the drive, gravel crunching satisfactorily under my feet. I stopped at the far edge of the drive and turned to stare up at the flat face of Elysium Hall. It looked so boring from the outside, so predictable and cold, but inside was a mess of lies and secrets and frustrations.

Eric came running towards me across the gravel.

'What are you *doing*?' he asked. 'You've upset Nuala.'

'Good!' I said.

'No, it isn't,' said Eric. 'Stop it. She's doing her best to be helpful. She's just ruled out one of the suspects! We'd never have thought of the knitting alibi on our own – you know that.'

'That was a fluke,' I said.

Eric glared at me. 'It wasn't,' he said. 'She's just as clever as we are. You know a re-enactment is a good idea. You just don't like her because she's another you.'

'She is not!' I gasped. 'She's stuck-up and opinionated and rude and—'

'And so are you.'

'I am not stuck-up!'

'You told me once that your father could buy Elysium Hall without even thinking about it.'

I hate Eric sometimes! I actually think he might be even worse than Nuala.

'Look, we have to work together. And I do think her idea was good. Both of your ideas are. But I'll help you first because you're right about us needing to find the papers. Where do you want to start?'

I felt sulky. I didn't know. All the fight had gone out of me, which is not usual. How was I supposed to think about the murder when I was also busy thinking about Nuala?

Just for something to do, I marched us round the side of the house, to the old stables that are now full of cars and tools and chopped firewood. Beyond the stables was the beginning of the gardens, all green and damp and scattered with dead leaves. I stamped across the grass, and behind us someone yelled. I whirled round, sure that it was Nuala.

But it was Annabelle Olivia.

She was shouting something, her mouth a big wide O in her silly pale face. She got closer, and at last I could hear what she was saying, even though it made no sense. Nothing Annabelle Olivia ever says does.

'—the GHOST?' she yelled at us.

'WHAT?' called Eric.

'DON'T SAY WHAT, SAY PARDON!' screamed Annabelle Olivia. 'IT'S COMMON! I SAID, *are you looking for the GHOST?*'

'There isn't a ghost!' said Eric.

'Yes, there *is*,' said Annabelle Olivia, lowering her voice at last as she came up to us. 'I know Daddy told me there wasn't, and I shouldn't tell anyone else about it, but there *is*. I saw it last night, after I was sent to my room. I couldn't sleep and when I went to the bathroom I looked out round the blackout curtain and saw it by the old well.'

'You're making that up!' I said.

'I'm not! I'm just trying to help! Why won't anyone believe me? I think Uncle Neil is right: the ghost killed Uncle Sidney.'

'The ghost didn't kill Sidney,' said Eric. 'Annabelle Olivia – you were hiding behind the plant pot, weren't you? Last night.'

Annabelle Olivia made a face. 'Yes,' she said. 'The game scared me. People kept running by, but no one noticed me.'

'Do you know who went by you?' I asked, excited.

'No, it was too dark,' said Annabelle Olivia. 'Someone dropped something in the plant pot, though. And I *did* see the ghost later, by the well. I promise!'

I growled because this wasn't helpful. But Eric was looking suddenly lit up from the inside, the way he gets when he solves a puzzle.

'Now go inside,' I told Annabelle Olivia. 'I heard your mother saying she needed you.'

That was a lie, obviously, because I could tell from Eric's face that he'd worked out something important. My heart sped up.

Together, Eric and I ran towards the well next to the kitchen-garden wall. It's got a little stone hat on it, to protect it from the weather, and there's a bucket that you can still just about raise and lower, even though there's no water at the bottom any more. (I know – I checked with some stones when we first arrived.)

I dug out my torch and played it down into the dark gap. At first, I saw nothing.

But then the beam of light caught on something. Something pale and rectangular, in the bucket about halfway down the well.

Something that looked quite a lot like a wrapped-up bundle of papers.

'Look!' I cried.

Eric beamed at me, and then we grabbed each other and danced around wildly. I wanted to yell with delight, but I didn't because that would have completely broken our cover. We couldn't draw anyone else's attention to what we'd found.

Then I stuck my head under the well's little stone hat. I bumped the rope that held up the bucket with my torch (I didn't mean to, it just happened) and the bucket wobbled and the bundle trembled.

'Careful!' said Eric.

'I know!' I said.

I didn't let on to Eric because even friends need to have secrets from each other sometimes, but it's not just air-raid shelters I don't like. A bad thing happened to my brother, Teddy, in a lift once, and ever since then I hate small spaces. Even before the war, I had nightmares about getting stuck in a dark little box with no air to breathe. Anyway, the point is that seeing the papers in the well made me feel all wrong.

'Can we winch them up?' asked Eric.

I felt dizzy. 'You do it,' I said.

Eric gave me a funny look, which I'm not surprised about because that wasn't like me, and said, 'All right, then.'

He took the frog he'd found in the air-raid shelter out of his pocket and put it tenderly on the ground. Then he tied his torch round his neck with a bit of string, stuck his chest over the lip of the well and began to haul up the rope.

And then I heard someone behind me say, 'What are you *doing*?'

38

From the diary of Fionnuala O'Malley, continued

Annabelle Olivia came running to find me. 'The evacuees are climbing down the well!' she said. 'They're *going* to *kill* themselves.'

So, even though I was still mad at May, I went to look. For a second, when I found them, I thought May was pushing Eric *into* the well. I was kind of shocked.

'What are you *doing*?' I asked.

May's head turned towards me like a snake, and she hissed, 'None of your business!'

'What's happening?' called Eric, his voice hollow and echoing.

'It's Nuala!' May called down to him. 'She's sticking her nose in again!'

'I am not!' I said, carefully stepping round Eric's frog, which was crouched in the mud at my feet.

'Quiet!' hissed May, glaring at me. 'We've found *the papers* in the well! We're getting them out.'

'I've got them,' called Eric. 'Only – I think I'm stuck.'

'Oh, come on!' said May. 'You won't die!'

'Now that I think about it, I might if I fall on my head,' said Eric. 'Could you pull me out, please?'

At that, May's face went red, and she started huffing and puffing, which I realized meant that she couldn't, but she didn't want anyone to know.

'Here, I'll help,' I said, and I took Eric's right ankle, and we both heaved.

'OW!' said Eric, and up he came like Winnie-the-Pooh out of his hole. His arms were scratched and raw, and he was bright red and gasping from being upside down. But he had the bundle of papers.

'It's what was stolen from the study, isn't it?' I asked, sitting back on my heels.

'Yes!' said May, sounding almost grim, even though I knew she was excited. 'And it's more proof that the murderer came from *inside* the house.'

So I've worked out why there aren't many kid detectives who solve murders in books: it's really hard to investigate crimes *and* do all the stuff that kids have to do.

We went inside to look at the papers, but then Granny came storming out of the drawing room to give out to us for being in the garden at the wrong time. Annabelle Olivia had obviously snitched. I had to stuff the papers inside my dress before she noticed, and keep them in there, crackling uncomfortably, while we sat in the library and did quiet reading until dinner. (I didn't do quiet reading, but I did keep quiet while I worked on the project I'd decided to make.)

Then it was bedtime, and I had to get myself ready because Mam was having one of her bad days. It wasn't until the house was totally quiet and the clock in the hall downstairs had struck twelve that May bounced out of the bed next to me, nightie buttoned up wrong, and said, 'Time for a meeting!'

I sat up and shoved on my glasses. May rapped on the wall between our room and Eric's, and after a couple of seconds he rapped back.

When we crept out onto the landing, he was already waiting, rubbing sleep out of his eyes and yawning. He had Emil the hedgehog in his dressing-gown pocket. Together we tiptoed down the poky back stairs, holding our breath in case we disturbed someone, and snuck into the night meeting room on the first floor.

Elysium Hall feels bigger and scarier at night. There are corners full of shadows and strange creaking sounds, like the whole place is suddenly a little bit alive. And it didn't help that I kept thinking about Uncle Neil seeing Leonard's ghost coming out of the same spare room – the exact room we were using.

I was really glad when we were sitting down in our usual

places. But, when I reached for the papers, May jerked them away from me with a hiss.

'These are highly classified!' she said. 'You can't look at them – you don't have clearance!'

'You don't, either! Anyway, they're *my* family's papers,' I said – and I knew I sounded exactly like the snob May thought I was.

'All right, then, take them and give them back to *your family*,' said May, glaring at me. 'We'll never solve the mystery, and Eric and I will fail our mission. And we can't fail. We *can't*. I'd have to go back to school.'

'Don't you like school?' I asked.

'NO!' May said. 'It's awful.'

I took a deep breath and remembered what Ruth had said to me, about May missing her family.

'Look,' I said, 'I'm sorry. It doesn't matter that they're my family's papers. They're not really *my* family, anyway. The Company was – Da was. You have as much right to look at them as I do. More, probably, because you found them. Just – you can't leave me out.'

'We're not going to,' said Eric, glaring at May.

'Oh, all right!' said May. I think she looked a little surprised. I was kind of surprised at myself.

May spread out the papers on the dirty wooden boards of the spare room, and we all crouched over them. And sat back again.

'Is this really what was stolen from the study?' I asked, confused.

I'd expected important-looking stuff, Diary, after what Uncle Hugh had said. But it was just dull papers full of Uncle Hugh's columns of numbers, with some of the little planes he doodles in the margins when he's bored. Then there were pages of ordinary Elysium Hall bills in Grandfather's handwriting, and some letters and telegrams. Nothing important. Nothing worth taking.

Eric kept poring over the papers, but May was frowning. 'I thought they were Hugh's things,' she said to me.

'They are,' I said.

'No, they aren't,' said May, shaking her head. 'This is Sidney's writing. I know it is. Look. Here's the piece of paper I found in his room.'

She held out the crumpled-up page, and I stared at it. There was the doodled plane, and there – there was real, serious, classified information, a map of Uncle Hugh's factory in the same handwriting.

'That's not Uncle Sid's writing,' I whispered. 'It's *Uncle Hugh's.*'

'Look at this,' said Eric with a gasp. 'It's a telegram to Hugh Verey from four days ago.'

```
LOOKING FORWARD TO PERFORMANCE OF
MOONLIGHT SONATA STOP ORCHESTRA ARRIVAL
THIS WEEK IF ALL WELL STOP DO NOT MISS IT STOP
```

'Hugh is supposed to go to a concert?' asked May.

'But he doesn't like classical music!' I said. 'Remember, at the party, when he asked Aunt Pam to switch to jazz?'

Eric shook his head. 'It's a code!' he said. 'I'm sure of it.'

'Then Hugh Verey is the spy,' said May grimly. 'Not Sidney. *Hugh.* That's why I thought there was something strange about the writing in Sidney's appointment book. That *was* his writing, but the paper I found in Sidney's room, with the map of the factory, was Hugh's. Hugh Verey has been sending the Germans information about his factory, so they know where to bomb. And, if Sidney had this in his room, it means that Sidney *knew about Hugh.* And if that's true – then maybe Hugh killed him to shut him up.'

I suddenly remembered what Aunt Pam had said about lending Uncle Hugh's trousers to Uncle Sidney on the evening of the party, and how angry Uncle Hugh had been. That must have been how Uncle Sidney found the paper – in the pocket of those trousers – and worked out Uncle Hugh was spying.

I couldn't believe it. It didn't seem real. But it had to be.

'Hugh didn't seem suspicious!' Eric said. 'We didn't even notice him getting that telegram! We shouldn't have been so focused on Sidney.'

'But Sidney seemed so – oh, BLAST!' said May. 'We've been idiots! We knew Hugh was desperate for money! Oh, and he even told Annabelle Olivia not to talk about seeing the "ghost" by the well last night. That must have been him! He was only pretending to be worried about where his papers were. If he killed Sidney and hid the papers afterwards, that would absolutely fit!'

'But what'll we do?' I asked, and my voice sounded wobbly. 'Should we tell someone?'

'Yes,' said May. 'We tell the Ministry – but only when we're sure we've solved the murder. Why, if we'd telephoned before this, we would have told them about the wrong spy! So we have to wait until we know *everything*. In the meantime, we keep these hidden. We should wrap up the parcel again, filled with blank notepaper, and put it back down the well, just in case the murderer looks to see if it's still there.'

She had folded her arms and stuck her chin out. I'm learning that she does that when she's really focused on something.

'Listen,' she said. 'Sidney *talked* about the Germans invading as though he wanted them to, but maybe he was more loyal to the British government than he pretended to be. So he suggests a secret meeting to Hugh. Hugh pretends to want to hear him out, but then, when Sidney's telling him what he's discovered, he creeps up behind him and hits him with the poker. It answers everything!'

'But what about the French window?' I asked. 'How did he have time to break it open from the outside? If he and Uncle Sidney were talking, how would Uncle Hugh creep up behind Uncle Sidney? And why would he turn round and tell the police about the papers instead of pretending they don't exist?'

I felt mean, but I had to say it. I kept trying to tell myself the story of the crime, but nothing fitted.

'Oh, BLAST!' said May, clenching her fists and glaring at me. 'Why do you have to make things so complicated?'

'But she's right,' said Eric.

'What else is here?' I asked, pushing Uncle Hugh's scribbles aside to inspect the rest of the papers.

'Letters, mostly,' said May. 'The murderer must have swept up the papers on the desk and in the open drawers. It shows they were in a hurry – that must be why they didn't open the window the first time round. One from Neil Verey to Old Mr Verey asking how he is. *Father, I am thinking of you and hoping you remain well. If your condition deteriorates, I shall come home at once.* That's what we overheard in the orchard, isn't it? Old Mr Verey's ill.'

'He still hasn't told us,' I said. It upset me so much, thinking about Grandfather hiding that.

'Well, he wouldn't, would he?' said May. 'No one tells children anything. But your uncles know, obviously. Oh, here's a bit where Hugh's asking Old Mr Verey for money. Interesting. Is your grandfather rich?' She looked a bit doubtful.

'Maybe?' I said uncertainly.

I didn't know how to answer that. Sometimes when Da was alive we had money, and sometimes we didn't – I knew when we did because the food got better, and the paper Da wrote on got thicker, and we'd stay in hotels with inside bathrooms, and I knew when we didn't because we'd have to run out of the back of the hotels really fast without supper. But here at Elysium Hall money is another thing that no one seems to want to talk about.

'Look at this!' cried Eric. 'It's Old Mr and Mrs Verey's will!'

This was unusual. Why would this have been out on Grandfather's desk, instead of locked away safely?

'Excellent!' said May, pouncing on it. 'All right. It's quite simple, really. Once Old Mr Verey is dead, Old Mrs Verey gets to live in the house for as long as she's alive, but the ownership of it goes to her oldest living son – that's Sidney, isn't it? At least, it *was* Sidney.'

I nodded. I did know that.

'And then, to their other living children – I call that rude! – only ten thousand pounds divided between them!'

'Only!' I said. I'm getting more and more convinced that wherever May is from she's very, very rich.

'But Sidney's dead,' Eric pointed out. 'So what happens then?'

'Humph!' said May. 'Then – all right, the house and so on goes to the next son, and Sidney's share is divided up among the remaining children. Who's the next oldest?'

'Uncle Hugh.'

'So, now Sidney's dead, Hugh inherits this house, and he, Neil and your mother get more money. Well! That's a good motive for Neil, and an extra one for Hugh, isn't it, if Old Mr Verey really is properly ill? With Sidney out of the way, they both stand to gain much more. Excellent. We're getting somewhere, I think.'

She sat back, beaming at me and Eric.

I had a thought then. We'd got to the bottom of the pile of papers, but there was still one missing.

'What about the ripped piece of paper that was in Uncle Sidney's hand?' I asked. 'The one mentioned in the policeman's notes that said *Warburton*. None of these pages are ripped.'

'Oh!' said Eric.

May was making her angry face again, so I knew she hadn't thought of it.

'Perhaps it – it – *blast*!' she cried. 'I don't know. We'll carry on looking for it. Why do you keep making up problems?'

Oh, I was raging, Diary.

'Wait,' said Eric softly. 'There's something else. Look.'

May had brushed the will aside, but Eric's careful hands had uncovered another piece of paper beneath it.

It was a cheap, thin sheet covered in carefully printed words.

SIDNEY AND WILLIAM VEREY. YOU KNOW WHAT YOU
DID. YOU TOOK A LIFE TEN YEARS AGO. I WON'T
FORGET. I'M BACK NOW, AND YOU'LL PAY.

C. SCOTT

39

From the report of May Wong

Every time I thought I understood this case, it went in a strange new direction.

Mr Scott was sending threats to the Vereys. But why? Why was he working for them if he hated them? And why would he write *I'm back now* when he'd worked for them for years? Did this mean that Scott was the person who'd killed Sidney? Nothing about this made any sense.

As I was thinking this, Nuala said, 'I need a break.' Then she got up and walked out.

'But we were just getting started!' I said to Eric.

Eric shrugged at me. 'This is a lot to think about,' he said. 'For her and us. We made a mistake, May. We thought that the wrong person was the spy.'

'But we've got it right now!' I said. 'It doesn't matter so long as we get it right in the end!'

'I don't know,' said Eric, tucking his bottom lip in and frowning. 'It's nice to be able to say that, but it's not always true. Did I ever tell you what I thought of the Nazis when I first saw them?'

'You hated them,' I said promptly. 'They made you leave Germany.'

'That was later,' said Eric. 'That's how I feel now. When I *first* saw them, before I knew anything about them, I wanted to be just like them. I thought their uniforms were beautiful. I asked Papa to let me be part of the Jungvolk, and when he told me he wouldn't allow it I was so angry at him. We left before I was old enough to join, but of course they wouldn't have let me, anyway, because of the colour of my skin.'

'Then they *are* horrible!' I said, not understanding.

'Yes, but I *wanted* to join,' said Eric miserably. 'I hate them, but in the beginning – I admired them.'

'Don't be stupid,' I said angrily. 'Everyone gets things wrong at first, before they learn, but that's not important. What's important is how you *fix* the mistakes you make. You're saying sorry now, aren't you? You're doing everything you can to stop the Nazis now you know what they're really like. It doesn't matter that we were wrong about who the spy was at first. It only matters that we're trying.'

'All right,' said Eric, picking up Emil the hedgehog and softly petting his spines. 'If you want to talk about fixing mistakes, will you go and speak to Nuala? You upset her earlier.'

Grumbling, I went out into the corridor. I could see Nuala in the darkness, a darker lump perched at the top of the stairs.

I sighed and went to sit down beside her.

'You don't really make up problems,' I told her. 'I was just saying that.'

'Grand, so,' said Nuala coldly.

'Do you really feel like the Vereys aren't your family?' I asked after a while. I was thinking about what she'd said earlier.

'I wish I didn't,' said Nuala. 'I'm trying to like them, but – they don't like me. And I miss our theatre company. We used to travel all over the world with them before Da died, and now I feel stuck here. I miss – *doing* stuff. I keep nearly running away, but sure, I don't know where I'd go.'

I almost told her how England feels like four walls squeezing together round me, and how I don't actually belong here and won't ever come back once I've helped win the war. For a moment, I didn't see her as my enemy: I saw her as someone just as trapped as me.

And, as we went back upstairs to bed, I felt as though we were finally getting somewhere. We could solve this case, I knew it. We were getting close – which was a good thing because I worried that Hazel must be getting closer to finding us.

40

From the diary of Fionnuala O'Malley

Sunday 10th November 1940

At supper this evening, Aunt Pam told us that she wanted to leave Elysium Hall.

'I shall be taking Annabelle Olivia with me,' she said, a bite of stew trembling on her fork. Her ring finger was still empty, just a pale dent on her skin where it should be, and I stared at it and felt weird. 'It's not good for her to be here.'

'You will most certainly not!' stormed Uncle Hugh. 'It's not safe in Coventry! The bombs!'

'Nowhere's safe!' Aunt Pam snapped back at him. 'We're at war, in case you haven't noticed. And Sidney was *murdered* here. What are the police doing about it? Have they caught the person behind it? Bombs or no bombs, I won't have Annabelle Olivia living in a house where she might be killed at any moment by marauding thieves.'

We were in the dining room at last, by the way. The police had come back this morning and taken Uncle Sid's body away. May tried to sneak into the van to have a look at him, but she was spotted by PC Cuffe and given out to for being a disgusting child. She's still raging about that, obviously. I don't know what she was hoping to find – we know exactly what happened to him. The only question is who did the hitting and why. Anyway, the dining room is clear, but not exactly clean. It smells *almost* normal, until you breathe in wrong and get a gust of something at the back of your throat that makes you want to gag.

Aunt Pam's right that the police still haven't caught anyone. They didn't even look in the abandoned cottage today, which makes me disappointed because it proves that May was right. We tried to go back to it, twice, but both times we were stopped by Scott, who's been stomping around, digging up the victory beds and setting traps for rabbits in the field. He glared at us out of his one eye, and we ran away, scared. We only just managed to hide a replacement packet of papers in the well without him seeing. He's certainly mean enough to have sent that message – but why would he?

Uncle Hugh was grumbling about his papers again, and how no one was trying to find them. May, Eric and I all looked at each other. I felt kind of guilty because I'm sitting on them right now as I write this diary entry. They're under my mattress. But then I remembered that they're proof that Uncle Hugh is after sending information to the Nazis. If he got them back, we'd all be in trouble. It's weird to know his secret. It makes me wonder what everyone else is hiding.

'It's still raining,' observed Granny, in an attempt to change the subject. Grandfather made a grunting noise of approval. 'But the weather is supposed to clear up in a few days, which is something.'

There was a pause, and then—

'If anyone would like to come to my seance, it'll be in the study at ten tonight,' said Uncle Neil. 'I'm convinced that Leonard knew that Sidney was going to be murdered, and he was trying to warn us with the poltergeist activity in the days before Sid's death. I want to know if my hypothesis is correct.'

'NEIL!' Grandfather burst out. 'That's ENOUGH! You are in MY house, and you will certainly not be doing anything of the sort.'

'Isn't your leave up soon?' asked Uncle Hugh quite meanly. 'I didn't think you had time to waste.'

'DO leave me alone, Hugh,' said Neil. 'Just because Sidney's dead doesn't mean that you can pretend to be him. And holding a seance isn't wasting time! The veil between worlds is still thin, especially given Father's condition, and I believe we could learn something crucial.'

Grandfather made a choking sound. 'Please stop talking about me as though I were dying,' he said. 'I haven't the faintest idea what you mean by *my condition*, but I am certainly not ill.'

Uncle Neil looked confused, and I thought Uncle Hugh had turned rather pale too.

'But – I heard – Hugh told me about it!' Uncle Neil stammered.

'Whatever you heard, you grievously misunderstood the situation,' Grandfather snapped. 'I don't want to hear another word about this. I want to eat my dinner in peace. Is that too much to ask?'

'No, Father,' said Uncle Neil after a pause.

We all murmured agreement, like the chorus in a play. But I was so confused. *Was* Grandfather sick or not? I realized that I hadn't actually heard it from Grandfather himself – just Uncle Sid telling Uncle Hugh.

Then I looked again at Uncle Hugh and Uncle Neil's stunned faces, and realized something else. I'd believed what Uncle Sid had said about Grandfather, and Uncle Hugh and Uncle Neil had too. And, if they'd thought Grandfather was dying, it would have made sense for either of them to kill Uncle Sidney so they'd get more money in the will. But now, if it turned out that Grandfather wasn't sick after all, they might have killed him for nothing. If that was the case, what would they do next?

PART EIGHT

WE DISCOVER SOME
UNPLEASANT TRUTHS

41

From the report of May Wong

Neil Verey was late to his own seance. This did not surprise me. I remembered his room and was amazed that he managed to get anywhere on time at all.

The seance was being held in the study, which gave me the shivers in a good way. There was still blood on the rug next to the desk, and even though Ruth had spent hours scrubbing away at it and it had darkened to a brown smear, we all knew exactly what it was.

Eric, Nuala and I were supposed to have gone to bed at nine, which we obviously ignored. We'd lain down in our beds, with the bedclothes tucked up round our necks and dark clothes on underneath, and as soon as Ruth had been round to turn off the lights we jumped up and crept downstairs to get into position. We were hiding in different bits of the room: Eric behind the sofa, Nuala under the table that had been dragged into the middle of the room, and me behind the blackout curtain next to the French window. I liked being able to feel the sky behind me, even if it was still raining.

As I waited and listened to the people on the other side of the curtain cough and mutter and shuffle awkwardly, I thought about the murder again. How had the outside of the French window been so scratched if the murderer was inside the house the whole time? I knew there was a fact we were missing, and it made me itchy.

I heard the door to the study open and close again, and then Pamela Verey's voice say, 'Hello, Neil.'

I was surprised that she'd come. She kept going on about leaving, but I suppose she was curious like us. Ruth was there too, and Old Mr Verey (disapprovingly – I think he wanted to keep an eye on what would happen). Old Mrs Verey had refused, but Hugh had turned up, and so had Nuala's mother, Mrs O'Malley – for once, she hadn't gone to bed after dinner.

'A good turnout!' said Neil, sounding pleased. 'Now, everyone, please gather round this table. Someone, put out the lights – we shall want nothing more than a candle lit. For this to work, I need you to keep your minds open to the Beyond. We shall be channelling the spirits and—'

The study door opened again. 'Hello,' said a gruff voice. 'If I may? I know it isn't usual, but—'

'What are you doing here, Scott?' asked Old Mr Verey.

'I was thinking about Master Leonard, sir, and my two. So many boys dead, and – I wanted to remember.'

I thought again about the note that Mr Scott had sent to Sidney and Old Mr Verey. Nothing about it felt right. It had been so angry, but the way Mr Scott had just spoken to Old Mr Verey was calm and respectful. And surely, if Old Mr Verey had read that note, he'd have fired Mr Scott? I couldn't make sense of it.

'Excellent, Scott!' said Neil, sounding excited. 'The spirits speak to those they feel a connection to, and of course they'll be close to you.'

A squeak as a chair was moved. Then everything was quiet again, but I could feel the tension in the air.

'Join hands,' said Neil Verey. 'Close your eyes. Now—'

There was a pause, then a gasp. 'Who blew out the candle?' snapped Old Mr Verey. 'Neil—'

'The spirits are here,' hissed Neil. '*Quiet*, Father, you'll spoil it!'

I think it's funny how young grown-ups sound sometimes when their parents are nearby.

Pamela Verey gasped. 'The table moved!' she said, her voice trembling. 'I felt it!'

'Don't let go of the hands you're holding!' cried Neil. 'There's a presence in the room! It speaks! It's – *IT IS I, LEONARD.*'

I had to squeeze my fingers over my mouth not to laugh. Neil Verey had put on a deeper voice that went booming through the study. It was still quite clearly Neil, though, and it was so stupid to listen to.

'*SIDNEY WAS MURDERED!*' he intoned. '*I WITNESSED IT!*'

'Oh no!' wailed Pamela Verey.

'*Thieves!*' howled Neil in his silly voice. '*They came through the French window, attacked Sidney and left him dead, before fleeing the way they came!*'

This didn't make any sense, of course – if the thieves had come through the French window, they'd have left muddy footprints all over the rug – but none of the grown-ups pointed that out. I heard Pamela Verey gasping again, and making a silly sort of panting noise.

'They?' asked Scott. 'How many were there?'

'*Two! Three! I can't say!*' moaned Neil. '*Oh! They took what they came for and left!*'

He really was being silly, and I wondered what his motive was. Was he trying to make himself less of a suspect by going on and on about thieves?

Pamela Verey began to cry then. Neil stopped, and there was an awkward pause as everyone tried to work out what was going on.

'Pammy?' said Hugh at last.

'It's nothing,' she sobbed. 'Oh – oh – I'm sorry—'

'Can't you be quiet, Pam? You're ruining the message,' said Neil crossly, in his normal voice.

'It's just . . .' blurted Pamela. 'I – I – I can't stop thinking about it! I was so CLOSE. I – it was almost me who died! It could have been ME!'

'Nonsense, Pammy, you were in no danger!' snapped Hugh.

'You don't know that!' The words tumbled out of her in a rush. 'You don't! You see – I was *there*! I went into the study during the game – I was trying to leave the house that night! I just wanted – I couldn't *be* here any more! I was almost at the French window when I heard someone behind me. I dived behind that sofa and then crept out of the room as quietly as I could. I thought it was just one of us, but I know now that it was the thieves! The murderers! I was so *close*!'

More nonsense! If Pamela had heard someone *behind* her, then they couldn't have been thieves coming through the French window in front of her. But was she telling the truth – or was she trying to trick us all?

'Very interesting, Pam, but could we get back to the seance?' asked Neil.

'I'm sorry,' Pamela went on wildly. 'It's just so dreadful! I'm sorry!'

'Pam, please, this *isn't* important. There's another spirit trying to come through! IT IS—'

Neil was getting ready to put on another ridiculous voice, and I was rolling my eyes, when someone else cut through the noise he was making.

'*I'm here,*' the voice said simply.

The tiny hairs on the back of my neck bristled.

'Who is it?' asked Neil, cross again. 'Look, if one of you is trying to—'

'Frank?' asked Mrs O'Malley. 'Oh, is that you, Frank?'

'*Edmund,*' said the voice.

I heard a low gasp and then a sad little sigh from Mrs O'Malley.

'What?' asked Neil, and now his voice was tinged with alarm.

'*You know who I am,*' the voice went on. '*Mr Verey and Sidney know what they did to me. Sidney deserved what he got. But this is a message for D. I send love and two warnings. C is in danger. And Mr Sidney Foley's murderer is in this house now. Protect C – do you hear me? PROTECT C!*'

A chair squealed, I heard footsteps and then a door banged.

'Who was that?' cried Pamela Verey. 'OH! There's something on my lap! HELP!'

Several other people shouted too.

'Turn on the lights, Neil!' snapped Old Mr Verey. 'This is too much! It ends now!'

But I wasn't paying much attention to the seance any more. I heard the front door of Elysium Hall creak open and slam – and then, through the French window, I saw a dark figure striding across the grounds.

I felt like a bolt of electricity was running through me. I reached up as quietly as I could and fiddled with the handle of the French window. After a bit of shoving, it swung open. I eased myself out into the flower bed – and then quick as a flash I was away, running through the dark garden, on the trail of the person I had seen.

42

From the diary of Fionnuala O'Malley, continued

So here's what happened at the seance. I believe in ghosts – Da taught me to be careful of them – and it makes me nervous to hear one being called like a dog. But when I got into the study I realized there was something else going on. I know when something's being stage-managed, when someone wants the audience to look one way and not the other, and when we're being told to focus on one thing so we won't think about another.

The table had been dragged out from its usual place on the right-hand wall of the study. It's a hexagonal shape and it looks really sturdy, but when I crept under it to hide I saw a piece of wood wedged against one side of its base, right where Uncle Neil could kick it away and make the table rock as soon as it was dark. And, when he *did* sit down, and the main lights were turned off, and everyone closed their eyes, I heard the rush of air that could only come from someone (Uncle Neil) puffing out the candle in the middle of talking.

It was all a set-up.

I was crouched with my knees up to my chest, staring at Aunt Pam's skirt on one side of me and Scott's dirty trousers on the other. Ruth had been next to Aunt Pam until Scott came in, but she shuffled across to make room for him. Scott's clothes smelled like cigarettes, and I wrinkled up my nose. Mam was on the opposite side of the table. I knew why she was there. She thought there might be a message from Da. He was always after telling her what to do while he was alive, and I know she still asks him for advice now. I couldn't cope with her disappointment if he didn't come through.

Then the seance began. And I knew it was all fake – until that second voice started speaking.

I could tell that Uncle Neil was shocked. It hadn't been part of his plan. And I could *also* tell that someone else was shocked too – Scott. His knees clenched and shook, and I could suddenly hear these weird soft sounds that I know (I wish I didn't) are the way adults sound when they're crying and they don't want you to know about it.

I tried to work out where the voice was coming from as it was talking. It was tough – we were all pretty close together. It definitely wasn't Uncle Neil, or Scott, or Aunt Pam. It almost sounded like—

Then Scott shoved his chair backwards, jumped up and charged out of the room. The front door creaked and then banged behind him, and I felt something cool and damp scatter down from the tabletop and flutter against my face.

I yelped and then clapped my hands over my mouth, scared that I'd be found out, but the adults were yelling too, and then the lights came back on to reveal a shower of leaves across the floor. I could see that they were from the apple orchard, and a lot of them were kind of rotten. There was a horrible dying smell in the room all of a sudden that made me heave.

When I saw those leaves, I knew that there was only one person who could have thrown them after Scott had left the room. Then I knew for sure who the voice had been coming from.

But that wasn't the most important thing that I noticed. There was a tiny squeak and creak, over by the blackout curtain, exactly the noise that'd be made if someone pushed open the French window and crept out.

I was almost impressed. It was about the quietest I'd ever heard May being. Maybe she wasn't such a bad spy, after all.

I waited for a second, until I was sure the adults were too busy yelling at each other to notice me, and then as fast as I could I rushed out of the room, heading for May and the garden.

43

From the diary of Fionnuala O'Malley, continued

It was still raining hard, and everything was dark around me. I had to take another deep breath and pretend that I was in the hot, close backstage of a theatre, using all the extra senses you need not to crash into a person or a piece of scenery. I calmed down then, and took off my useless glasses, and started using my feet and my hands and my skin to work out where I was.

I went round the side of the house as fast as I could, and ahead of me I heard panting and the heavy thump of feet that had to be May. Past the the victory beds and the box hedges, past the rose garden. I tripped once and caught my arm against a thorny branch. I felt my dress snag and rip but I kept on running, into the long grass of the field.

Obviously I'd worked out where May was going by now. The only thing I wanted to know was *why*.

Then, for just a second, a flashlight snapped on in the window of the abandoned cottage.

I was so shocked that I slammed hard into something solid in the dark. I yelped, and the something growled and swung round, arms flailing.

'May!' I hissed, ducking backwards. 'It's *me*!'

'UGH!' grumbled May. 'What are you doing here? You're ruining everything!'

'Oh, stop being so mean!' I said. 'We're on the same team, aren't we?'

May made an angry noise. 'Perhaps,' she said at last. '*Fine.* I saw someone running through the grounds just now, so I'm following them. I think something important's happening.'

I realized then that I knew information she didn't. 'It's Scott!' I whispered. 'He ran out of the seance when he heard all that weird stuff from Edmund about C and D. Why's he *here*, though?'

'How should I know? Fine, let's split up. You go round the left side, and I'll go round the right. That way, if one of us is caught, we can pretend we're on our own. Get as close as you can and listen in. Do you understand?'

I really hate the way May sometimes acts like I'm stupid. I'm not, Diary. I think I'm as smart as she is.

'Grand,' I snapped.

'Good,' said May. There was a pause, and then she said

something that was almost drowned out by the whipping wind.

'What did you say?' I asked.

'I said THANKS!' roared May. 'I was being NICE. Obviously I won't bother again.'

'GRAND!' I shouted at her.

'GR— FINE!' shouted May.

You know, Diary, I've started to realize that she doesn't actually mean half the stuff she says. She's only doing it for show. And when I yell back at her, I think I'm doing it for the same reason.

Anyway, off I went, to the left.

As I got closer, I could hear voices. I crouched down and crept even closer, until I was right under one of the hollow windows. The first voice I heard was Scott's.

'—safe,' he was saying. 'You need to go.'

'I don't understand why,' said someone else. This voice was younger, a man – and not French or German but English.

'Who told you?'

'Edmund,' said Scott.

The other man swore. 'Come off it. Don't say that.'

'You don't understand—'

'Of course I do. You've got the wind up because of some stupid thing you heard. I'm safe here—'

'The police have been snooping around! Mr Sidney's murderer hasn't been caught – and, if they find you after that letter you sent, what are they going to think? You need to move on. The message from Edmund convinced me. It was him. He said things – things about what happened with Mr Sidney and Old Mr Verey.'

'I hope he said that he's glad Sidney's dead. *I* am. Hope Old Mr Verey's next. So you're turfing me out, are you? Very nice, I must say. Running out of excuses to bring me food?'

'Please, Clarence!' cried Scott, and he sounded really desperate.

'You told me you'd look after me, Dad! But if that's too difficult now I'm a deserter—'

Dad! I covered my mouth with my hands. Of course – Dad. *D.* Clarence was C – he was Scott's son, and so was Edmund. I remembered Eric and May telling me about the photograph in Scott's bedroom. Three boys: Arthur, Edmund and Clarence.

'Of course I'll look after you, but you have to tell me the truth. Did you do – *something* to Mr Sidney? When I came here the other night, where were you?'

'Oh, lay off, Dad. Of course I didn't. I've told you – I was in the village. I was starving, and you hadn't turned up. I had to take matters into my own hands, didn't I?'

'So it wasn't you I saw by the kitchens?'

'Of course it wasn't! Can't you—'

'Wait!' said Scott fiercely. 'I heard something – don't move! THERE!'

I heard the noise of a scuffle, and a furious yell, and then Scott said, 'Well, missy? What are *you* doing here?'

44

From the report of May Wong

I still can't believe what happened next. I'd been careful, but I had to get closer so I could hear what was being said – and then Mr Scott shouted, and I was grabbed by my collar and dragged out of my hiding place. Mr Scott was yelling in my face. I was frightened, and that made me furious.

'GET OFF ME!' I screamed, striking out with my fists. 'LEAVE ME ALONE!'

Mr Scott shook me like a rat, and I could feel my teeth clack together. I howled with rage.

'WHAT ARE YOU DOING HERE?' he shouted. 'WHO SENT YOU?'

I spat at him. That made him even angrier, but it was worth it. I hated him.

'Who is it?' the other man, Clarence, asked.

'One of the evacuees,' said Mr Scott grimly. 'She won't be a problem. Don't worry.'

I couldn't believe it. I am always a problem! How dare he!

'She *looks* like a problem,' said Clarence.

Exactly!

'She won't talk,' said Mr Scott.

Yes I would!

Mr Scott glared at me. 'You've got to leave at once. Now look, does anyone else know you're here?'

Not being stupid, I said, 'Everyone! I ran away from the house and they're all looking for me. And when they find me, you'll be in *huge* trouble. I'll tell them Clarence sent that letter!'

'She won't,' said Mr Scott to Clarence. 'Listen to me, girl – you *can't* tell anyone about what you've seen. It's important! Old Mr Verey and Sidney – they did a wicked thing to my son Edmund years ago. Clarence wanted to remind them of it by sending that letter. He only meant to scare them. He didn't do anything else. This is all a misunderstanding. If you promise to be quiet, you can go. Do you *promise*? Will you keep mum?'

I struggled and kicked, but gardeners are *strong*. I began to get a bit afraid, despite myself.

And then someone knocked at the broken old door of the cottage. Mr Scott and Clarence both froze.

'Who's there?' called Mr Scott.

'Scott?' called Old Mrs Verey's voice. 'What's going on?'

This was a surprise to me. I thought she'd gone to bed

before the seance. What was she doing all the way out here?

'Nothing, Mrs Verey,' said Mr Scott, gesturing frantically at Clarence with his free hand. He was just as surprised as I was.

'I heard a commotion, Scott,' Old Mrs Verey's voice went on. 'Is there someone in there with you?'

'No, Mrs Verey,' said Mr Scott. 'I mean – I found the evacuee girl. She was running away.'

'*Was* she?' asked Old Mrs Verey. She was standing back a few paces in the field, so we could only hear her voice and make out her dim, slightly stooped shape.

Clarence was rushing round the room, shoving things into his bag. At last he began to climb out of the empty window opposite the door. I wanted to yell, but I also wasn't sure what Mr Scott was going to do next.

'Send her out, Scott,' said Old Mrs Verey. 'Hurry up.'

The hand holding me unclenched, and I was free. I leaped backwards and rushed towards the door. And, as I did, I realized what was going on. I knew someone who could change their accent and sound like another person. I knew someone who'd been taught to act.

I got through the door and a hand reached out to grab me – a hand that I knew perfectly well.

'*Run!*' hissed Nuala.

45

From the diary of Fionnuala O'Malley, continued

I don't think I've ever acted so well. I was really proud of myself. My heart was pounding, and I was shaking all over, shaking so hard that I felt like I couldn't run at all. But I also kept wanting to scream with laughter.

May dragged me in a zigzag across the field, Scott bellowing behind us. The rain was coming down harder than ever, and I couldn't see a thing. I almost slammed into a tree face first, and May pulled me down onto the ground and we hid, panting, as Scott raced by us. Then the only thing I could hear was our breathing and the rain.

'That wasn't bad,' May whispered at last.

'Don't you mean *thank you*?' I asked.

'Fine! Thank you. I would have got out of it without you, though.'

'Sure you would.'

We were both quiet again. Then we both said, *'Clarence is Scott's son!'*

'He *did* desert, just like Eric said! He's the soldier who's been hiding in the cottage. *And* he's the person who sent the threatening letter we found – signed with his last name, which is why we thought his father had written it,' said May.

'That's why Scott asked how many murderers there were, in the seance,' I said. 'He's been worried that Clarence did it.'

'So you think Mr Scott *didn't*?' asked May.

It was the first time she'd ever asked me something like that, like she actually wanted to know what I thought. It gave me a warm glow in my stomach, even though the rest of me was icy from the rain.

'Definitely not. The thing he's been hiding is *Clarence*, not the murder. And he hid him in the abandoned cottage because he could check in on him without raising suspicion. No one would be surprised to see the gardener out in the field – that's where he's been disappearing to for the last few weeks!'

'That's why he had that wheel of cheese in his room and those pickles! He's been smuggling food to Clarence! And – wait. That's his alibi, isn't it? Mr Scott came out of the kitchens just after the body was discovered, and he was still wearing his coat!'

'Yes!' I said. 'He must have headed for the cottage straight after he turned off the generator in the stables. But of course we know now that Clarence was in the village,

267

looking for food. Scott must have arrived at the cottage and found it empty. He came back – and he saw the *real* murderer going back inside the house through the door into the kitchens. He's been terrified ever since that it was Clarence!'

'So we've ruled out Mr Scott!'

'And I know something else,' I said. 'The second voice at the seance – it was *Ruth*. She knows about Clarence hiding in the cottage, and she must know about . . . whatever it is that Sidney and Old Mr Verey did, years ago, that Clarence wrote about in the letter. She was warning Scott that she knew about Clarence, and that other people might find out too if he's not more careful. And – after you'd gone – she played a trick with leaves that was exactly like something the poltergeist would do. I think *she's* the poltergeist, and she was scaring Sidney to punish him. Remember what Neil Verey said in his notebook? He said that the ghost seemed to be targeting Sidney more than anyone else.'

'Come on!' said May, her eyes glittering. 'We have to get back to the house. We need to tell Eric what we've found out – I think it's time for a detective meeting.'

46

From the report of May Wong

But when we got back to the house, all the grown-ups were still awake and very angry that Nuala and I were also up, as well as soaked to the skin and muddy. We were shouted at and put to bed in disgrace at once. Being a child is so annoying.

I knocked on the partition wall between our room and Eric's to let him know what was happening. He's taught me some Morse code, which we'll need to know when we become proper spies, and so I tapped out MEETING 1 A.M. USUAL PLACE and settled back to wait.

Then Ruth came to see whether we were both asleep, so we had to lie down flat in our beds as quick as we could and pretend to breathe evenly. It was hard because of everything we'd discovered about her. She was pretending to be the poltergeist! And she really might be the murderer.

*

Nuala set the alarm clock under her pillow to wake us up, and at 1 a.m. we all crept downstairs to the spare room to hold our meeting.

'What happened at the end of the seance?' Eric asked, as soon as we'd sat down – Nuala cross-legged on an old cushion on the floor, Eric on a low table, and me against a battered old iron bedstead with big, lumpy brass bedknobs. 'You ran off – I was stuck behind the sofa and couldn't follow.'

I felt guilty then because Eric and I are partners, and I shouldn't have left him – but I couldn't help it, could I? Not when there was such an important lead to be chased.

Before I could explain, Nuala pulled out a bar of chocolate from her dressing-gown pocket. I knew she had it – I'd seen her get it out of a dusty old suitcase underneath her bed – but Eric gasped. It's strange to think that chocolate used to be an ordinary part of all our lives, when it's so rare now. I haven't seen it in a shop for months, and I haven't eaten it for almost as long, and so, when Nuala broke it into pieces and gave us each a bit, I thought I'd never had anything so good. It was a bit melted at the edges and had gone whitish with age, but it still tasted as rich as Christmas.

'I've had it for a while,' said Nuala. 'I've been saving it, but I thought it could help us.'

And, funnily enough, the way she said that made me realize that it meant something to her, to share the chocolate with us – and that was when I understood just how hard Nuala was trying.

Nuala and I explained what had happened. She's good at telling a story, I have to admit, and Eric's eyes were wide as we got to the bit where she'd pretended to be Old Mrs Verey to get me out of Mr Scott's clutches.

'It's good you know how to act so well,' Eric said, and Nuala's face suddenly changed.

'My da taught me,' she said shortly, and she took off her glasses and rubbed them against her nightie.

I had the same sort of feeling I'd had before, of suddenly understanding how much it meant to Nuala that her father wasn't here, and couldn't ever be.

'We ruled out two suspects: Mr Scott and Pamela,' I said, as fast as I could.

'I think we can only be sure about Mr Scott,' said Eric, licking chocolate off his fingers while Emil the hedgehog snuffled hopefully in his lap. 'We can rule him out because he was in the cottage during the murder. But what Pamela said at the seance – she could have been making it all up, to trick us.'

'And I worked out something important about Ruth too,' said Nuala, while I was still grumbling. Eric was right and I hated it. 'The person behind the second voice at the seance and the hauntings – it was *her*, Eric. That's why she had all those things in her room. She must have collected them, ready to fling at Uncle Sidney when she got the chance – using tricks and misdirection she learned from her time at the circus. She's the poltergeist – and I think Uncle Sidney had worked it out just before he died. That's why he had his own collection of objects in his room! He must have been saving them up as evidence against her. What if he was going to tell someone, and she killed him to shut him up?'

'But why?' asked Eric. 'Why pretend to be a poltergeist in the first place?'

'To frighten Uncle Sidney. She hated him. Sure, her family's still in Austria, in danger. She's angry that Uncle Sidney and MPs like him have the power to help people, but choose not to. Her motive for being the ghost – well, it's the same as her motive for murder.'

Nuala had jumped up in excitement as she talked, and as she delivered her final sentence she shook the brass bedpost for effect. It was a silly theatrical gesture that made me snort – but then something happened that left me breathless with shock.

One of the round, knobbly bedknobs came loose and fell to the floor – I had to dodge away from it to avoid getting hit. I flashed my torch on it, and we all saw that, although the top of it was brassy clean, the long handle bit that screws into the main frame was rusty and dark, a long-dried stain that looked just like—

'Blood,' said Eric, his voice wobbling.

I bent over it, almost knocking heads with Nuala as I did so. Now that I was squinting straight at it, I could see a dim stain on the round part.

'Why's there blood on it?' asked Nuala. 'I mean – who'd do this?'

'Someone who wanted to hide it,' I said, and I heard my voice shaking. It was silly and weak of me, but I couldn't help it.

'But why? It's not like this has anything to do with the murder – does it?'

'What if it does?' I asked. My mind was whirring as it tried to put everything together. 'We thought – we've thought all along – that the murder weapon was the poker in the study. It was beside Sidney Foley's body, after all. But what if this was the actual murder weapon?'

Eric hunched up his shoulders. 'But if it was, then why would the murderer pretend it was the poker?'

I had the answer to that too. Suddenly all the clues were falling into place. 'Because they wanted to make it look as though a thief was behind it, and they'd just picked up the poker without planning anything. But this is heavier than the poker, a much better weapon. Remember what Neil Verey told PC Cuffe? That he'd seen what he thought was Leonard's ghost coming out of this room? There are only two options now: either the murderer was him, and he wanted to throw the police off the scent, or he saw *someone else* leaving this room – on their way to meet Sidney and kill him.

'Finding this proves that the murderer *planned* to kill Sidney. They planned to meet him, after all, and they planned to come here, get this weapon, go back downstairs and kill him. The murderer set up the broken French window beforehand too. It was *all* a set-up to *look* like the murder happened on the spur of the moment – to make everything seem like a burglary. So we're looking for a murderer who's very clever indeed, and very good at hiding their cleverness!'

Nuala and Eric were both gaping at me. At that moment I felt just as clever as the murderer, perhaps even more so.

47

And that was when we heard it. Stealthy footsteps outside on the landing.

'Who's that?' I whispered.

'*Shh*,' said Eric and Nuala together.

We listened as the steps went pacing past the door to the spare room – and then Nuala stood up as though she'd just thought of something. Before we could stop her, or say anything, she rushed to the door and flung it open, switching on her torch to shine it on – Mr Scott.

He was framed in the glare, a bag on his back and his eye screwed up in surprise.

'Who's there?' he whispered.

'Where are you going?' hissed Nuala. She'd changed her voice again – this time she sounded like Pamela.

'Nowhere,' said Mr Scott – then he raised his hand to shade his eye, and I saw his expression change. 'Hey, you!

You're not Mrs Pamela. It's you blasted kids again, isn't it? Why aren't you in bed?'

I realized I was still cross and hurt about being caught by him earlier. 'Why aren't *you*?' I snapped, coming to stand next to Nuala.

'I don't have to explain myself to you. Go up to bed where you belong.'

'Shan't,' I said.

'Are you off to see Clarence again?' asked Nuala.

'See here! Don't you mention that name – you leave him out of it. Whatever you think you know, you don't.'

Mr Scott was angry at us, I could tell, and something else too. He was *afraid*. Afraid of what we could do to him if we told one of the Vereys.

'That he's your son? That he deserted from the army, and you've been looking after him in that cottage for weeks?' I asked. But my heart wasn't really in it.

'BE QUIET,' hissed Mr Scott, looking anxiously around. 'Please. I'm – I'm getting him out. We'll be gone by tomorrow. I'll give you – I'll give you a shilling if you don't say anything.'

Bribery! I was impressed.

'Wait,' said Eric, coming to stand next to me and Nuala. 'We don't need a shilling. We won't tell.'

'*Why* don't we need a shilling?' I asked. Eric elbowed me.

'But why were you hiding him?' he went on. 'It's illegal, isn't it, if he's deserted?'

'He's my son,' said Mr Scott heavily. 'My last son. My eldest, Arthur, died in the last war, along with Mrs Verey's boy Leonard. They were best friends, grew up here together. The mischief they caused, running through my vegetable patches! After Arthur died, I thought if I stayed at Elysium Hall I could – stay close to him. Even when Mr Sidney told Old Mr Verey that my middle boy, Edmund, had been poaching, and Old Mr Verey sent him to prison for it, I didn't leave. I should have, but I didn't. Not even – not even when Edmund caught pneumonia and died in his cell.

'But now, with Clarence – well, he refused to stay and fight, to die young like his brothers. He's never got over Edmund, and he blames the Vereys for what happened to him. He's rash and hot-headed. But he's still my boy, and I mean to protect him. And, like I told you earlier, if you try to stop me—'

'We won't,' said Eric. 'Will we?'

I sighed. 'We won't,' I said. 'I promise.'

'Me too,' Nuala agreed.

And we stood and watched as Mr Scott crept down the stairs. It seemed to me that, even though we'd ruled him out, we were finding more and more reasons why someone might have wanted to kill Sidney Foley.

48

From the report of May Wong

'All right,' I said when he was gone. 'Your idea, Nuala, from before. The re-enactment. We should do it.'

Nuala sat up. 'Really?' she said.

'It's not a *bad* idea. You were right.'

What I *meant* was that it was quite a good one. I hoped she'd understand.

'Thank you!' said Nuala. 'Ah, well, I've been making something that might help. I'll show you.'

Which is how the three of us ended up in the library five minutes later, ready to re-enact the Murder in the Dark game that had ended with Sidney Foley's death.

I couldn't believe it when Nuala showed us what she'd made.

'It's a paper set,' she explained. 'Orla used to make them in the Company for every new play so the actors could block their movements. Look, here's the house, all three floors of it, and here we are.'

I shone my torch on the thing she'd unfolded from the middle pages of the *Encyclopedia Britannica*. It was the most perfect scale model of Elysium Hall, done in careful paper cut-out shapes. I could peer into each little room, and every floor was connected by two sets of delicately folded paper stairs. Nuala had even made paper people, each of them wearing a tiny crayoned version of their costume from the night of Sidney Foley's murder.

'This is beautiful,' said Eric wonderingly. 'You're so clever.'

I stared at her. 'But this is good, Nuala.'

Nuala shoved her glasses up her nose and beamed shyly at me.

'I thought we could move everyone round the set – I mean the house – to see if they could have been where they said they were. Look, we can start with where everyone was just after ten, when the lights went out. Scott had gone outside to the generator in the old stables, and we know he went to the abandoned cottage from there. Mam was upstairs—'

She was moving the little paper people round her set: the bearded Mr Scott doll outside, and slender, sad Serena O'Malley up to the top floor.

'And the rest of us were in the hallway,' agreed Eric, scooping the other dolls in a heap into the space where the front hall was. 'Then the lights were turned off. Sidney Foley went into the library, and I followed him in.'

'I went upstairs past Old Mr Verey,' I said. 'On the first floor I heard Hugh and Pamela arguing outside their room, and Old Mr Verey going into his. Then I heard Old Mrs Verey and Neil come up the stairs behind me before I went into Sidney's room.'

I moved all five little paper dolls up to the first floor, and dropped the Old Mr Verey, Hugh and Pamela dolls into the right rooms.

'Granny went back downstairs once Uncle Neil had caught her,' said Nuala. 'And from the evidence of her knitting we know that she was in her chair by the door until Eric raised the alarm. I went into the drawing room and hid there until almost the end of the game. What about Ruth and Annabelle Olivia?'

'Ruth told the policeman she was in the kitchens, but told us that she was in her room. She came down the stairs at the end of the game, so let's put her up there,' I said, moving her doll upstairs. 'Annabelle Olivia was behind the plant pot on the stairs.'

'That's the end of the first scene, then,' said Nuala. 'Uncle Sid, Eric, me, Granny and Ruth on the ground floor; Annabelle Olivia halfway up the stairs; Scott outside; May, Grandfather, Uncle Hugh, Aunt Pam and Uncle Neil on the first floor; and Mam asleep on the second floor. What happened next?'

'I came out of the library,' said Eric, picking up his doll and moving it into the downstairs hall. 'I was going to the study to get Papa's watch, but I heard someone coming down the stairs. I hid next to the clock and they went past me to the study. They were in a hurry. I went back to the library to follow Sidney, but he wasn't there. I went into the drawing room, and then ended up back out in the hall. That's when I heard the voices in the study, and I knew Sidney was in there with someone.'

'Oh!' I said. I'd realized something. 'We know that Sidney's appointment with the murderer was at ten fifteen, and we know that the murderer came down around that time and almost caught Pamela in the study.'

'Unless the murderer *is* Pamela,' said Eric. 'All right, we just need to work out where everyone was between . . . let's say twelve minutes past ten and ten fifteen.'

'Yes!' said Nuala. 'Lookit, Uncle Neil says that he was on the first floor, and he saw Leonard's ghost coming out of the spare room and going downstairs. But it wasn't a ghost. It was the murderer, getting the bedknob to kill Uncle Sid – so it was Grandfather, or Ruth, or Aunt Pam or Uncle Hugh.'

'Or it was Neil, and he only pretended to see a ghost to cover up the fact that he was in there getting the bedknob,' I said. '*Five* suspects.'

But Nuala had paused, and was staring at the dolls on the first floor. 'Wait,' she said slowly. 'I've noticed something. It isn't five, it's four. Grandfather couldn't have done it.'

'Why not?' I asked.

'Think about the costume he was wearing. Uncle Hugh, Aunt Pam and Ruth had dark clothes with a bit of white on them, but Grandfather's siren suit was light blue all over. And it was new and starchy too – remember how it crackled when he moved? You heard him going up the stairs, May. If he'd crept back down to murder Uncle Sid, you'd have heard that too, Eric.'

'Oh!' said Eric. 'You're right!'

'I know,' said Nuala happily. Her freckly face was going pink and intense with excitement, and her glasses were flashing in the light of our torches. 'Grandfather said he was in his room until he heard the commotion downstairs, and I guess we've proved it's true. We have *four* suspects: Aunt Pam, Ruth, Uncle Hugh and Uncle Neil. We just have to work out which one of them it was!'

Suspects:
– Hugh Verey. May heard him talking angrily to Pamela Verey outside their room on the first floor at the beginning of the game. Nuala saw him come out of the dining room as the alarm was raised. He says he was in his room for the whole game, but this has to be a lie! He is in need of money. Could this be his motive? He is the spy sending information to the Germans! His motive for that is money – and he'll also get more after Old Mr Verey's (William's) death now that Sidney is dead. It's very likely that he's the person Sidney was meeting, and therefore the murderer.

— Pamela Verey. May heard her talking to Hugh Verey outside their room on the first floor at the beginning of the game. Nuala thinks she heard her crying in the drawing room just before Eric stumbled across the body. She turned on the oil lamp after Eric raised the alarm. She says she was in her room for the whole game, but this has to be a lie! Her ring was in the plant pot and her hairgrip was in the study – she must have been in there at some point on the night of the murder! Did she try to leave the house and was caught by Sidney? Did she kill him because of that? She has confessed to being in the study during the game as she tried to leave the house – she was frightened away by someone else, and ran out again! Is this true or is she the murderer?

— Neil Verey. May heard him talking to Old Mrs Verey (Iris) on the first floor at the beginning of the game. He was the murderer in the game. (Was he the murderer in real life?) Nuala saw him come out of the library as the alarm was raised. He says he saw his dead half-brother's ghost just before Sidney's murder. Is this a lie, to throw the police off the scent? Or does he really believe this – and did he kill Sidney as revenge for Sidney's cruelty to him as a child? He might also have killed Sidney to get more money from William Verey's will.

— Ruth the maid. Came rushing down the back stairs after the end of the game. She found the body and telephoned the police. Her apron had blood on it, even though she says she didn't touch Sidney, and she did not help clean up

Eric, either. She says she was in the kitchens during the game – is she lying? Her room had items stolen from the Vereys – why? Could the murder be revenge on Sidney – a politician – for not allowing her family to come to England with her? She's the person behind the hauntings – we think they were to punish Sidney for what she thinks he has done to her family and people like them. She also knows about Clarence Scott – she is clever and secretive, and she might very possibly be the murderer too!

- Mr Scott the gardener. Came from the kitchens with bandages after the end of the game. Still wearing his coat. Motive as yet unclear! He didn't do it! He was at the abandoned cottage, looking for his son who has been hiding there for weeks!

- Iris Verey. May heard her talking to Neil Verey on the first-floor landing close to the beginning of the game. She went downstairs and was still by the front door, knitting in her usual seat, when the alarm was raised. Motive still unclear – why would she kill her own son? She seems sorry that he's dead! She couldn't have done it – her knitting gives her an alibi!

- William Verey. May heard him go upstairs and into his bedroom at the beginning of the game. Nuala saw him come downstairs after the alarm was raised. Motive still unclear – why would he kill his own stepson? He seems sorry that he's dead! We have ruled him out – he was not wearing the right clothes to have either moved quietly or been the person Neil Verey saw!

49

From the report of May Wong

The next morning, the eleventh, Mr Scott was gone.

Everything was cleaned out of his already bare room, which echoed when Eric and I went to look at it, and he'd taken a side of bacon and a loaf of bread from the kitchen, so there wasn't enough for breakfast.

'SO unlike him,' said Old Mrs Verey.

'Most unhelpful,' said Old Mr Verey.

'What if Scott – well, what if he was working with the thief?' asked Hugh Verey, poking at his fried potatoes. 'Are you sure there's no more bread?'

'Hugh dear, *please*,' said Old Mrs Verey. 'Let's not talk about that. Eat up, can't you?'

'I think I might go back to bed,' said Mrs O'Malley. 'You don't need me, do you, darling?'

'No,' said Nuala shortly. 'I'll be all right.'

'That's my girl,' said Mrs O'Malley vaguely.

She drifted away. Nuala stared down at her plate, her cheeks pink.

After breakfast, there were supposed to be lessons. I hoped that we'd be let off with another free day, but then Old Mrs Verey came by, lips pursed up thin as a line and a new scarf on her knitting needles, and told us that there was *no excuse not to learn*. She shepherded us into the drawing room, sat us down and told us all to write a composition on someone heroic. Obviously, she meant us to write about Lord Nelson or Charles I and so on – this is always what they mean at Deepdean, and then they get angry at me when I refuse to care about anyone who let themselves get murdered by their enemies – but since she wasn't clear I began to write about the very best person I know from history.

Ching Shih was a lady pirate who terrorized everyone she met and commanded 400 junks.

I looked over at Eric's exercise book.

Tom Shark is not real, but he is a very famous detective.

'What is it, Fiona?' asked Old Mrs Verey.

'Can I use a book from the library?' asked Nuala, her hand up.

'What do you need that for?'

'I want to write about Grandfather,' said Nuala.

Old Mrs Verey looked pleased. 'Of course you may,' she said. 'Go on.'

Nuala beamed and trotted out of the drawing room. I knew she was up to something, but I didn't know what. It made me itchy.

'May I use a book in the library too?' I asked.

'Certainly not,' said Old Mrs Verey without even looking at me. 'Annabelle Olivia, don't press so hard on your paper, dear, you'll ruin it, and there's a shortage.'

'Please?' I asked. 'I've forgotten when Charles the First was executed.'

'It was 1649,' said Old Mrs Verey.

I'd made a mistake – English people always know that date.

'*And* I can't remember how many people were at the Battle of Edgehill,' I went on.

I thought this might be better, and I was right. Old Mrs Verey sighed hard and clicked away at her scarf. 'Very well,' she said. 'Go on then. But be quick!'

I ran off to the library to see what Nuala was doing.

50

From the diary of Fionnuala O'Malley

Monday 11th November 1940

What I know about detectives from books is that they never miss an opportunity to be smart. You have to grab every chance you get, and I guessed that this was mine.

I'd been thinking again about the papers we found down the well, and the one that had to be missing. We didn't know much about it, but we did have a clue: *Ed Warburton MBBS*. If we wanted to find out who he was, then we had to look for him – and the best place to do that was in the library.

The only problem was, apart from that name, I had no idea what I was looking for.

I checked in the family Bible first, in case Warburton was related to us somehow.

The Elysium Hall Bible has everyone's names in it. Before she got married, Granny's name was Iris Arden.

Her family, the Ardens, are the ones who owned Elysium Hall, so you can see her parents and grandparents and on and on up. The Bible also contains the date she married her first husband, Henry Foley (1897), and the date he died (1899). Their first son, Leonard, was born the same year as their marriage – 1897 – and died when he was twenty in 1917.

Then there was the date Uncle Sid was born (1899, just a few months before Mr Foley died), and the date Granny married Grandfather (1902). Then there came Hugh, and Neil, and Mam, and Uncle Hugh marrying Aunt Pam, and Annabelle Olivia being born. There's nothing next to Mam's name, though, because Grandfather and Granny didn't want to believe she'd really run away to America to become an actress and married Da while she was there. If you believed this Bible, I don't exist.

That made me realize that historical books sometimes don't tell you everything. It's a weird thought.

But I was still nowhere close to finding Warburton.

I looked up and found myself staring at an old photograph of Grandfather's regiment hanging on the library wall. They had tall, round hats and were all clutching old weapons.

'They look so silly,' said May, behind me. I'd heard her come in, but pretended I hadn't. I knew it'd annoy her if I said anything.

'They do, don't they?' I said. 'Like they're wearing costumes.'

'Which one's your grandfather?'

I squinted. It was really hard to tell. Everyone's faces blur together in old pictures, like they're all one person.

'That one,' I said. 'Ah, no, that one. I do know who the man next to him is – Granny's first husband, Henry Foley.'

'How *did* she get two husbands?' asked May. 'She didn't have them at once, did she?'

I laughed. 'Mr Foley died,' I explained – which obviously isn't funny. I wasn't laughing at that. 'During the war they were fighting. He was killed in a raid by some Boers.'

'Boars?'

'No, *Boers*. The people they were fighting against. Grandfather was really brave – he tried to fight them off, and almost managed it, but Mr Foley was too injured. Grandfather got a medal for it, and when he came home Granny was so grateful that she turned round and married him.'

'She married him for *not being able to save her first husband's life*?' said May, her face twisted up in confusion. 'I don't understand grown-ups sometimes.'

'She knew him before,' I said.

Honestly, this story doesn't make much sense to me, either, Diary. I can't imagine even having a husband, but if I did, and he died, I don't think I'd ever want to see anyone who was there when it happened, let alone marry them.

'They were all friends when they were kids – Henry Foley's family owned the big farm on the other side of the village, and Grandfather lived in one of the cottages next to it. He'd always been in love with Granny, but him trying to save Mr Foley proved it.'

'*How?*'

'I don't know!' I said.

I could feel my face flushing. I'd heard Grandfather telling the story, and it always sounded so wonderful, but now I was trying to explain it to May it was all going wrong.

'What if your grandfather has a dark secret?' asked May. 'What if – what if the real William Verey died in the attack and this ... Henry Foley person was the one who came home, only he pretended to be him so he could marry your grandmother again?'

'That makes *no* sense,' I said. 'And I told you – he'd lived here all his life. Granny knew who he was. Sure, *everyone* knew who he was.'

'Gah!' said May, taking down the picture from the wall and turning it over. 'I'm just trying out ideas.'

'Well, try out better ones.'

'All right. What if Sidney was stealing money from your grandfather, family money, and Old Mr Verey killed him because of that?'

Sometimes May really annoys me, Diary, and this was one of those times. 'Arra, would you stop!' I said. 'You don't have any evidence. Grandfather's been ruled out, and anyway why would Uncle Sid steal money from him? He thought Grandfather was dying.'

'Blast!' said May. 'Fine. We're wasting time. What did you come in here for?'

'To look for Ed Warburton,' I said. 'I thought there might be something about him here, but there's not.'

May goggled at me. 'But he's there,' she said.

'What?' I asked. 'Where?'

May pointed – to the back of the picture of Grandfather and his regiment.

'There,' she said. 'Look. Top row: *J. Beamis, M. Mahmood, T. Spenser, F. Warburton*. He's there.'

I stared. I couldn't believe it. I'd been so busy looking at Grandfather that I'd missed it. *We'd found Warburton*. I'd been expecting an Edward or a Theodore, but of course it wasn't *Ed*; that was just the second part of the name, the part that had been ripped off in Uncle Sid's hand. It was *Fred*.

And that was when we heard footsteps outside the library. We didn't have time to think. We both dived for the sofa and rolled under its fringed bottom. It was dusty under there, and I had to squeeze one hand over my mouth, so I wouldn't sneeze, and hold onto my glasses with the other. I was pressed up against May, and her hair tickled my chin – and I could tell that mine was bothering her because she whacked at it with her palm. I shoved her in the ribs.

'Good,' said Uncle Hugh's voice, far above us. 'We're alone.'

51

From the diary of Fionnuala O'Malley, continued

'I still don't know why you wanted to talk to me,' grumbled Uncle Neil.

Next to me, May elbowed me in excitement. She's got really pointy elbows for someone so small.

'Because I have to ask: where *did* Sidney get the idea that Father was dying?'

Uncle Neil made a sharp, upset noise. '*You* were the one who told me!' he said.

'Sid said he overheard Father and Mother talking, and Father saying that his health was failing.'

'He *said* that?'

'Well, I don't know. I wasn't there, was I? Sidney was. But apparently Father was talking about cancer, and Mother asked what could be done, and Father said he'd write to that doctor friend of his, you know, from his old regiment. Warburton.'

I gasped. Warburton. There he was again! So he wasn't just a soldier, he was a *doctor*.

'Perhaps it was only a scare. But I was so sure it was real. And, when I spoke to one of my spirit guides, they said—'

'Don't give me that nonsense! So Sidney heard Father talking about *someone* with cancer, and decided that meant Father was about to die. And, being Sidney, he went around bragging that he was going to inherit Elysium Hall. What an idiot! Well then, it's his fault, isn't it?'

'His fault?'

'That he's dead. Asking for trouble, just like always. He had to use up his lives sometime, didn't he?'

'I don't know what you mean,' said Neil with a wobble in his voice.

'Rot. Of course you do. You hated him.'

'I had good reason! I *asked* you for help when he was awful to me, but you just laughed at me. You always took his side when we were boys. And then he shut himself away in this house while I put myself in danger by enlisting. Disgusting.'

'Oh, don't think I don't know why you enlisted – to make Father proud of you at last. But of course it didn't work.'

'What, and you think Father's proud of *you*? What have you been up to lately, by the way?'

Now it was Uncle Hugh's voice that went wobbly. 'I don't know what you mean,' he said.

'I've seen the look on your face,' said Uncle Neil. 'It's just like the time you sold my marble collection to Julian Peters for a go driving his dad's motor when you were ten. You've got a secret – only I don't think it's just marbles and cars this time. Am I right?'

'Oh, be QUIET!' roared Uncle Hugh. 'You have no proof. I am your older brother, and—'

'So you are,' said Uncle Neil quietly. 'But who knows what might happen next?'

'What the devil do you mean?'

'Tragedies usually come in threes, that's all. Serena's husband was the first. Sidney was the second. So who will be the third?'

'Oh, not your spiritualist nonsense again.'

'My spiritualist nonsense has been right more often than you'd like to admit! Look at the seance!'

'Oh, rubbish. You don't believe in the thieves any more than I do.'

'What do you mean?'

'*If* it was a common thief who surprised Sid while committing a burglary, that's all well and good. That's what the police think. But – well, is that what really happened? When there are so many people in this house who had a motive to get rid of Sid? *You*, for example. Sid was cruel to you, and now he's dead. And with Father dying, as you assumed, you'd suddenly stand to inherit more. And you need it. Ghost hunting doesn't pay, does it?

I almost gasped again. I felt proud of us, at that moment, hearing our theory coming to life like this.

'We *both* assumed Father was dying!' cried Uncle Neil. 'And I don't care for money. But *you* do, don't you? You're desperate for it, in fact. And you're in line for the house now.'

I was trying to take slow, shallow breaths. The dust under the sofa tickled my nose and made my eyes water, but I didn't want to make a single sound – I had to know what was going to happen next. May, beside me, was vibrating with excitement.

'If you dare say any of this to the police, I shall – I shall – oh, you have no *idea* what I could do,' said Uncle Hugh.

'Greater forces than you have tried to hurt me! I'm protected all around by my spirit guides. You, on the other hand – well, just you wait and see.'

'Is that a *threat*? Weak sauce, Neil.' And, with that, Uncle Hugh snorted and stormed out.

Uncle Neil stood still for a moment, and then he sat down on the sofa with a thump that made the springs above us sag. Dust burst into our faces and May coughed – but Uncle Neil was still shifting about angrily and didn't hear. I was just like Nancy Drew, hiding in the closet from the thieves. I imagined as hard as I could that I was smart and brave and totally safe, and it almost worked.

'This family never listens to me,' said Uncle Neil at last, to the empty room. 'Well, I shall make them.'

Then he got up and strode out after Uncle Hugh, leaving me wondering exactly what he meant.

PART NINE

WE COME UPON
ANOTHER MURDER

52

From the report of May Wong

The next day I was certain something was about to happen, but I didn't know what. I had a bad feeling – but feelings aren't facts, and so I ignored it. We had proper leads to chase down – we'd found Ed Warburton, after all. We looked through *Who's Who* until we found his entry (Frederick Warburton, MBBS, former member of the Royal Warwickshire Regiment, now of Harley Street). We wrote him a very nice letter (at least I thought so, even though Eric and Nuala rewrote the first version I did) asking why Old Mr Verey had written to him, and why he thought his name might have been at the crime scene, and then we handed it to the postwoman and waited.

And then the second murder took place.

Here are my observations of exactly what happened. I wrote them down in my notebook straight afterwards, so I wouldn't forget anything, and I'm copying them here.

*

We were at dinner on Tuesday night, which was the twelfth of November. It was late – there'd been an air raid earlier, one with planes properly overhead, and we all had to run to the shelter. The Germans were definitely back that week, and for a while I thought that was what my feeling was about. I hate going into the shelter, and being jammed up against so many other people. It makes me feel as though I can't catch my breath.

When we got back to the house after the all-clear, it was almost nine, and the dinner had burned. Around the table were Old Mr Verey, Old Mrs Verey, Hugh, Neil, Mrs O'Malley, Pamela Verey (Hugh still wouldn't let her leave, so she was spending most of her time in her room, sulking), Annabelle Olivia, Nuala, Eric and me. Ruth had just brought in the pudding (bread-and-butter pudding, with no butter, only dripping) when Mrs O'Malley gave a little shriek.

'What's that noise?' she cried.

'What's what?' asked Hugh Verey, a spoonful of pudding halfway to his mouth.

'Is it the planes again?' asked Annabelle Olivia, eyes wide.

'No, no, there's something tapping at the window,' said Mrs O'Malley anxiously. 'I keep hearing it – I was sure I was imagining it, but there it is again!'

Everyone shut up and listened. I half closed my eyes so I could hear better, although the room was fairly dark, anyway, with only a candle lit. And I heard it. A tap-tap, tap-tap-tap on the glass of the dining-room window. The blackout was up, obviously, and it came softly through that.

'It's a branch,' said Hugh, putting down his spoon. 'Serena, come on—'

'No, there aren't any trees near that window,' said Neil. 'What *is* it?'

The tapping came again. It gave me goose pimples all up and down my back, and I shuddered angrily. I *hate* not knowing the answer to mysteries, even small ones, and I knew Neil Verey was right. There were no branches close to the window.

'Snuff out the candle,' said Neil. 'I'm going to look behind the curtain.'

'NEIL!' said Old Mrs Verey. She was upset because of having to sit in the air-raid shelter. 'I'm sure it's nothing! Please sit down.'

'*I'll* do it,' said Old Mr Verey, particular about the blackout as always.

There was a hurry to blow out the candle, and we sat in darkness for a moment. Suddenly the room felt much warmer and smaller.

I heard footsteps, and then Old Mr Verey twitched aside the curtain. It was dark outside (obviously) and the clouds were low and scattered, wind blowing them across the sky in waves. But there was just enough moonlight to see

303

that there was *someone at the window*. The pale oval of a face was peering in at us.

Pamela Verey screamed. Hugh Verey swore. Eric and I gripped hands underneath the table.

Old Mr Verey flung up the window sash with a cry, and leaned out into the night. Whoever it was vanished in the slam and clatter of the window going up.

Pamela was still screaming (and so was Annabelle Olivia, the noise she made weaving in and out like an air-raid siren), Old Mrs Verey was gasping in horror, Mrs O'Malley had her eyes tight shut and her lips pressed together – and then Neil Verey leaped up from the table and ran out of the room. We all heard the slam of the front door.

'Neil!' cried Old Mrs Verey. 'Ruth, Ruth! Come here!'

There were more heavy footsteps, and then a pause and a flare of light. Ruth appeared, holding a candle in her hand. The curtain was closed again, and now Neil *and* Hugh were missing.

'They've both gone after the thief!' gasped Old Mrs Verey. 'Oh, they'll be killed!' She began to sob, and Mrs O'Malley stood next to her, gripping her hand.

I've learned that it's always worth looking away from the excitement, though, to see what's really going on behind it all. So I turned and stared at Ruth. And her face was – strange. It was all twisted up, half angry, half . . . thoughtful? Surprised? Or – no, not surprised at all. And that was the strange thing about it.

'I'll follow them,' she said shortly.

'And so shall I,' said Old Mr Verey.

'Really!' cried Old Mrs Verey. 'Ruth! William! Don't be ridiculous!'

But they both ignored her, hurrying out of the room and leaving the rest of us in the dark again.

53

From the diary of Fionnuala O'Malley

Tuesday 12th November 1940

Sharp little fingers grabbed my elbow. 'We have to go after them too!' hissed May in my ear. I could tell she was standing on her tiptoes.

'Ow!' I said. 'That hurts!'

'QUIET!' growled May – who was obviously *not* being quiet because she just can't be.

I'll admit I was kind of scared about whoever had been outside the window. Was it Clarence? Had Scott come back? Everything felt possible, and nothing felt real now that we'd seen that weird face.

But here's the thing: when May tells you to do something, she's infectious about it. You somehow find yourself following her lead, even when the thing she wants you to do is nonsense. So it kind of made sense for the three of us – me, May and Eric – to duck out of the dining room and race for the front door – which was hanging wide open again, letting in the wind and a few flying specks of rain.

'Go left! I'll go right – Eric, straight ahead!' cried May, and then we were all out and running, for the second time in a week. My shoes slipped and slid on the grass, so I kicked them off and took off my glasses too. The ground was icy cold, but I didn't care. At least I knew I wouldn't fall over.

The moon had gone back behind the clouds, but I heard noises up ahead. I mean, I think I did. It's hard to know when the wind's all around you and you're in the countryside. I never realized it before I came to Elysium Hall, but sometimes the country's as noisy as a city. There are always animals screaming and scuffling, and the weather makes the trees shake. So it's hard for me to say *what* I heard – I think there were voices, someone shouting, and then a kind of grunt, cut off.

I got even more scared then. I hung back – sure, I feel bad saying this, but it didn't sound right, and I didn't want to get mixed up in whatever was going on. I know May would be raging at me if I admitted that to her, but she didn't hear that noise.

Someone went by me in the dark, I think – there was a rustling sound and breathing. Then I heard yelling.

'Help!' they shouted. 'Help! Quick! HELP!'

Suddenly the garden was shot through with a beam of light from behind me – a flashlight, held low to the ground, the way we're all supposed to if anyone absolutely needs to see during blackout. The light gleamed around – on the box hedges of the garden, on the grass, on the gravel pathways – and on Uncle Neil, standing over two bodies lying on the ground.

Ruth – she was the one holding the flashlight – cried out and ran past me. I followed her. Everything went kind of weird, like I was watching a movie and they'd cut out some frames from it. I was staring at the bodies from a few feet away, and then I was kneeling beside them. I didn't want to look, but I did, anyway, right into Grandfather's face. His eyes were closed, and I really thought he was dead, until he groaned.

The other body was Uncle Hugh. One of his eyes was open and one wasn't, and he was – I don't want to talk about it, Diary, but he was definitely dead. He was only the third dead person I've ever seen.

I crawled away backwards, covering my face with my hair. Ruth was kneeling next to the bodies, shining her flashlight on them, and so was Uncle Neil. They both had blood on them, and I wondered if that was a clue.

Then I wondered how I could be thinking about clues right now, and whether there was something wrong with me.

The flashlight flickered again, and I saw something lying on the gravel path next to Uncle Hugh and Grandfather. It glittered, and I realized that it was a knife, a thin silver one. It was clean, with flecks of rain on it, and I realized that it must have been wiped. There really has to be something wrong with me to be able to think like that, absolutely clearly, as if I was watching a movie instead of actually sitting in the rain in the garden where two people – my own family – had just been attacked.

May was shaking me, and Eric was saying, 'Are you all right? Are you hurt?'

'I'm not the murderer,' I said, and then (this is really embarrassing, but I do have to say this part, Diary) I fainted.

54

From the report of May Wong

I was a bit embarrassed for Nuala when she fainted – but I supposed this was still her very first murder case. I waited next to her until she came round (and I only poked her a bit, in the arm, until Eric told me to stop), and then I said, 'What did you see?'

'Uncle Hugh's dead,' said Nuala, breathing through her nose. Anyone could have worked that out.

By this point, Old Mrs Verey had arrived with Mrs O'Malley. When Mrs O'Malley saw Old Mr Verey and Hugh, she sat down on the gravel path and screamed.

'No, no, no, no!' she said. Nuala got to her feet and put her hand on her mother's shoulder.

'Come on, Mam, it's all right,' she said nonsensically.

'I can't – I can't – not AGAIN!' cried Mrs O'Malley, and she jumped up and went running back towards the house.

'It reminds her of Da,' said Nuala to us, white-lipped. 'She found him.'

I thought to myself that, whoever found him, it wasn't very fair of Mrs O'Malley to forget that a dead body might upset Nuala too. Then I thought that I really was getting soft because I was feeling sorry for Nuala again, and very much on her side. And I didn't even mind about it.

Then Pamela Verey and Annabelle Olivia came out, and there was more screaming and sobbing. It made me feel sick. Even though I hadn't liked Hugh Verey much, it was still horrible to see people so upset. It reminded me that this wasn't a game – Eric and I might be here to prove ourselves as spies, but we'd got mixed up in a real murder case, with real people in it.

Old Mrs Verey was crying too, and making a fuss. The only person who wasn't was Ruth, who was working quickly to bandage up Old Mr Verey. I watched her. She was very calm as she worked, and she seemed to know exactly what to do. I thought this was suspicious. I think if you're good at putting someone back together, you're much more likely to be good at taking them apart. That's just common sense.

I tried to get a good look at the injuries on Old Mr Verey and Hugh. It seemed as though they'd both been badly injured by something – a knife? That was all I could tell, really. I was annoyed.

'Is Old Mr Verey going to die?' I asked Ruth.

'I don't know,' she said, bandaging away. 'Perhaps. We need to telephone for a doctor.'

'I'll go!' said Eric quickly. I knew he wanted to get away from the crime scene, but I didn't tease him about it. I'd be able to do that later.

'Let me!' said Neil Verey, and he went running back to the house.

This made me remember him, and remind myself to be suspicious of him as well. He'd been standing over the bodies when Eric and I had arrived. When had he found them? Why hadn't he started to help them? All four of them – Ruth, Neil, Hugh and Old Mr Verey – had been outside during the time Hugh and Old Mr Verey were attacked. So what had Neil Verey been doing, if he hadn't been busy attacking his brother and father?

I sat back on my heels and thought. We'd had another murder – actually, an attempted double murder, only it hadn't gone right. And, since Pamela had stayed in the dining room during the second crime, we only had two suspects left – Ruth and Neil.

55

From the diary of Fionnuala O'Malley, continued

The doctor was called, and Annabelle Olivia was taken upstairs, still screaming. I felt so bad for her it made me sick. I thought about the day Da died, and my hands shook and I had to squeeze my lips together to stop myself crying.

May, Eric and I were supposed to go upstairs too, but obviously we didn't. We crept outside into the dark and rain and crouched under the dining-room window.

'I don't know why they always send us away,' grumbled May. 'Plenty more awful things than this happen to children all the time, especially now there's a war on. We ought to be allowed to see them if we want.'

I could tell that Eric was just as upset as I was, even though it was for different reasons. He'd looked a bit grey in the hall lights, and his teeth were chattering. I put my arms round him, and we leaned together until we were both calmer.

'Oh, come ON!' said May impatiently. 'Stop being so wet. Hugh Verey's dead, and we have to work out who killed him.'

'And they tried to kill Grandfather too,' I said. I squeezed my fingers into the fabric of my dress so that beads of water leaked out of it. 'Sure, I saw the knife. Did you? It was lying on the path. I think it was one from the kitchens.'

May ground her teeth. 'You should have picked it up!' she said.

'No, she shouldn't!' said Eric, careful as always. 'If she had, the police would think the murderer ran away with it, and keep believing that someone outside the house did all this.'

'But they didn't! It's all a trick! It has to be! I just don't know *how*.'

'Shh!' Eric said to her.

'It's obviously a trick,' I said, 'and don't we know who's doing it? There were only four people who went outside before Uncle Hugh was murdered – Uncle Hugh, Grandfather, Uncle Neil and Ruth. Uncle Hugh and Grandfather were both attacked, so the murderer has to be either Uncle Neil or Ruth. And Ruth knows how to do illusions. She's behind the poltergeist tricks, after all!'

'Well, Neil's good at illusions too,' May pointed out crossly. 'He pretended to be a spirit and made the table wobble. Anyway, aren't you the one who knows all about theatrical tricks? You ought to be able to work out what happened.'

'I know,' I said, 'but I just *can't*. I keep thinking about the face at the window, but I can't work out how it was done!'

'All right, stop moaning and let's look at the crime scene.'

I glared at May, and she looked a little embarrassed. 'Feelings don't matter when you're a detective,' she said, sticking out her chin at me. 'Anyway, you're ruining the crime scene again. You've stepped all over where the footprints ought to be.'

'Are you sure there were footprints?' asked Eric, taking a deep breath and pulling himself upright.

'There must have been! Come on – let's look.'

I pushed a draggle of hair out of my eyes. 'What's that?' I asked. It was hard to see anything without a flashlight. I reached out to the thing I'd seen, a pale, roundish lump in the dark dirt. My fingers sank straight into it.

'Ah!' I said, louder than I'd meant to. I was just shocked.

'What?' asked May.

'Someone left a ball of paper on the ground,' I said. 'Look! It's soaking.'

'Huh,' said May.

'Can I see?' asked Eric.

I held it out to him, and he took it gently and tried to smooth it out on his hand. Even more of it fell apart as he did so, but he shook the fragments into his notebook and closed it carefully. Then he stood up and started to stare at the window itself.

'Careful!' I said. 'You'll get caught!'

'There's no one in the room, and the blackout's up again,' said Eric.

He had his nose up to the glass, peering at it, and then he started to work his way round the sides.

'What've you got?' asked May.

'Nothing much,' said Eric. 'There's a string here, hanging down – but I don't think it's anything. I don't know.'

'Well,' said May, 'never mind that. The doctor's here now, and so we ought to go back inside and see if we can find any more clues. We only have two suspects left, and they are both exactly the sort of person who would do this!'

56

May was right. There was an extra pair of gumboots by the front door, and a shaken-out umbrella, and we could hear voices in the kitchens.

May and Eric went rushing towards the voices, but I said, 'Wait! I'll go. You stay out here.'

I knew that sounded kind of mean of me, but I knew that none of the adults would want any of us kids in there – so the fewer the better, especially since I could say that I wanted to find out how Grandfather was.

The kitchens were chaos. The range was pumping out hot air and steam as a huge pan boiled and hissed. Ruth was running around with towels and extra bandages while the doctor (round and old, with little gold glasses on his nose – the kind young doctor we had when we first arrived had enlisted months ago) bent over the big table where Ruth usually chops vegetables and prepares food. But Grandfather was laid out on it now, just like a piece of meat. That made me feel sick to think, but it's what he looked like. Granny was next to him, crying, and Uncle Neil and Mam were hovering anxiously, Uncle Neil with his arm round Mam.

'He's lost a lot of blood,' the doctor was saying grimly as I tiptoed in. 'It'll be touch and go. Lucky he was found when he was – and doubly lucky that the knife caught him where it did. A few inches lower and there'd be nothing I could do. And you didn't get a look at the assailant?'

'It was dark,' said Ruth briefly. 'The family heard someone at the window. Mr Hugh and Mr Neil ran outside, and Mr Verey and I followed, but I lost him – the person must have struck Mr Hugh and Mr Verey when they had the chance.'

'And there were no warning signs? You didn't see anyone hanging about earlier? I've heard there are thieves in the area.'

'I didn't see anything unusual at all,' said Ruth. 'I was in the kitchens the whole afternoon. I can only see the back of the house, the study and drawing-room windows, from here – the dining room's in the wrong place.'

I don't know how to explain it – I'm still trying to work it out, Diary – but the way she said that was weird. Her face was blank, and even her voice was stiff. It was like – I've got it – the way someone talks before they've learned their lines. Like she didn't believe what she was saying.

'I heard them both shout,' said Uncle Neil. 'Hugh – my brother – he yelled out, and then Father shouted too. I ran

318

towards them, but I was too slow. God! This is – it feels like a nightmare! Do you think Father will be able to identify the person who did this?'

And that sounded weird too – *more* emotional than it should have done.

'I should think so, if he recovers,' said the doctor, nodding. 'More hot water, please. Hugh Verey was struck from behind. A surprise attack. But Mr William Verey here was *facing* his assailant. Wounds on his hand and arm, and his cheek, as well as the deeper cut to his abdomen. He must have come upon his son being attacked and tried to stop the violence. Poor man! To lose two sons *at home* – what a dreadful thing.'

Mam noticed me then. She blinked at me, as though she couldn't remember how I fitted into the scene, and then remembered that I wasn't supposed to be there.

'Nu— Fiona!' she said. 'Do go away, quickly! You shouldn't look at this!'

She'd called me the wrong name, and I was so mad at her. She hadn't cared about me seeing Uncle Hugh's body earlier – she'd just been thinking about herself.

'I've already seen it, Mam,' I said because I wasn't going away without a fight. 'I want to *help*.'

'Tidy up Mr Verey's clothes, then,' said Ruth. 'I have to clean them before they can be mended.'

This was really suspicious as far as I was concerned. They were evidence, weren't they? The police should want to see them. But no one else seemed to be thinking about that. Maybe Ruth thought she could use me to help her clean up Grandfather's clothes before anyone else noticed, but she didn't realize that she'd given us a chance to take a look ourselves.

'Grand, so,' I said.

'Say *yes*, Fiona, not *grand*,' said Granny automatically.

'Sorry, Granny,' I said in my nicest Fiona accent, and I gathered up Grandfather's trousers and jacket and shirt where they were lying in a heap on the floor and ran for it before she could tell me off again.

57

From the diary of Fionnuala O'Malley, continued

I laid out Grandfather's suit and shirt on the floor of the laundry room and stared at them. May was breathing heavily, right over my shoulder, which was distracting. Eric stood back, holding a notebook, and said, 'Did the doctor tell you anything about his injuries?'

'He cut his cheek and arm and hand trying to fight the murderer off,' I said. 'And then the murderer got him in the abdomen – which is the stomach, right? And I guess then Uncle Neil arrived, and the murderer ran away.'

'Unless the murderer *was* Neil,' pointed out May. She was still way too close, and I elbowed her. She elbowed me back and kept talking.

'So all we really know is that the killer threw the knife down and pretended to be shocked to find a murder taking place. Is it a clue that the knife came from the kitchens, by the way? I suppose that fits with Ruth more than Neil, but

Neil could still have helped himself to a kitchen knife quite easily. All right, what do the clothes say? There's a cut on his shirt, here, a big long one that's bled all over the place. That fits with what the doctor said. What else?'

I stuck my hand into the right-hand pocket of Grandfather's jacket. I had to bite down on my lip as I touched something that was tacky and wettish.

'What is it?' asked May.

'There's – ugh! – his handkerchief,' I said, pulling it out like a really bad magic trick and trying to talk and hold my breath at the same time. It was covered in red, and it smelled like pennies. 'He must have put it against his stomach to stop the bleeding and then put it back in his pocket.'

'Anything else?' asked May.

She was trying to sound calm, but I could see her face wrinkling up as she smelled the blood. I was kind of glad to know that she could be disgusted by something like that, after all.

'A pen,' I said, digging. 'A box of lozenges. A piece of string. A pebble. A piece of paper and a cufflink. And that's it.'

'Blast,' said May.

'What did you expect to find?' I asked her. 'Sure, he didn't know he was going to be attacked.'

'I know, I know,' said May, sighing.

We crept out of the laundry room, and even though I knew everything was completely horrible – Uncle Sidney

322

and Uncle Hugh were dead, and Grandfather was injured –
I felt kind of hopeful. I liked being part of something. It
buoyed me up. And I know I said that I'd never be friends
with May, Diary, but it's nice to be working with her and
Eric for a while, anyway.

58

The next morning I woke up, and the police were here again. Nuala and Eric and I crept down to the curve of the stairs above the hall, still in our nightclothes, and listened in.

'Terrible business,' said PC Cuffe. I caught a glimpse of his high blue hat before Eric pulled me backwards, out of sight. 'I'm very sorry, Mrs Verey. We ought to have – well, we're very stretched at present, but we are doing the best we can. I have men combing the countryside for the thieves – we had a tip-off about a deserter in the area, and we're following that up. We'll get to the bottom of this.'

'You had better,' said Old Mrs Verey, her voice shaking. Pamela Verey was sobbing. 'This is not good enough. You promised us we were a *priority*, and now look! Because you've been so slow, another of my sons is dead, and my husband is at death's door. Their blood is on your hands. You are supposed to keep us *safe*.'

'Mrs Verey—'

'Enough. I want them caught, do you understand? You seem to be treating this like any other case when it is not. My husband is a *magistrate*. He is *respected*. I'd like to see him treated as such.'

'Yes, Mrs Verey. I understand, Mrs Verey. Many apologies.'

'And I want you to speak to Ruth again. *She* was outside last night. What if she was helping the thieves? She can't be allowed to get away with it! I had doubts when she was hired, but, you know, it's so difficult to get staff at the moment.'

This was horrible, and I was shocked.

'*My* husband was respected too,' said Pamela Verey thickly, blowing her nose into a handkerchief. 'What about him? The important work he was doing – doesn't that matter to you? He was a hero! What are we going to do without him?'

There was an awkward English pause. I thought about what we'd worked out – that Hugh Verey wasn't a hero at all but someone selling secrets to the Germans for money.

'I'll go and speak to the maid again,' said PC Cuffe. 'She's certainly been holding something back. And the knife was from the kitchens too, wasn't it? Well, perhaps this can be wrapped up soon, after all.'

There was a rustle of skirts, and I turned to see Annabelle Olivia tripping down the stairs. Her face was pale and her hair was sticking up in a very un-Annabelle Olivia way.

'Daddy's really dead,' she said. It wasn't a question.

All three of us tensed. But Annabelle Olivia just bit her lip and sat down next to Nuala.

'Aren't you going to cry?' I asked.

'It's too serious to cry,' said Annabelle Olivia.

Nuala gave her a very complicated look. 'Come here to me,' she said. 'I know.' She put her arm round Annabelle Olivia and they sat together, with Annabelle Olivia's eyes closed and her head on Nuala's shoulder.

Eric and I stared at each other. You can't apologize for having alive parents, can you? The fact is that some people have them and some people don't, and there are lots of ways to be unhappy about it whether you do or not. But it's hard to think what to say when you see someone so sad, and you know that you can't possibly understand how it feels. It's like a door shut in your face, one you never want opened.

And I know that I wanted to solve this case because Eric and I needed to prove ourselves. But at that moment, even though the Vereys were pretty awful people, I realized that we also had to crack the case to stop anyone else looking as miserable as Annabelle Olivia did then.

We were still waiting for the letter from Dr Warburton. One of us had to hang about in the hall every day at post time to intercept the postwoman before any of the Vereys could get to it, and it was my turn that day.

I saw someone coming up the drive and rushed to open the door. But it wasn't our postwoman. It was a young woman wearing overalls, her shiny yellow hair tied back in a kerchief and a bag in her hand.

My heart sank to the bottom of my toes, my face turned red and I ducked back round the door frame – but not before I'd been seen. I'd been expecting Big Sister Hazel to find me. I'd imagined how she'd look when she arrived. But what I hadn't imagined was that she might send someone else.

Footsteps crunched towards me, tapped up the stone steps, then paused.

'I know you're there, May,' said Daisy Wells.

59

From the report of May Wong

I took a deep breath and stepped out of my hiding place. Daisy was staring down at me, her eyes very blue and fierce.

'I've been looking for you,' she said. 'I've been *all over the country* looking for you.'

I balled up my fists. 'You didn't need to!' I said furiously. 'We've been doing absolutely all right on our own. We found our way here, didn't we? We found a case, and we've almost solved it!'

'You little idiots,' said Daisy. 'Really! You ran away without telling anyone, you haven't sent us any messages to let us know you're all right, and now you've got yourselves caught up in a murder mystery. You're lucky that I haven't told Hazel about this yet.'

'You haven't told Hazel?' I asked.

Twin pink spots suddenly appeared at the top of Daisy's cheeks.

'I – well – I thought it best not to, until I'd found you,' she said quickly.

My heart was racing. Big Sister Hazel didn't know! She wasn't angry at me yet! It felt as though a weight had been lifted off my chest.

'If you don't let us into the Ministry, I'll tell Hazel that you *abandoned* us for weeks,' I said experimentally.

'*Don't* try it! I've told you, you're too young! The Ministry is serious business, May, not a game for children.'

'Children can be serious! I told you – we've almost solved this case!'

'I don't call two murders and an attempted murder *almost solving the case.*'

'You – hypocrite!' I hissed at her. 'When you were our age, you solved *plenty* of murders.'

'I was *thirteen*!' snapped Daisy.

We were both breathing crossly, glaring at each other. It's just like a grown-up to think that everything they did when they were younger was perfectly all right, while everything children do now is all wrong and much too old for them.

'Who's there?' said Old Mrs Verey from the hall behind me. 'Who are you? May, why are you talking to this person?'

Daisy's face changed immediately. 'Mrs Verey,' she said, bobbing a curtsey. 'My name is Poppy Poe. I've been sent by the Ministry – of Agriculture, you know. I'm here to assess the property for official war use.'

329

She's as good at acting as Nuala is, I thought.

'Today? Don't you know what's happening here? We –
my sons are *dead*!'

'I'm terribly sorry for your loss, madam,' said Daisy.
'But I really must insist.'

Old Mrs Verey gave a wobbly sigh. 'This is too much,'
she said. '*Too much*. I wash my hands of you. Take
whatever measurements you need, but please do not
disturb us further. May, go to your room at *once*.'

I rushed upstairs, feeling a new whirl of despair. If
Daisy was here, that meant the adventure was almost
over. I didn't know how much time we had left, but I
knew it wasn't much at all.

I went outside just after lunch and found Daisy in the
garden. She was sitting on the lip of the well, squinting in
the thin November sunshine and eating a sandwich
wrapped in brown paper.

'What do you want, Daisy?' I asked.

Daisy wrinkled her nose at me. 'Who's Daisy?' she
asked. 'My name is Poppy—'

'I don't care *what* your name is supposed to be,' I said
crossly. 'I asked a question, and you might at least answer
it. Are you here to take us away?'

Daisy paused, and I could feel the blood pounding in
my ears.

'Not immediately,' she said. 'The case – well, it is

interesting. And, besides, there *was* a reason why Hazel had written down this address in the note that you most inconveniently found.'

'Oh, because someone here was selling secrets to the Germans?' I asked.

I saw Daisy's face change.

'We know who it was,' I went on, '*and* we know what they were selling. It was quite obvious.'

(It hadn't been, but I wasn't going to tell Daisy *that*.)

'But—'

'I told you,' I said, as witheringly as I could, 'we worked out who the spy was, and now we're solving the murders. We're proving to you that we'd be good spies so that you'll let us into the Ministry.'

'No!' said Daisy. 'How many times do I need to tell you, May? You're too young!'

I pulled the most horrible expression that I could. It was babyish of me, but that was how I felt.

'Oh, now, who's this?' asked Daisy, looking past me.

I turned and saw Nuala, feet bare as usual (I don't understand how she can when it's so cold in England all the time) and hair pulled up in a scraggly knot at the back of her head. She had on an ugly purple dress that was too big for her and coming down at the hem, and an old knitted jumper. When she saw I was with Daisy, I watched her pull into herself. Her back straightened, and her shoulders went up, and her face turned stiff and cold behind her glasses.

I remembered the first time we'd met her, out on the drive on our first morning. I'd thought I was so good at knowing whether people were nice or not, but I'd been tricked by an act. The girl we'd met that day wasn't the real Nuala at all.

'Good afternoon,' said Nuala coldly to Daisy, putting out her hand.

'Wotcher,' said Daisy, winking at her. 'My name's Poppy. I've come to requisition your house.'

'No she hasn't,' I said to Nuala. 'This is Daisy – she's a spy.'

'May!' said Daisy.

'It's true!'

'Is it?' asked Nuala.

'That's top-secret information,' said Daisy, sighing. 'May's being bothersome, as usual. She oughtn't to be spreading such things about. Careless talk and all that. D'you know I've known her since she was practically a baby? She's always been this annoying.'

'I HELPED YOU SOLVE THREE MURDERS!' I said, my voice getting the better of me.

Nuala unbent. She almost laughed – but I knew she wasn't laughing at me. 'Are you actually a spy, so?' she asked quietly. 'I mean – a spy for *us*?'

'That is classified,' said Daisy firmly – and then she raised one eyebrow and gave Nuala another wink.

'Then I think you should have this,' said Nuala,

shrugging off her jumper. It gave out a strange crackling noise, and she put it on the lip of the well between her and Daisy. 'There's papers in here – a map and a telegram – we found them in the well after the murder. They help prove that my uncle Hugh was a spy for the Germans. We've hidden fake ones back in the well to trick the murderer if they go looking.'

'Nuala!' I said.

'You need to show her what you've been doing!' hissed Nuala. She looked at Daisy. 'May and Eric are after doing a great job, they really are. They've almost solved the case – I know they can do it. You should let them into your spy organization.'

I was astonished – and a little bit guilty. 'It wasn't just us,' I admitted. 'Nuala helped.'

'I am not letting you in *anywhere*,' said Daisy, snatching up the papers. 'I shall look at these later. Now, listen. I am going to tell Hazel where you are—'

'NO!' I wailed. 'Please! She'll make me go back to school!'

'*Will you wait a moment*,' said Daisy, holding up one finger. 'I am going to tell Hazel where you are during my next sked. That's a top-secret scheduled radio transmission, by the way, which happens to be in *two days*. I'll say that you're safe, and I'm bringing you with me when I go back to the Ministry. I've got to get to Cairo next weekend, and I can't be late.'

'What's in Cairo?' asked Nuala.

'Oh, very boring work,' said Daisy. 'You wouldn't be interested.' The top of her cheeks had gone pink.

'Now, what you do with those two days is up to you. You've got this far, so it only seems fair – but after that, May, yes, you will have to go back to school, you young idiot.'

'Thank you!' said Nuala.

'*Don't* thank her,' I said. I was smarting from being called an idiot. When I had helped unmask a spy! Rude!

'Right,' said Daisy, 'I must get back to work. Ministry of Agriculture, you know. If you need me, I'll be poking around in the garden, digging things up. Just like detection, really.'

Nuala laughed. Why had I ever thought she was cold and rude?

'Now go away,' said Daisy.

And she waved us off and went back to her sandwich. As we left, I saw her begin to leaf through the bundle of papers.

60

From the diary of Fionnuala O'Malley

Wednesday 13th November 1940

Once we were back inside, I tried to ask May how she knew the spy so well, since it seemed kind of unlikely – Daisy's *so* English, and May's just *not* – but May just frowned and growled and said, 'She's my sister's friend. Don't ask.'

I looked out of the drawing-room window and saw Daisy walking away quickly through the grass, clutching the papers I'd given her under her arm.

'Where's she off to?' I asked.

'No idea,' said May. 'Probably to tell my sister about us so she can take us away.'

That made my heart jump strangely in my chest. I thought I wouldn't care about saying goodbye to Eric and May, but now that it was really happening I realized I'd actually miss them.

'We just have to hurry, then,' said Eric. 'Come on. What's next?'

I knew what we had to do. We needed to see Grandfather as soon as possible, to find out if he could tell us anything now that he was healing up. That meant getting into his room.

We hung about on the stairs until Ruth came along, a tray in her hand, and saw us. 'Fiona, will you take this to your grandfather?' she asked. She was looking strange too, really anxious, and she kept smoothing down the pocket of her apron. I guessed the policeman had scared her.

I took the tray from her, and realized it was Grandfather's supper – a piece of white fish in sauce, with pale tapioca in a bowl. I stared at it.

'What's wrong?' asked Eric, as Ruth walked back to the kitchen.

'Sure, what if it's *poisoned*?' I whispered. 'Ruth might want to finish Grandfather off!'

I know it sounded made up, but ever since Uncle Sidney died I've been stuck in a world where anything really can happen.

Eric didn't laugh at me or tell me I was being ridiculous. He just nodded and said, 'You're right. May?'

'Why don't you feed it to Annabelle Olivia?' asked May.

'*Here!*' I said. '*No!*'

'All right, fine, that was a joke,' said May, scowling. 'Here, give it to me. I'll lick it, and if I don't die it's all right.'

I felt like this wasn't the best plan, and Eric's face agreed with me.

'That's not how poisons work,' he said.

'Well, at least I'm willing to try *something*!' snapped May. 'If you won't let me do that, then use it as a distraction. Go up, pretend to trip over something once you get into your grandfather's room, and spill it. It gives you an excuse to talk to him, and Ruth'll have to make up another plate. We'll watch her while she does that. All right?'

I wanted to disagree with her, but I couldn't because honestly that was a great plan. Even when May's being rude and sulky, she's still smart, and she never gives up. I really am going to miss her. I hate admitting that.

'Fine,' I said, taking the tray, and up I went to Grandfather's room.

I knocked on the door, and Grandfather called, 'Come in!'

It was scary, actually going inside. I didn't know how Grandfather would look. When I pushed open the door, the feeling got worse. It was dark, and quiet, and hot, like it was underground.

'Shut the door!' snapped Granny at once, and I jumped.

I'd been expecting that I'd really have to act to make the tray spill, but it wasn't hard at all. I let my hand wobble and my knee buckle as I turned to close the door, and the tray dropped to the floor with a crash.

'RUTH!' cried Granny. 'Whatever's wrong with you today?'

A match was struck, and Granny's face appeared above me, hovering in the darkness next to a globe of yellow light.

'Fiona! What are you doing? You silly girl! Why, it's quite ruined! Go and get Ruth – no, I will. Honestly, can't anyone in this family do anything right?'

She put the lamp down next to me and whisked off towards the door. 'Stay here! Don't move. You silly, *silly* girl!'

And then I was alone with Grandfather. I could hear his wheezy breathing in the bed.

Then: 'That was very careless of you, Fiona,' he said. I jumped again.

'Grandfather, I'm sorry—' I began.

'Shush. Stay still. You don't want to cause any more mischief, do you?'

I almost said no, before I decided it was probably better not to say anything else.

So I stood still and stared round the room. I looked at the cabinets full of Grandfather's war medals and important papers, and the little sculptures that Granny collects. Grandfather was a lump under his bedsheets – I could just make out his white froth of hair, and one arm, bandaged, draped over the blanket.

The lamp was dim, and everything flickered with it. Da taught me the trick of staying really still, even when you're itching all over to move. You have to imagine that your arms and legs have turned to stone, and you couldn't move them even if you wanted to. Sometimes I'm so good at imagining that my whole chest and throat turn stony, and I almost forget to breathe. I stood quietly and heard Grandfather's breathing thicken.

Then my eyes went to the bottle of medicine on the bedside table, and the rolls of bandages laid out ready. How badly hurt *was* Grandfather? I'd been so worried he was dying, and then I'd found out that it wasn't true – but now he might be dying for real. It was a scary thought, and it made me forget about being a stone.

Grandfather's breath changed again.

'What's wrong?' he rasped. 'Why are you sniffling?'

'Are you really sick, Grandfather?' I said. 'I don't want you to die too.'

'Nonsense!' said Grandfather gruffly. 'I won't, my dear. I've survived worse. In South Africa, Foley and I were set upon by ten men. I couldn't save him, but I fought them all off. Ironic, isn't it, that the same thing should happen to me again, with Hugh? I tried, but it was too late. All I can seem to do is save my own skin.'

Grandfather sounded so sad. I realized that Uncle Hugh dying must have felt like losing Mr Foley all over again. It was awful.

'I'm sorry,' I said. 'I really am.'

Grandfather sighed. 'You're a good girl, Fiona. Thank you. I wish it hadn't been that way.'

'Did you see who did it?' I asked, glowing from being called good.

'I saw the knife,' said Grandfather. 'I heard Hugh shout, and then I saw the knife flashing in the moonlight. Didn't see a face, though. I couldn't stop them. I'm getting slow in my old age, eh? Come here, Fiona.'

He reached out with his right hand, the uninjured one, and held mine. I took a deep breath and tried not to cry.

'What exactly happened with Scott's son Edmund?' I asked, to try to distract myself. It had been bothering me, what Scott had said.

'Edmund?' asked Grandfather. 'Where on earth did you hear about that, Fiona? A bad business. Sidney discovered him poaching, and I sat for his case. Scott hoped I'd be lenient, I know, but the rules are for everyone, and they're not to be broken. I had to give his son the sentence I'd give to anyone else. He died in prison – pneumonia, caught it in his cell – but I couldn't have foreseen that.'

'Oh,' I said. 'Poor Scott!'

'The law is the law,' said Grandfather severely. 'Never forget that, Fiona.'

I knew he was right. But, all the same, maybe the law should be better, if following it can make such bad things happen.

61

From the report of May Wong

When Nuala came downstairs again, she looked upset. I thought that this was at least partly because she'd got splashes of disgusting white fish sauce all over her dress. The things English people do to fish are horrible.

'What's wrong?' asked Eric, and Nuala started babbling on about her grandfather seeing the knife in the moonlight and people dying in prison.

'Yes, but did he see who did it?' I asked.

I'd been stuck in the kitchen, watching Ruth remake Old Mr Verey's dinner – and not poison it, as far as I could tell – so I was cross and bored.

Nuala took a deep breath and told us what her grandfather had said to her about Edmund.

And then Neil Verey came striding across the hall. He was waving a thin piece of paper that fluttered in his hand – a telegram – and he looked upset.

'Hi! Hi! Hello!' he shouted. 'Anyone about? I've been ordered back to barracks. On Friday! Ridiculous.'

Mrs O'Malley came wandering down the stairs. 'What's wrong, Neil?' she asked.

'I've been called back,' said Neil. 'I shall have to leave soon.'

'Surely not? After – all this?'

'I'm sorry, Serena. I did try. Now who'll take care of Elysium until Father's better? *If* he gets better. You never know – well, you never know what might happen next.'

Pamela Verey and Annabelle Olivia left that afternoon at last, Pamela crying and Annabelle Olivia still with the same white, shocked expression. I thought I'd be glad to see Annabelle Olivia gone, but now that it'd happened I felt blank and disappointed with a funny current of something underneath it that might have been guilt.

Their car pulled away, and Ruth closed the door behind them with a bang.

'There's a letter for you three on the table,' she said. She was still looking strange, nervous and pale around the eyes.

Eric rushed over to the hall table and scooped up an envelope. I saw his eyes widen.

'It's from *Warburton*,' he said in a whisper, with a nervous glance over at Ruth.

'Come upstairs at ONCE,' I said fiercely. 'Now!'

I was excited all over again, my heart thumping. We ran upstairs, I slammed the door of the spare room shut behind us, and Nuala and I bent over Eric as he carefully peeled the envelope open. He's always so measured and careful, and it made me want to tear at my hair, but at last he pulled out a sheet of paper.

'*Dear Eric, Fenella and May,*' he read. 'Sorry, Nuala, he's misspelled your name.'

Then his voice changed.

'*I regret to inform you that my father passed away a week ago, after a long illness. I am a little surprised by your request – the second such from Elysium Hall this autumn. I would recommend speaking to Mr Sidney Foley, whom my father wrote to in early November this year, just before his health failed him. Yours, Lucinda Warburton.*'

We stared at one another.

Fred Warburton had written a letter to Sidney. This was what Sidney had been holding when he died. But what did it say? And . . . where was the rest of it?

PART TEN

WE SOLVE THE CASE, OF COURSE

62

From the diary of Fionnuala O'Malley

Thursday 14th November 1940

Dear Diary,

Something's happened. Something big.

The air-raid sirens went off just as we were sitting down to supper this evening. We all ignored them at first because Granny's lips pursed when she saw us twitching, and there was no point doing anything else. I had to tell myself that they won't come here, there's nothing to bomb, it's just dark countryside, and then I could calm down.

Ruth was bringing in the first course when the door to the dining room opened and Grandfather came in.

He'd been outside that afternoon, frowning and poking at the beds Scott had only half finished before he left, and Grandfather had insisted on checking the blackout, but we'd thought he was going to have supper in his room. But here he was. He was limping, and holding his hand over his stomach protectively. In the candlelight, he looked like a ghost. Mam let out a small gasp, and Ruth almost dropped the tureen of soup.

'Please don't fuss,' said Grandfather.

Uncle Neil jumped up and went to help him into his chair – I watched him, closely, and I could see May and Eric were too.

'I'm so glad we're all together,' said Granny emptily.

I couldn't help it. I started giggling. It was just so ridiculous. We were still pretending – even though Uncle Sidney and Uncle Hugh had been murdered, and Grandfather had almost died – in the middle of a war, with air-raid sirens screaming. What was the point of any of it?

'Shush, Fiona!' said Granny.

And that was when it started.

The top drawer of the sideboard slammed open. Then the one below it, and the one below that. Cutlery bounced out onto the carpet, Mam screamed and Uncle Neil jumped up.

'Leonard! He's back!' he cried eagerly.

'Nonsense, Neil. Sit down,' snapped Granny. 'It was just—'

She stopped short. I knew what she was thinking: that it was the reflected rattle from *a bomb* – but I knew she'd never say that. And then, like she'd conjured the idea up, we all heard the thrum in the sky, starting tiny and getting bigger and bigger in waves, *whoosh, whoosh, whoosh*. Planes. And it sounded like hundreds of them.

That was when the tapping on the window started. It was just a fingernail-scratch of sound at first, and then it got louder and louder, until it sounded like a fist was hammering on the glass, fighting with the roar of the planes' engines above us.

The hammering at the window went on and on. I couldn't work out what was happening. Mam had her ears covered, Uncle Neil was pacing frantically round the room, Granny was sitting up very straight, her hands clenched round her knife and fork as though they were weapons, and Grandfather was leaning forward in his chair, breathing heavily. Ruth darted her eyes between them all, and I saw her shoulders shake.

The planes were still thrumming the air. I looked down at my hands, and they were trembling. I don't think I was scared then. I don't know. I remember thinking, *Here we go, this is it,* and being amazed at how *real* everything looked. That sounds weird, but I can't explain it any other way. Everything in the dining room was almost glowingly perfect, and everyone's faces were clear and lovely, and I suddenly felt as though I might belong here, after all.

May had both hands lightly resting on the table, but her whole spine was tensed like a cat waiting to pounce. Next to her, Eric looked anxious, but was trying to hide it.

The rapping on the window went on and on – and then, somewhere off in the distance, the first bomb fell.

63

From the diary of Fionnuala O'Malley, continued

Mam stood up so quickly she scared me. I hadn't seen her move that fast for months.

'That's enough,' she said. 'We're going to the shelter. *Now.*'

'Serena—' said Granny.

'*No,*' said Mam. 'You heard it. I am not letting the children stay in this house when there are bombs falling. Nuala, May, Eric: go outside at once.'

She almost sounded – well, right then she almost sounded like Da. She put out her hand and squeezed mine.

'Come here to me,' she said. 'Hurry up – don't dawdle.'

It felt so good to see her taking charge.

We'd just got out of the front door when the next bomb hit.

It was far away, I knew, but it sounded like it might have landed in the orchard. Everything telescopes in when a bomb falls. Your ears get like a bat's and every hair on your body tingles, and you can feel the dropping *scream* right through you – and then the *crash* as it hits.

The next second there was a juddering, spitting noise, *dat-dat-dat-dat*, and thunderous booms from the anti-aircraft guns, and then more screams-and-crashes. Sparks of bright light flung into the sky.

'That's Coventry,' said Mam, still holding my hand. 'They're hitting Coventry.'

Across the dug-up lawn Mam and Eric and May and I went, and then ducked into the air-raid shelter. It smelled of dirty water and stale earth and rusting metal, and even though the night was cold it felt warm inside – and warmer when Uncle Neil and Ruth followed us in, and then Granny and Grandfather. Grandfather was clutching his stomach – I could see that it still hurt him to walk, and I felt guilty, even though the air raid wasn't my fault at all.

Everyone was quiet, and I could hear us all panting over the *scream-crash boom scream-crash boom dat-dat-dat-dat* from far away. It was like someone had cupped a hand over all of us – like we were all being held together in the dark.

And then Uncle Neil lit the storm lamp – and we all realized that there was someone else in the shelter with us.

The light shone on a head of gold hair, blue eyes and slightly dirty overalls.

'Wotcher,' said Daisy.

Granny gasped and put a hand on her heart. Mam shrieked and pulled me to her. She was still convinced that there was a thief somewhere near Elysium Hall who wanted to murder us all.

'It's just the woman from the Ministry,' said May scornfully. 'She's all right.'

'Indeed, I am,' said Daisy, staring round at all of us. 'Didn't you hear me knocking on the window earlier? I should have come sooner, but I was trying to speak to the police, and then events overtook me. I am sorry, I really am.'

'That was *you* knocking on the window?' I asked, before I could stop myself.

'No, no, it was Leonard,' said Uncle Neil. 'I'm sure—'

'It was definitely me,' said Daisy. 'I wanted to warn you.'

'About the bombs? But we heard the air-raid siren,' said Eric.

'Oh no, not that,' said Daisy. 'I'm too late to do anything about that. I had to warn you that there was going to be another crime.'

64

From the diary of Fionnuala O'Malley, continued

'Don't be ridiculous,' said Granny. 'What on earth are you saying?'

'It isn't ridiculous,' said Daisy apologetically. 'I wish it was, but it isn't. I saw the preparations for it this afternoon when I was coming back from – well, never mind what I was doing. I telephoned around to make certain, and, as soon as I was, I knocked on the window.'

'You saw the thieves?' asked Mam.

'There were never any thieves. I saw the *murderer*,' corrected Daisy.

'But whatever nonsense is this?' cried Granny. 'Really, this is unbelievably unpleasant. I shall telephone your supervisor and lodge a complaint.'

'I'm aware this is unwelcome, but I'm afraid it's all absolutely true. There is a murderer in this house, and I'm here to tell you who they are.'

'It's Ruth!' rasped Grandfather. 'I spoke to the police

this afternoon – asked them to come back and interview her again – but now that the raid has started they'll be delayed until tomorrow!'

'Will you wait a moment?' asked Daisy crossly. 'I'll tell you everything if you just *wait*. But—' Here she paused, and sighed through her nose, as though she was remembering something annoying. 'Well, as a friend reminds me constantly, it's important to give credit where credit is due. Although I know the solution to this case, it was mostly unravelled before I arrived by someone – a few someones – else. So I ought to let them speak. May, Eric and Nuala?'

'What – Fiona and the evacuees?' said Uncle Neil. 'What do they have to do with this?'

'Don't be ridiculous,' said Grandfather. 'They're children! If you know it was Ruth, she mustn't be allowed to get away! She's been working with the thieves!'

'Please,' said Ruth. 'That isn't true.'

'Will you *wait*?' said Daisy again. 'And – really. Why *do* people always underestimate children? Now, come along, you three. Hurry up. We're waiting.'

Even in the dim, weird light, I could see May flush red as all the adults turned to stare at her. I'd never seen her like this. She'd always been so noisy and confident – and somehow knowing that she could be shy made me realize that we're all just pretending, all the time. It's not just me – we're all actors. No one's actually who they seem to be.

I couldn't think what Daisy wanted us to say. *Had* we unravelled the case?

'She's right. Ruth can't be working with the thieves because there aren't any,' said Eric suddenly. 'We've known that from the beginning. When I went into the study, during the Murder in the Dark game – when I found Sidney Foley's body – the French window wasn't open.'

'Don't be silly!' said Granny.

'What were you doing in my study?' snapped Grandfather. 'I told you children not to go in there!'

'I wanted to get my watch,' said Eric.

'Watch?' cried Grandfather. 'What are you talking about?'

'The watch that you took from him,' said May. Her face had gone even redder – but I knew that now she was angry on Eric's behalf. 'Do you remember? The policeman found it and thought it proved there was a German gang. But it was Eric's.'

'You're German?' cried Granny, staring at Eric. 'But – good Lord! We trusted you! Wait – are *you* working with this gang?'

'No!' said May crossly. 'There is no gang! What I'm trying to say is that, because Eric went in to get it back, the murderer's plans were ruined. Eric found the body before anyone was supposed to, when the French window was still closed – when the murderer was *still in the room*. It was open when we all went in just a few minutes later, but Eric knew that it hadn't been open when Sidney was killed.

'According to the police, the thieves were supposed to have broken the latch, come in from the outside and hit Sidney Foley with a poker when he disturbed them stealing papers. But what Eric saw – and the fact that there weren't any muddy footprints on the rug, even though the ground outside was wet and dirty – meant that the murderer might have *left* through the French window, dropping the watch on the way out, but they'd come in from the hall.'

'But they stole those papers!' said Grandfather.

'No, they didn't. At least they weren't really stolen. We found them put down the well – actually, Annabelle Olivia told us about that. She saw the murderer hiding them on the night of the murder, only she thought she'd seen the ghost. So you see, someone here was just *pretending* that there were thieves, to throw the police off the scent.'

May stopped and nudged Eric. 'Go on!' she whispered. 'You do the next bit!'

'First, we thought that Pamela Verey might be the murderer,' Eric said, his voice getting more confident as he spoke. 'I found her hairgrip by the desk in the study, even though she told everyone she hadn't been in there. She was acting suspiciously, and she was lying about where she was while Sidney was being killed. Nuala heard her in the drawing room at the end of the game – she wasn't upstairs the whole time the way she told the police she was.'

'Are you saying that Pamela killed her husband?' cried Neil Vercy.

'No,' said Eric patiently. 'She didn't kill Hugh Verey, or Sidney, either. During the game, she argued with Hugh and decided to run away. So she threw some things into a bag and came down to leave through the French window in the study. Only she got disturbed – by the murderer coming to meet Sidney. She panicked. She ran out of the study and tried to go towards the front door, but someone else was sitting there. So she hid her bag in the plant pot on the stairs – dropping her ring in it by mistake – and rushed down again into the drawing room, where Nuala heard her crying. That was where she was when I discovered Sidney's dead body. She didn't do it, and she stayed in the dining room during the second murder, so she couldn't have done that one, either.'

'And who did she hear by the front door?' asked May. 'Well, Nuala can tell you about that.'

I was surprised. 'It's your case,' I said.

May stared at me as though I was being stupid. 'You were the one to work out the next alibi,' she said. 'We wouldn't have got it without you.'

I could feel myself blushing now. 'Granny's knitting,' I said, clearing my throat. 'She – it – she'd started a stripe just as the Murder in the Dark game began, and she'd almost finished it when Aunt Pam lit the lamp. I know how long a stripe takes – she couldn't have done the murder *and* knitted all those rows. We had to rule Granny out.'

'Goodness me,' said Granny. 'This is all quite ridiculous. Ruling me out! What a silly game you're playing!'

'It's not a game!' said May severely. 'We had four suspects left – Neil, Mr Verey, Ruth and Hugh. And then the second murder happened.'

65

From the diary of Fionnuala O'Malley, continued

'The second attack helped us rule out almost all our suspects,' said Eric, hunching his shoulders nervously. 'Hugh Verey died during it, and Mr Verey was badly injured – so that left us with Ruth and Neil Verey.'

'Now really, this is all nonsense!' said Grandfather. 'We *were* attacked by the thieves that you say don't exist – and it seems obvious to me that they were being helped by Ruth. As I've said, I have called the police this afternoon to ask them to interview her again and search the grounds – I've been suspicious of her for several days now. Who knows what they'll find? Fiona saw someone in the trees the day after Sidney's death, after all.'

'No!' I said.

I couldn't help it. I could feel everyone staring at me, shocked. I pulled myself up and tried to be Gráinne with ice in her spine, Nancy Drew at the end of a book, Fiona with her English confidence. I suddenly felt like all of them together – not three people, but one.

'No, I didn't. I was lying. I couldn't have seen anyone because there wasn't ever a thief. And you're – you're not listening. It *had* to be one of those four.'

'It wasn't me!' said Uncle Neil shrilly. 'When I arrived on the scene, Hugh was already dead, and Father was injured! It was Ruth! It has to have been!'

'No, no, no,' said Daisy, breaking in on us suddenly. 'Ruth is extremely important to this case, but she isn't the murderer. The one thing the children don't know is that Ruth is the *victim* of the third crime. Or she would have been, at least, if I hadn't stepped in.'

Ruth gasped. Her face in the lamplight was pale and haunted. 'What do you mean?' she asked. 'I didn't do it, I swear.'

I couldn't understand. Ruth was one of our final two suspects! If she wasn't the murderer, did that mean it was Uncle Neil?

'Because you know something,' said Daisy. 'Something about the first murder. Don't you?'

'No, I don't,' said Ruth, shaking her head. 'I promise. I don't know *anything*.'

'Oh, come now,' Daisy went on. 'Be honest.'

'Ah, so you admit she's lying!' said Grandfather. He pointed angrily at Ruth – and I suddenly realized something.

360

I remembered seeing Ruth run into the study, and I remembered the pause before she screamed, and the blood on her apron.

And I thought of what PC Cuffe had found in Uncle Sid's hand.

'Sure, *you* found the letter – the letter from Dr Warburton!' I exclaimed. '*You* took it out of Uncle Sidney's hand. That's why we haven't been able to find it. You've got it! It – it's in your apron pocket!'

Ruth was shaking. 'No, I didn't,' she said. 'Please. You don't understand.'

'I don't understand why you're still lying,' said Daisy severely. 'You quite obviously know several things of great importance to this case, and what's more, from what I saw this evening, the murderer knows you do. Come clean!'

'I didn't mean to hide anything,' said Ruth in a rush. 'But when I went into the study I bent down next to Sidney, and I put my hand on his. I wanted to see if he was really dead. That's when I felt the paper and I – just – took it. *Then* I screamed.'

'You thief!' cried Granny. 'Taking things – why, how dare you!'

'I'm sorry, Mrs Verey. But I couldn't put it back! PC Cuffe was already suspicious of me – he thought the thieves were a Nazi gang, and I knew he suspected *me* of helping them. Even though I would *never* work for the Nazis, never in my life! So I kept quiet. And anyway,' she added quickly, 'I don't know much.'

'I should say you know quite a lot,' said Daisy. 'You've read the letter, after all. And – why, you're the maid. You see everything that goes on, don't you? And you tidy up after everyone else. You clean the household's clothes, and you brush the household's shoes. You know whose shoes were muddy the day after Sidney's death, and you know what that means. All that was enough to make you the target of the second attack, and now the third. Will you show us the letter?'

She put out her hand, and after a pause Ruth reached into her apron pocket and pulled out a folded piece of paper.

'Read it to us,' said Daisy.

She's the kind of person you just obey, Diary, so Ruth bent her head and began to read.

Dear Mr Sidney Foley,

In your last letter, dated 27th October, you asked for particulars of the incident. I have not spoken about this since it occurred, feeling that my memories would not be helpful – and may indeed be harmful – to the living, while not benefiting the dead.

However, I am now at the end of my life, and I find that, as you say, I do not want my account to die with me. Please

know that what follows is merely my own recollection. I hope
you will make careful use of it – I would not want a good
man's reputation ruined.

On the evening of 25th November 1899, I was on patrol
near Mafeking with Private Mahmood when we heard faint
but desperate shouting in a small coppice of thorn trees, some
five hundred yards away. We ran towards the noise, but
Mahmood tripped and fell on a rocky outcrop, meaning
I arrived in the coppice first and alone. The sun had gone
down, and the air was dark – it was hard to make out what
was happening. Someone on the ground was crying out,
'He got me! He got me!' and someone else was running away
from me. I thought at first it was the enemy, and let off a shot
from my rifle, before that person shouted, 'Sir! It's me, Verey!
Foley's down! They got him!'

When I heard that, I went to the person on the ground,
whom I realized was your father, Captain Foley. He had been
grievously injured, with stab wounds in his back, arms and
legs. I tried to help, but after several minutes he ceased crying
out and thereafter died. A minute more, and Sergeant Verey
came back to kneel beside me. I saw that he was also
injured – a gash on his leg, and another in his shoulder and
his cheek. He was bleeding quite badly.

He told me that he and Foley had been set upon by a group
of Boers, who had attacked them both without warning and
then run off. He tried to chase them, but his injuries were too
serious, so he returned to see what could be done for Foley.

This is the official story – this is what Command heard, and why Verey was given his medal for bravery. But, in the years that followed, I have wondered. I never saw any Boers. The dust around Foley's body was disturbed, but I cannot swear I saw the marks of any other footsteps but Verey's, Foley's and my own.

And finally – I am aware that Verey went on to marry Foley's wealthy widow, your mother. He often talked to me about Elysium Hall and Iris Arden – I am not sure which he loved more.

None of this is evidence, of course. But many times, over the years, long after I left the army and took up my current profession, I have wondered what I really saw, and what really happened that evening.

That is all.

I remain,

Yours,

Fr

The paper was ripped, right through the signature. It was what was missing from Uncle Sidney's hand. And the story in it—

Everyone in the room turned to look at Grandfather. Everyone was silent.

Granny had turned pale.

'I won't have this,' said Grandfather. He had gone almost purple, and his eyebrows were working furiously.

'I won't – this is baseless supposition! That man was out to ruin me! I won't – give me that letter!'

'Absolutely *not*,' said Daisy crisply. 'Isn't it interesting? Foley was stabbed in the back. Rather similar to what happened to Hugh Verey when you think about it.'

'It was not!' roared Grandfather. 'How dare you! I am a respected member of this community. I will NOT BE SPOKEN TO IN THIS WAY! Investigate *her*, I say.'

And he pointed, finger trembling, at Ruth.

66

From the diary of Fionnuala O'Malley, continued

'I wasn't telling the truth before,' said Ruth suddenly.

'HAH!' said Grandfather. 'You see? She can't be trusted. I happen to know she worked in a circus before she came to England, which we kindly overlooked when hiring her – but who knows what she's capable of?'

He stared round at all of us wildly. I could feel myself trembling – or maybe it was just the ground shaking. I felt like the whole world was tilting and crumbling.

'Yes, you *don't* know what I'm capable of,' said Ruth. She was breathing heavily, her jaw clenched. 'The ghost you've been so afraid of – your precious poltergeist – it was *me*.'

'It was Leonard!' cried Uncle Neil.

'Leonard's *dead*,' said Ruth. 'I did it all – the plates, the cups, the eggs, everything. It's easy when you know the tricks. I learned them in the circus. I did it because I wanted *you* to be haunted by your dead the way my family haunts *me*!'

Her eyes were shining with rage. 'And I won't lie for you, Mr Verey. It wasn't just what I read. I *saw* you too. I saw you on the night of the party. I looked out of the kitchen window, just as I was doing the blackout, and I saw you in the garden beside the French window. I thought at the time you must have been fixing the latch, but – after Sidney died – I realized you were making it *look* like it'd been broken. And the next day you put out *two* pairs of muddy shoes for me to clean: the ones you'd been wearing during the day, and the ones you were wearing at the party.'

'This is a lie!' said Grandfather. 'This is nonsense!'

'If it's a lie, then how did you know where the murderer had hidden the papers they stole from the study?' asked Daisy. 'Because I watched you pull them up from the well and bury them in the beds behind the kitchen this afternoon.

'You were going to tell the police to dig there, weren't you, when you called them to come and search the grounds? That was the third crime: to frame Ruth for the murders, and pretend that she was working with a German gang of thieves.'

'You're evil!' cried Ruth furiously. 'I knew it! Oh, I wish I'd done worse than I did. I made up the haunting. But I didn't kill Sidney, and I'd never work with the Nazis. My family—'

'Ah, but what if you were exchanging information for your family's safety!' said Grandfather. 'They're still in Austria, aren't they?'

'We are Jewish. The Nazis wouldn't let them leave,' said Ruth angrily. 'And I don't know where they are now. I haven't heard from them for months. Don't you understand? I'm not a spy.'

'Of course Ruth isn't a spy! But someone else in the family was: Hugh Verey!' said May indignantly. 'We found papers in his handwriting, maps of his factory and details about what it makes – he was passing information to the Germans.'

I felt sick. Something had been bothering me about Eric's watch, and I finally realized what it was: if Grandfather had taken it from him, why had he let PC Cuffe assume it'd been dropped by the thief during the murder? It only made sense if Grandfather had *wanted* people to believe the story of the thief. And he'd only want that if he really was the murderer.

I suddenly *got it*. I saw the whole pattern of the crime, like a costume laid out in front of me, like a first night gone perfectly, like a beautifully told story. And I knew that, even though saying it would shake up my entire life, I couldn't stay quiet.

'Uncle Sid's murder was supposed to look like it wasn't planned,' I said. 'As if a thief broke in and did it. But it *was* planned – really carefully planned. The latch on the French window was broken before the crime. The poker wasn't the murder weapon, a bedknob from the spare room was. The murderer went out of the French window to make it look as though thieves had got *in* that way. It was

368

all a trick, misdirection, like a play. We thought the murderer must have been Ruth, or Uncle Neil, because they both know how to create illusions – but there's one person in this family who's taught everyone else to pretend. Grandfather pretends to Granny that everything's safe; he pretends to Mam that Da never existed at all – he's acting, pretending, every day of his life. And now we know why. He killed Granny's first husband so he could marry her. This house shouldn't be his. He shouldn't live here at all, or be a magistrate, or anything. He's been lying his whole life.'

'Fiona, BE QUIET!' roared Grandfather, so loud that the shelter's walls rattled.

'My name's not Fiona!' I said. I was shaking. 'It's Fionnuala! The murders all happened because Uncle Sid overheard Grandfather telling Granny that his friend Dr Warburton was dying, and misunderstood, and thought *Grandfather* was ill. Uncle Sid got excited and thought he was going to inherit Elysium Hall, so he wrote to Dr Warburton, thinking he'd get information about how long Grandfather had left. But Dr Warburton wrote back and told him about Mr Foley instead. When Uncle Sid read the letter, he realized that everything Grandfather had told us about what happened was a lie – and he decided to confront Grandfather about it. Uncle Sid made an appointment with him on the night of the party, and then he made up the game to distract everyone else and make sure they weren't interrupted.'

'That's what Sidney was getting from the library at the beginning of the game,' said Eric suddenly. 'Dr Warburton's letter! He must have hidden it in a book.'

I nodded.

'But he didn't know that Grandfather was planning something too. Grandfather takes the blackout very seriously. He goes round the whole house to check it each evening. He would have had the perfect opportunity to set up the crime before it happened – to fix the French window to make it look like someone had broken in from the outside.

'Even his costume was chosen so cleverly! He was wearing that pale siren suit that crackled – so everyone would hear him going upstairs in it and think he stayed there. But he didn't. He went into his room, took it off quickly, went to the spare room and picked up the brass bedknob as a weapon. He was in his shirt and trousers – and that's what Uncle Neil saw, not the ghost, but Grandfather's pale shirt coming out of the spare room. Grandfather put the bedknob in his trouser pocket and crept back downstairs. He needed something he could hide, see, not something big like the poker that Sidney might notice him holding.

'Grandfather went into the study, scaring off Aunt Pam, and a minute later Uncle Sidney joined him in there. That's something else we should have seen – Uncle Neil's always late, so it wouldn't fit for him to be in the study *before* Uncle Sid, before the meeting began. Grandfather turned

370

on a flashlight, and pretended to show Uncle Sidney something on the desk – I think it was his will, since we found it in the bundle of papers – but, while Uncle Sid was bent over, he hit him on the back of the head with the bedknob. He got some blood on his clothes – I remember I saw Ruth hanging his shirt up to dry later. It didn't seem that strange at the time, but it was, because it was the siren suit that should have been bloody, not the shirt he was wearing underneath.

'Then Grandfather staged the crime scene. He grabbed the poker and put it next to the body, so it'd seem like the kind of murder weapon that a thief might use, and bundled up all the papers and the watch from the desk to make it look like a theft. But, before he could get the letter in Uncle Sid's hand, he heard someone else opening the study door.'

'*Me*,' said Eric. 'The room was quiet, so I thought everyone had left. Old Mr Verey must have hidden behind the curtain when I came in. I went over to the desk to look for my watch, and that's when I fell over Sidney Foley. I ran out to get help, and Old Mr Verey opened the French window and escaped. He went back in through the kitchens – he must have taken off his shoes so they wouldn't get mud in the house. Ruth didn't see him because she was upstairs in her room. The party was on Friday night, when Shabbat begins, and so I think Ruth was lighting the candlesticks May and I found in her room.

But Mr Scott saw him running into the kitchens and thought he might have been – someone else. Old Mr Verey went up the back stairs to his room, put his siren suit on again and shouted from his room, loudly asking what was going on.'

'This is all nonsense! I was nearly killed by an assailant from *outside* this house only a few days ago!' cried Grandfather. 'They knocked on the window, lured us all outside, and attacked in the darkness. My son – *my sons* – are *dead.*'

'That was what you wanted it to look like!' said May crossly. 'But Nuala worked it out again. She told us that the second murder felt like a play, and it *was*. It was all misdirection and clever props. We couldn't work out how you'd done it at first, but once we'd searched your pockets, and the space beneath the window, it should have been obvious. We found—'

'String, a stone and some wet paper,' said Eric, his face lighting up. 'None of them seem very suspicious, but when you put them all together . . .'

He scrabbled in his pocket and pulled out his notebook, unfolding something from it very carefully. It was a piece of paper, crumpled and torn, shaped like an oval.

'This bit of paper was stuck up against the window. When the blackout was pulled aside, everyone further back in the room would have seen it – but not very clearly. You knew that the room would be very dark, with only a candle to light it. And, just like you planned, everyone would have thought this paper was a face.

'And the tapping we all heard? A stone tied to a piece of string, jumping in the wind that evening, would have made that noise. You could have put everything up when you went round to check the blackout again. Once everyone was in the dining room, the wind would have started up the illusion without you having to do anything else. Then, when Hugh and Ruth went running outside, you followed the person you thought was Ruth, and attacked them from behind. You didn't realize until it was too late that you'd caught Hugh instead of Ruth in the dark. You must have been horrified – but you couldn't stop. You cut yourself in a few places, to make it look as though you'd been attacked as well – just like you did when you killed Foley. Then you wiped the knife with your handkerchief and threw it away on the path.

'When you talked about the crime later, you mentioned catching sight of the knife in the moonlight – which should have told us you were lying. The moon had gone behind the clouds when we came outside. *There wasn't any moonlight.*

'You'd killed the wrong person this time, and you still weren't safe – but you had managed to rule yourself out as the murderer *and* convince the police even more that there really was an outside attacker, instead of someone in Elysium Hall being behind the crimes.'

'This is simply silly,' said Granny, but I could hear the wobble in her voice. 'William wouldn't kill his own flesh and blood!'

'Of course there's a reason,' said May, blinking at her. 'Didn't you hear us? First of all, Mr Verey thought Hugh was Ruth – he didn't mean to kill him. And second – yes, he killed Sidney on purpose, but Sidney was about to reveal the truth about him. He killed Mr Foley, your first husband, Sidney's father. His whole life was a lie. He shouldn't be the owner of Elysium Hall; he shouldn't be married to you; he shouldn't be a magistrate. His precious reputation is based on something that never happened – he's not just and fair and all that nonsense. He's a murderer.'

'Those are stories!' said Grandfather. 'They don't prove anything!'

'But the way you reacted to them does,' said May. I couldn't believe how brave she was being, standing up to Grandfather like that. 'Nuala was right, you know. She said if we told the right story we could catch the killer. And we did!'

I stared at her. I didn't think May had been listening to me when I'd said that – I didn't think she listened to anyone.

'If Nuala hadn't been here, we wouldn't have got as far as we did,' said Eric. 'Right, May?'

May made a grumbling sound. 'I suppose,' she said at last. 'Yes. She was quite helpful.'

I felt like there were bubbles inside my chest.

I hardly noticed that Grandfather had jumped up so his head almost hit the top of the shelter. 'I won't stand for it! I have a reputation! You have no proof!'

'Haven't you been listening?' said Daisy. 'We have blood on your clothes where it shouldn't be, a letter from a witness to a murder you committed forty years ago, Ruth's evidence that she saw you jemmying the French window and found mud on your dress shoes, and mine that I saw you burying the papers – which, when we dig them up, will be blank pages, since the children gave me the originals. There most certainly is proof.'

And she reached out and grabbed hold of him, twisting his arms round behind him and upward.

The thing I really remember was how weird it was to see Grandfather being held onto like that. He was writhing around in Daisy's grip, but he couldn't get loose. I'd always thought he was tall, but right then he looked much smaller. Maybe it was because his shoulders were hunched, or maybe because of the look on his face – like a little kid caught stealing candy.

Then Grandfather gave a yell, twisted out of Daisy's grip and fled. He was out of the shelter before we could even think. Daisy rushed after him, and the rest of us followed her.

We all stumbled out into the night – but it wasn't dark in the garden, like I expected it to be. It should have been – the sun had set hours ago. But the whole sky above the trees was orange, as bright as a sunrise, glowing and flickering and beautiful. The clouds were lit up from beneath with searchlights like flashlights under a face.

'Oh my God,' said Uncle Neil. 'It's the end of the world.'

With my feet on the ground, it felt like being in an earthquake or a storm. The echoes shook through my whole body. The anti-aircraft guns were rattling, and I could see the planes dropping bombs, *pop, pop, pop*, like marbles falling out of someone's pocket.

'"Moonlight Sonata",' said Eric quietly. 'We didn't understand what it meant before, but we do now. Hugh Verey knew this was coming. That's why he didn't want Pamela and Annabelle Olivia to go back to Coventry.'

Annabelle Olivia and Aunt Pam. They couldn't be *there*, could they? They had to be safe. I suddenly felt like I couldn't breathe properly.

Daisy caught Grandfather then. She wrestled him to the ground, with him groaning as he fell on his wounded side, and put handcuffs on his wrists. 'You – distraction!' she snapped at him. 'Do be quiet. I really am too busy to be catching murderers. I need you to know that you are *not* a priority.'

'How dare you!' cried Grandfather. '*How dare you!* You have no right! I was – this is *my* house. I would never have hurt *my* son. I thought – I thought it was *her*, in the dark!'

'But you knew it was Uncle Sid!' I shouted.

Grandfather's face twisted. 'No Foley will inherit *my house*,' he hissed. 'Iris! Help me!'

'Help you? This is *my* house,' snapped Granny. '*My* boys. They should have been safe here. I don't want to hear another word from you.'

And she turned away from him.

Someone put their arms round me. I turned and looked up and saw Mam standing behind me, her face all lit up red and yellow and orange, and her eyes shining. 'Shh,' she said. 'It'll be all right, Nuala. You're safe. And you're a brave girl. I think your da would be proud of you.'

May took my hand. Eric was clinging onto her other arm.

And we stood like that and watched as, far away, Coventry burned.

Usually when your life changes, the world doesn't seem to care. But sometimes the whole universe really does feel like a play, and you're the hero – no, I mean the heroes. And that was me, and Eric, and May, Diary. We uncovered the spy, we solved the murders, and we saved Ruth from being framed for them. And the long and the short of it is I don't think my life is ever going to be the same.

67

From the report of May Wong

So that's the story of how we caught the murderer at Elysium Hall, and how we finally became part of the Ministry of Unladylike Activity. After what we'd done – me, Eric and Nuala – not even Big Sister Hazel could prevent us from becoming spies.

She was quite upset, though, when Daisy called her and she finally came to collect us the day after Coventry was bombed. She kept on saying that I might have been hurt – which, obviously, I wasn't – and that I'd been very stupid. I *felt* a bit stupid then. I should have telephoned her. I should have told her about the 'Moonlight Sonata' telegram we found. If we had, we might have been able to help stop the bombing.

But when I said this to Hazel she cried, and squeezed me against her. 'No one could have stopped it, May,' she said. 'But you *did* help.'

That made me feel pleased. And now I knew that,

although everyone *was* quite angry, they were all very grateful too. I'd proved myself – we all had – and we absolutely deserved to join the Ministry.

Hazel took us back to London, and we finally walked through the red door of 13 Great Russell Street, where the cat Eric had found was watching us thoughtfully from a basket in the hall. ('I'm going to name her Pfote,' Eric told us. 'It's German for *paw*.') Then we were rushed back out of it and off to the country again, to Fallingford House, the Ministry's out-of-London headquarters while the bombings carry on. We're being trained up at last – we're being taught codes and spycraft and self-defence and lots of excellent secret things that I can't *wait* to use in real life.

When I say 'us', I do mean all of us. Nuala is going to be a spy too. She might be annoying sometimes, but the fact is that she is actually a good detective. And *actually* sometimes annoying people can still become your friends.

Eric is teasing me about this part because I know it's not exactly what I was saying when I first met her. But, when I think about whether I'd prefer to be friends with Nuala or the other girls in my form at Deepdean, I'd rather Nuala every time. She's clever, and brave, and she's even stranger than I am.

Old Mr Verey was arrested, by the way. I was telling the truth at the beginning of my report, you see, about evil looking like anything – he seemed so respectable, but underneath he was really horrible. Daisy had alerted the

Ministry – not the Ministry of Agriculture, obviously; the *spy* Ministry – before we all went down into the Anderson shelter, and the Ministry called the police and told them what Daisy had seen and what we had found, and the next morning PC Cuffe in his tall hat arrived and very apologetically took him away in handcuffs.

'You can't do this!' Old Mr Verey protested as he left.

'But the rules are for everyone, Grandfather,' said Nuala angrily. 'That's what you told me.'

She'd pulled herself up tall, and she glared at him as he left. I think it really hurt her to find out the truth about him, but she hasn't said much about that to me and Eric.

The Ministry also knows now about Hugh Verey and the secrets he was passing to Berlin, and they have the papers we found. I feel quite proud about that.

Ruth has been hired by the Ministry too. Daisy said that anyone who can make such convincing illusions as she managed with the poltergeist will be very useful to them. Ruth's going to help them invent more clever things to help spies while they're on missions.

Elysium Hall is going to be requisitioned for the troops (Daisy's cover story turned out to be true, after all) and so everyone has to leave. Mrs O'Malley and Old Mrs Verey are moving to a house in the village, and Nuala's going to stay with them – when she's not at Deepdean, that is. Daisy and Hazel arranged it, and Old Mrs Verey agreed. I think she's finally realized that nowhere is truly safe, and so there's no point hiding from the world. So Nuala will be at school with me.

Eric is going to go to a school called Weston, which is like Deepdean but for boys, and we're all going to pretend to be normal – until the Ministry needs us to go on another mission. I think I can cope at Deepdean if Nuala is there to talk to about the Ministry and how we're going to make the world better, and if I know that it's not forever.

There is one more thing to say about the Elysium Hall case. I've left it for last because – well, because I didn't really know how to talk about it, and I still don't. The night we solved the case, the night of the raid, Coventry Cathedral was hit – and Pamela Verey and Annabelle Olivia's house too. When people went looking for them the next day, their whole street had been flattened into rubble. There was nothing to find. They were all just – gone. Pamela Verey's ring is almost the only thing left of them.

Thinking about it makes me feel like I'm stuck in a tiny box and can't breathe, so I try not to. Annabelle Olivia was extremely annoying, but now she just doesn't exist any more. She's not in another town or another country. She's not anywhere, and there's no reason for it, apart from the fact that some Nazis far away in Germany circled Coventry Cathedral on a map and sent planes to smash it to pieces.

That's what we're trying to stop, isn't it? People shouldn't just be allowed to *die* like that, for no reason.

They shouldn't die at all. They should be able to go on living, even if they are sometimes annoying and silly like Annabelle Olivia was.

Everyone matters, but in a war that gets forgotten. But *I* won't forget, and neither will Eric or Nuala. And that's why we have to end the war. Once it's over, Eric's father will be able to come home, and I'll be able to *go* home, and everything will go back to the way it was before – or, no, *better*.

I know it feels like we're very small and the war is enormous, but we can do a lot to help. We've already proven that, and we're going to do it again. We outwitted a murderer, didn't we? We uncovered a spy. If we can do that, then we can do anything.

68

From the diary of Fionnuala O'Malley

21st December 1940

Dear Diary,

How are you? I haven't been writing in you very much lately, have I? It's just that life is so interesting now that I don't really know where to start. We're being trained to be *spies* – real, serious spies. And I guess – since that moment on the night of the raid – maybe I don't feel as lost and split into pieces any more. My life's not bad these days. Sure, I'm Irish, and I'm American, and I'm English too, and I can be all those things together here.

Here is Fallingford. It's a big house in the country that belonged to Daisy's family before the war, and now belongs to the Ministry, and we're going to stay here until the next school term starts. Mam and Granny are letting me go to *school*! It's the same one May goes to, Deepdean, and it sounds wonderful. I know May's excited that I'm going to be there with her, even though she pretends not to be. May is usually a lot more excited by everything than she pretends she is.

Eric's mother and his sister, Lottie, came up to visit us yesterday in a big burst of laughter. They're both so fun and bright, but it's weird – Eric is much quieter around them. I guess it's not just me who's different with my family.

Mrs Schlossbauer found out that Eric wasn't with Lottie at the beginning of November – 'I didn't tell her!' said Lottie. 'I swear I posted that letter you gave me for her! She just *knows* things sometimes . . .' She spent weeks calling round everywhere she could think of, convinced that Eric was dead, until the Ministry wrote her a letter explaining that Eric had been chosen for a special scholarship programme. She obviously doesn't believe that – she's like Eric, too smart to get taken in by tricks – but she is carefully not saying anything.

I think she's very proud of him. When she looks at him, her face lights up just the way Eric's does when he's looking at a piece of code. She even gave him a letter from his father. Eric grabbed hold of it and ate it up with his eyes.

'Papa's all right,' he told us. 'He thinks they might let him go soon. He's been writing a newspaper with some of the other people in the camp, and they're going to put on a concert next month. He's *all right.*'

I'm so glad.

At the Ministry, Daisy and May's sister Hazel are in charge of us. This makes May mad, but Hazel keeps pointing out that none of us are thirteen yet and so we need to have someone paying attention to us.

'You've all done excellent work, though,' Daisy told us this morning, a little grudgingly. 'You ought to be proud of yourselves.'

'No thanks to you!' May said.

'Do be quiet, May,' said Hazel.

'And you were years older than us when you solved your first case,' May pointed out. 'So we're actually better than you when you come to think of it.'

'You are *not*!' said Daisy instantly. 'But I grant that you've made a good beginning.'

They always argue like this. May just can't help it.

'When do we go on our next mission?' I asked. That was what I wanted to know.

'When there's a mission for you to go on. Honestly, in my day we waited until murders happened. We didn't go hunting them out,' said Daisy.

Hazel made a face at her. 'Didn't we, though?' she asked.

'SHUSH,' said Daisy. 'ANYWAY, what I WANTED to say was that – well – you remind me of us. And so we were thinking— Hazel, tell them.'

'We were thinking,' said Hazel, suddenly grinning, 'that you deserve rewards. These were given to us when we began, and so it seems only right that we should pass them on to you. We asked our friend Beanie to lend us hers for you, Nuala. She's doing her nurse's training, so she doesn't have much use for it at the moment.'

She held out her hand, and three silver discs glinted in it.

'They're detective badges,' said Daisy. 'Now, you must look after these properly! No losing them. Being given them is an honour, and I hope you understand—'

'We understand,' said Eric fervently. 'Thank you.'

'What do they say?' I asked. I peered at mine and saw faded letters scratched into it. 'Detective—'

'Detective Society,' said Hazel. She'd gone a little pink. 'It was just a silly name that we called ourselves when we were younger.'

'"Silly"?' said Daisy, outraged. '"SILLY"?'

'It isn't silly!' said May. 'Detective Society Forever, right?'

Hazel beamed at her. 'That's exactly it,' she said. 'Detective Society Forever.'

I looked at May and Eric. I remembered what I'd thought of them when I'd first seen them: that they weren't who I was expecting, that I wasn't going to like them – and that I was sure they'd hate me and then leave. I was wrong, Diary, so wrong about all of it, and I'm really glad about that. May and Eric aren't horrible at all, and they haven't left me. They've become my friends.

I still miss Da so much, but I finally feel like I have something to do, something that isn't just make-believe, and somewhere to be. The Ministry is real, after all, and I'm part of it – and now I'm part of this Detective Society thing as well. Me, and Eric, and May. Together.

And I knew then that I couldn't wait for our next mission.

Nuala's Guide to Elysium Hall

So Daisy asked me to write this guide, to help explain some of the words that people might find confusing from May's and my accounts, in case people read them in the future. And now I'm imagining this being read by people we don't even know – maybe even people from the 1960s, and that makes me feel kind of dizzy. So hello, person from the future. I hope this helps.

- **Ah Yeh** – what May calls her grandfather.

- **amah** – May says that this is a kind of maid she has in her house in Hong Kong. May really must be rich.

- **Anderson shelter** – an air-raid shelter that sits in the garden, under the earth. They're really uncomfortable, but I guess they keep you safe.

- **arra** – my da used to say this when he was mad, to tell me that I'd better stop *or else.*

- **banshee** – an Irish fairy woman whose screams mean someone you love will die. I've dressed up as one before.

- **barrage balloon** – a huge silver balloon that hangs above buildings to protect them from bombs.

- **bold** – naughty or bad.

- **buck up** – an English way of saying cheer up.

- **Ching Shih** – a pirate queen that May loves.

- **classified** – absolutely top secret!

- **coalition government** – a government made up of people from different political parties. England has one now because of the war.

- **dripping** – a kind of fat that you use in cooking.

- **eejit** – an idiot.

- **fifth columnist** – someone who is secretly working for the other side.

- **French window** – a kind of a cross between a window and a door; it has panes of glass in it, but you can open it like a door and step outside.

- **give no quarter** – show no mercy.

- **give out to** – tell off.

- **Gráinne Ní Mháille** – an Irish pirate queen I love. You might know her as Grace O'Malley, but this is her *real* name, just like mine is Fionnuala, not Fiona. You say it a little like Grawnya Nee Wallyeh.

- **grand** – an Irish word that can mean yes or no or anything else, depending on how you say it.

- **gumboots** – boots you wear when it's raining or muddy.

- **Home Guard** – a volunteer defence force made up of English people.

- **Jerry** – a mean nickname for German people.

- **Jungvolk** – Eric says that all kids in Germany have to join this group, to prove that they love Hitler and they believe in what he's doing.

- **Kipferl** – Austrian cookies made of almonds and sugar.

- **Liebchen** – *darling* or *sweetheart* in German.

- **magistrate** – an English kind of judge who isn't paid.

- **Oma** – a German word for grandmother.

- **Pfote** – Eric says that this means *paw* in German.

- **the pictures** – another way of saying the cinema.

- **ration book** – a book full of stamps you can exchange for foods like meat and sugar that we don't have much of right now.

- **Sassenach** – an English person. It's usually rude.

- **scrump** – to steal fruit from a garden or orchard.

- **Shabbat** – the day of rest for Jewish people. It starts on Friday at sunset and ends on Saturday at sunset.

- **siren suit** – overalls that people wear on top of their normal clothes, in case there's an air raid.

- **sleeveen** – an Irish word meaning someone sly or cunning.

- **tower-watchers** – English people who stand on top of towers and watch for Nazis parachuting down to invade.

- **verflixt** – a curse word in German, meaning darn.

- **weak sauce** – pathetic.

Author's Note

The first thing to say is that the plot of this book, its locations, and all its characters, are completely invented.

The second thing to say is that the history surrounding it is as true as I could make it.

It is very easy in 2022, especially if you live in the UK, to see the Second World War as simply about right and wrong. The British and their allies (as I was taught in school) were good, and the Germans and their allies were bad. We, the goodies, defeated the baddies, so everything turned out well in the end. But the truth is much more complicated. Although the wickedness of the Nazi ideology cannot be overstated, what had to be done to defeat it was also vastly cruel.

The accounts of the Coventry bombing of 14 November 1940 made me cry when I read them in Juliet Gardiner's *The Blitz*. The destruction was so dreadful, and the death toll so high (officially, 568 people were killed in just a few hours), that the Germans invented a new word to describe it: *coventriert*, meaning 'flattened'. And that terrible night happened at least in part as revenge for the bombing of Munich by the British.

I went to university near Coventry, and walking through the city is an eerie experience – in many parts of it there is simply nothing built before the 1950s. My German publisher's offices are in Munich – and when I visited them in 2019 I experienced the same sense of dislocated eeriness to realize how new many of the buildings are, with the added stomach-dropping realization that *my* side did that.

There is no good side to be on in a war, not really, although there are some wars that have to be fought, against people like Hitler, for whom peace was never an option. I believe very strongly not in good or bad nations, but in good and bad people. One person can do absolutely extraordinary things, no matter how small or seemingly insignificant they are, and the real heroes of the Second World War for me are those people who risked, and often lost, their lives trying to help others.

Of course, Nazism wasn't – and isn't – confined to Germany. It's a rotten ideology that can infect anyone anywhere. It was important to me that Eric should have had a brief moment of being taken in by it, as most German people were, because that's often how evil operates. It seems exciting and true and right at first, until it's too late. And it also felt important to me to start this series by talking about *British* Nazi sympathizers. The ones in this book are made up, but Oswald Mosley and his fellow British Union of Fascists members were not. *Agent Jack* by Robert Hutton is a great account of Nazism in Britain in the 1930s and

1940s – and how UK government spies tried to uncover their whereabouts – though it's written for adults.

I also want to be clear that even British people who did not support Nazism did some very cruel things. The Holocaust was a systematic attempt by the Nazis to wipe out Jewish people, as well as Roma people, disabled people, queer and trans people, and Black people, among others, in the countries they controlled. Today Britain celebrates its part in ending it, and that is wonderful and true – but it is also true that when those terrified, targeted people were fleeing persecution in Europe in the 1930s the UK *set a limit* on the number of visas that could be granted to them. We were worried about too much immigration, and so we closed our doors to them. People died who could have lived because we decided we did not want to save them. And we are still doing the same thing. We capped visas available to desperate Afghans in 2021 and Ukrainians in 2022. We turned away from their suffering. Becoming a refugee is entirely a matter of random fate. It could happen to anyone. It *is* happening, increasingly, to anyone. And I think it is immoral not to try to help everyone.

Other things that are true: in the autumn of 1940, the British really did think that they were about to be invaded by the Germans. People were seeing Nazi spies everywhere and were preparing to fight off the invaders when they arrived. The invasion never happened, but the terror was very real, and I've used that in this book.

The nasal radio presenter that Sidney Foley listens to was also real. Nicknamed Lord Haw-Haw because he sounded so posh, he broadcast Nazi propaganda from Germany to the UK during the war, to try to depress British morale by making a Nazi victory seem inevitable.

Britain really did put Italians, Austrians and Germans living in the UK, mostly men and boys, mostly entirely innocent, into internment camps in places including the Isle of Man during the war. It's mentioned in Eva Ibbotson's gorgeous novel for adults *The Morning Gift*, but I haven't seen it in many other places – I really think it's important to talk about!

Ireland pursued a policy of neutrality during the war. Many Irish people served in the British army, but the country itself was officially uninvolved. This made British people deeply (and unfairly) suspicious of the Irish, just as they are in this book. And the feeling was quite mutual. Nuala's da's anti-English sentiment is also very accurate. The Republic of Ireland only became independent from the UK in 1922, after many bruising centuries of British rule, and the cultural wounds still exist to this day.

Finally, there really was a Ministry of Ungentlemanly Warfare, the joke name for the spy branch the Special Operations Executive. I first came across it on the podcast *Stuff You Missed in History Class* – a great place to discover lesser-known pieces of history – and just thought it was too perfect to be true. I read more about it in Leo Marks's

Between Silk and Cyanide (including the fact that the real Ministry had a Cairo office!) and started wondering what a spy agency for (mostly) women would be like. The WOE, of course, is my answer.

The two new detectives in this book, Eric and Nuala, have backgrounds that come from many different sources. Eric's childhood in Germany is based on the incredible memoir *Destined to Witness* by Hans J. Massaquoi (again, for adults, but absolutely worth a read), and his experiences as a refugee have echoes of *When Hitler Stole Pink Rabbit* by the wonderful Judith Kerr (this one is for children!). I borrowed his last name from a German fan who happened to email me at exactly the right time. Thank you, Fanny! By the way, many apologies to all my German early readers who commented, quite correctly, that Eric is not a German name. His real name is Erich, not Eric, but of course in England in 1940 it would not be safe for a German-born child to be called Erich. Hence the name change!

Nuala's mixed-up identity comes from my own family unit, but also just a little from Shrabani Basu's *Spy Princess*, a fantastic biography of my personal Second World War hero, Noor Inayat Khan. Like Nuala, she spent her early childhood travelling the world and then lost her father at a cruelly young age. Also like Nuala by the end of this book, she was firm on the importance of multiple parts of her identity, seeing her loyalties to England and India as not conflicting but complimenting each other. Sufiya Ahmed has written a great book on Noor for children, *My Story: Noor-un-Nissa Inayat Khan*, and I'd recommend that everyone read up on her.

By the way, although this is the beginning of a new series, I hope that some of you will also have read my previous books, the Murder Most Unladylike Mysteries, which star younger versions of Daisy and Hazel. May was first introduced in *A Spoonful of Murder*, and appeared again in *Death Sets Sail*. You can also read her very first solo mystery in *Once Upon a Crime*. Although she and Hazel share a father, they have different mothers – so the person who May calls Ma Ma is someone you may be more familiar with by the name Jie Jie.

It has been strange and hard to write this book during a time of both universal and personal suffering. I began work on it in 2021, the second year of the pandemic, just a few months after the death of my father and a few months before the birth of my child. I finished it in 2022 as we watched a new war in Europe unfold. History does not repeat itself, but it does rhyme. All I can hope is that each of you reading this book will keep on trying to make your corner of the universe a better place, just like May and Eric and Nuala. One person can do astonishing things, and I hope the world I have created will go with you as you do them.

Robin Stevens, Oxford, June 2022

Acknowledgements

I had a co-author for the early drafts of this book, so thanks must go to them first for setting the tone of this new series, and for inspiring certain aspects of both Nuala and Eric's characters. In later drafts, my co-author became more focused on rolling over and learning to crawl, and I am immensely grateful to the people who paid attention to these important activities and allowed me to spend time on my own in 1940: my partner D, my mother Kathie and my assistant Becki (with help from Poppy!). Huge thanks to Bennie (with help from Michelle, Emma and Charlie!) for taking Howl for so many walks so I could write.

I took some leave last year, halfway through the writing of this book. Thank you to the people who kept this show on the road while I was away: Fritha Lindqvist, Kat McKenna, my website designer Helen Wills (hire her – she's great!) and my accountants Kate, Sharon, Julie and Magda (thank you for knowing about taxes; I do not).

Thank you to my amazing early readers: Courtney Smyth, who made sense of Nuala and her world; Wei Ming Kam, May's number-one cheerleader; Andrea Henke, Scarlett Fu, Ellis Walker, and Pam Roberts, Eric's support team;

Mike Smith for his incredibly thoughtful and painstaking comments on my presentation of the Second World War and the murder plot (as well as Ngaire Bushell for connecting me with him, and Ross Montgomery for connecting me with both of them); Keren David for her very helpful read of Ruth's background; Kathie Booth Stevens for her wonderful comments as always; Louise O'Neill for being an absolute queen and reading this book when she really had no time; and Bethany Culbert for her advice on South Africa.

Thank you to the team at Puffin: Harriet Venn, Michael Bedo, Charlotte Winstone, Wendy Shakespeare, Jane Tait, Toria Hegedus, Sarah Hall, Stephanie Barrett, Kat Baker, Toni Budden, Francesca Dow and everyone else who has worked so hard to make this book a success. Thanks to Jan Bielecki, my designer-turned-illustrator, who has created the most brilliant cover, and Marssaié Jordan for her helpful input! And special thanks to my amazing editor Nat, who kept telling me that everything would be OK. I think I almost believe her now.

Huge thanks to my agent Gemma, who nine years after we first met is still tirelessly enthusiastic about my world and characters.

And finally, thanks to you, reader. I am so lucky to be able to write books for you. I hope you enjoyed this one.

© Chris Close, 2018

Robin Stevens was born in California and grew up in an Oxford college, across the road from the house where Alice in Wonderland lived. She has been making up stories all her life.

When she was twelve, her father handed her a copy of *The Murder of Roger Ackroyd* and she realized that she wanted to be either Hercule Poirot or Agatha Christie when she grew up. She spent her teenage years at Cheltenham Ladies' College, reading a lot of murder mysteries and hoping that she'd get the chance to do some detecting herself (she didn't). She went to university, where she studied crime fiction, and then she worked for a children's publisher.

Robin is now a full-time author and the creator of the internationally award-winning and bestselling **Murder Most Unladylike** series, starring Daisy Wells and Hazel Wong. She still hopes she might get the chance to do some detecting of her own one day. She lives in Oxford.

LOOK OUT FOR THE MINISTRY'S
NEXT **MYSTERIOUS** MISSION . . .

THE BODY IN THE BLITZ

COMING SOON!